Her Favorite Hot Doc

by

Barbara Lohr

Purple Egret Press

Purple Egret Press
Savannah, Georgia 31411

Cover Art by Kim Killion – The Killion Group
Editing by Nicole Zoltack

for

Ted

Chapter 1

"The baby's head is crowning. Amy, I see dark hair!" McKenna checked vitals for mother and baby. Both heartbeats remained strong with no signs of distress. Excitement spiked the moist warm air of the water birthing suite.

McKenna's best friend was having a baby. All systems were go. Well, except for Amy's husband. "Almost there, Dad," McKenna told Mallory as Amy's contraction eased. "Buck up, buddy."

He gave her a thumbs up, but both husband and wife looked beat. Amy's pretty hazel eyes were ringed with exhaustion and her lower lip quivered. "I don't know if I can do this."

"Amy, darlin'," Mallory crooned. "You are my princess. You can do anything."

"Oh, Mallory." Amy's head fell back onto his shoulder. Heck, that southern drawl could melt a rock. Catching her friend's attention, McKenna mouthed, "Be a babe."

Amy smiled into her husband's eyes. "McKenna wants me to be a babe. Was I a babe in Italy?"

"Is a bluebird blue, darlin'? You most certainly were."

McKenna swallowed hard. That mantra, "be a babe," had helped Amy through some wild adventures in Italy. Reaching over, she wiped her friend's forehead with a cool cloth. Amy thought she'd never have a baby. Tears prickled in the corner of McKenna's eyes.

Cripes, lately she'd been so darn emotional.

"Thanks, McKenna." Eyes closing, Amy pulled in a deep breath. "I am so ready to have this baby."

"That's my girl. Now we're back on track." Mallory smoothed back Amy's damp hair and kissed her forehead, looking at her as if this woman was his whole world.

A chill skittered down McKenna's spine. Would a man ever look at her like that?

Back to work. The lights in the water birthing suite were low. In the background played the sound of waves lapping a shore, punctuated by cawing seagulls. Most couples that decided on water birth at Montclair Specialty Hospital chose their own soundtrack. Usually, the music tapped into a personal memory. After Amy's trip through Tuscany with Mallory, McKenna could only guess what the beach background conjured up for the pair. They'd visited the Amalfi Coast. How romantic was that?

And today, here they were with McKenna. Felt so cozy. Mary Beth, the neonatal nurse, had been checking in periodically. At a nod from McKenna on the last visit, she'd stayed. Wouldn't be long now. A cool breeze hit McKenna's neck when the door whooshed open. She shot a quick glance over her shoulder, but the door was closing. Was that Logan Castle? Visitors weren't allowed, not even the head of OB.

"Oh, my gosh!" Eyes flying open, Amy grabbed Mallory's arms

so tight he jerked.

McKenna took another peek through the glass viewing panel on the pool. Excitement spiraled through her chest. Amy's baby. Could they ever have imagined this when they sat giggling in the cafeteria of Immaculate Heart of Mary High School?

Bearing down, Amy gritted out. "Come to Mama, Gianna."

"We are waiting for you, baby girl." Mallory looked like he just might faint.

McKenna's own pelvic muscles clenched when Amy's gutsy grunt filled the room. A wave of relief and then again. And again. One final sob, and Gianna Anne Thornton spun into the world, the umbilical cord unwinding behind her in the water.

"Welcome, little water sprite." McKenna scooped up the slippery baby. With a mewling cry, Gianna fanned her delicate hands. McKenna settled the baby into Amy's waiting arms and called the official time of birth. "Four fifty seven."

"Oh, my word. Why, she's just a tiny pollywog, Amy darlin'." Jamming one wet hand through his hair, Mallory blinked furiously. Wouldn't be the first time she'd seen a new father cry in this room. McKenna's throat swelled.

"Great teamwork, Mom and Dad." She handed Mallory the scissors to cut the cord. Once Amy was settled in a bed, McKenna delivered the afterbirth.

McKenna felt the usual adrenaline rush as she worked with the new family. Nothing topped this, in her book. Sure, she grumbled when a late night call wrestled her from a warm bed, but she loved her work. How she wished she could record the goofy sounds new parents made to play back years later, like when the kid wrecked the family car. But today her joy held a weird sadness.

This tug in her gut wasn't the flu. Lately, each birth reminded her how much she wanted her own family. She'd love to pump out a passel of babies. The Kirkpatrick clan called for nothing less. First, she needed the right man, and they weren't turning up in the yellow pages. Besides, the sad fact was, she didn't have a high success rate with relationships.

Time to chart. Rubbing her aching neck, she entered notes into the electronic medical record. Caffeine had to be the next priority. Thank goodness Logan had left. What was that interruption all about? This called for a conversation. Behind her, Amy and Mallory were getting all syrupy sweet with each other. Gianna took care of that with one outraged wail. When her friend began to nurse, McKenna's own breasts felt heavy. The words on the screen blurred.

Reality check. She could never picture this family intimacy with Nick, the last man she'd dated before "pulling the plug" – her brothers' words. They'd jumped all over her when she broke it off. She didn't want to mention that they were part of what Nick couldn't handle. McKenna and her siblings were a package deal. You either fit in or you didn't. Even after two years, Nick didn't. Not really.

The night nurse bustled in to move Amy to the OB floor before shift change.

"McKenna, thank you so much," Amy said as McKenna came close for one more look at the wonder child. "Your godchild thanks you too."

"McKenna, darlin', you are a wonder." Mallory wrapped her in a sweaty hug and she didn't mind one bit.

Warmth flooded McKenna. "I figure that new godmother title gets me to the top of the list when it comes to all family parties—where ever they may be."

Mallory hailed from Savannah and the couple planned to move back there following the birth. McKenna fought the unwelcome wave of sadness. She didn't want Amy and her baby to live that far away. Holding out one forefinger, she felt her heart hitch when Gianna's impossibly long fingers latched on. "Sleep well, little one."

Holding the door open, she followed the gurney into the quiet hallway. The night nurse trundled Amy away, wheels squealing on the tile floor. "Would you give Vanessa the news?" Amy called back, voice echoing in the early morning silence.

"You bet." Since grade school, the three had been inseparable.

McKenna could picture Amy and Vanessa swapping child rearing advice since Bo, Vanessa's little boy, was about four. So strange to be on the outside looking in, but that's exactly how McKenna felt tonight. Amy and her entourage disappeared into the elevator. The doors swished shut, leaving her alone in the cavernous hallway. Usually she was high on excitement following a birth. Tonight felt different. This time her patient was a good friend. Was that teensy pinch in McKenna's chest because they were the same age?

Enough. Picking up the pace, she headed for the lounge.

~.~

Outside the wall of windows, the rising sun tipped the Chicago skyline from gray blue to pink. The staff lounge was empty when McKenna slipped in. The cool air was a welcome change from the birthing suite. She felt tired, sweaty and restless. Burned coffee tinged the air and she got busy rinsing out the carafe and setting a fresh pot on to brew. Then she returned to the sunrise, pressing hands flat on the cool glass. This lounge gave such a great view of the city. Skyscraper lights dotted the semi-darkness and off to the east, Lake Michigan swelled with dark waves.

The scene might be serene but her thoughts raced. She couldn't get Amy and Mallory out of her mind. Heck, she'd coached Amy through that crazy trip. When Amy's engagement fell apart two weeks before her wedding, she'd decided to take the dream honeymoon to Tuscany anyway and used an Internet site to find a roommate. McKenna had totally supported her friend's adventure. What a surprise when Mallory turned out to be a man and an all-around good guy. Confusion had reigned, and McKenna had thoroughly enjoyed weighing in as a consultant. Now the traveling duo were parents. Could life get any better? Sucking in a deep breath, she pushed back from the glass. Were her raging hormones doing a job on her? The door behind her swept open and she pivoted.

"Mother and baby stable. Heart rate of adult female…" Logan was dictating notes for Medical Records, but he stopped short when he saw her. One click and he pocketed the recorder and flipped on the overhead lights. "McKenna."

"Hey, Logan."

Sweeping off his surgery cap, Logan stuffed it in his pocket. "Sorry about interrupting this morning. I thought someone had left the light on." He gave her a sheepish smile.

She swallowed a laugh. So, that had been Logan, saving on electricity?

Chicago Magazine had named Logan Castle one of the city's "Hot Docs." Sometimes she found him preoccupied, a physician who swept through the halls with a ready but reserved smile. Always impeccably groomed, this morning he looked rumpled. Cheeks and chin were edged with stubble. When he pushed one hand through his hair, his fingers left rebellious ridges that glinted blond under the lights.

"Hey, don't let me interrupt your dictation, Logan." McKenna's surgery cap felt tight and she swept it off, tucked it in her pocket and shook out her long hair. She threw back her head with relief.

"Not a problem. Ah, I was just finishing up. Kind of hungry." His eyes never left her hair. Was it oily? She combed her fingers through the mess.

With a jerk, Logan headed for the open box of doughnuts that filled the air with sugary sweetness. While McKenna pulled down a mug, Logan studied the assortment, hands on lean hips. "So what do you think? Chocolate? Plain? I don't want to take your favorite."

"I'm a chocolate freak." That was putting it mildly. She scooped up a chocolate doughnut dripping with chocolate frosting and topped by jimmies.

"Whoa, guess so."

"Never too much of a good thing." She sank her teeth in, and he went back to studying the remaining choices.

"Go for it. Thought you were famished," she managed around her second bite. Delivered in early morning darkness, the doughnuts were still warm. Icing coated her teeth but a quick flick of her tongue took care of that.

Logan had glanced up and his eyes followed her tongue. For a second his full lips worked in silence before, "Right. Well, too much chocolate for me." His hand landed on a plain sour cream doughnut. No frosting, nothing.

Now, what fun was that?

"I believe in quality calories." McKenna laughed, one hand over her mouth to avoid spewing crumbs. She licked a dollop of chocolate from one finger.

His doughnut sailed to the floor with a faint slapping sound. "Damn!" After tossing it in the trash, he grabbed another equally pathetic plain doughnut and took a big bite.

"Coffee?" She held up the pot.

He nodded. Her hand shook a bit as she filled her own mug, and McKenna tightened her hold on the plastic handle. Long night, and she was tired. He must be too, with those red-rimmed eyes. Still, that working man scent called to her. Just something about a guy who exuded heat and passion in his work. Kind of like her five brothers. Even though he could take things too seriously, Logan was probably like that. Dedicated.

But, man, sometimes the head of OB could be so serious.

Reaching into the cupboard, McKenna pulled out a mug that

read, "Snap out of it…smile." She poured Logan's coffee and handed it to him. Glancing at the wording, he grinned before taking a sip, laugh lines crinkling the corners of his eyes. "Interesting…and tasty."

She took a quick gulp that seared her mouth. Ducking her head, she kicked off her clogs in front of the brown tweed sofa and sank down, folding her legs under her.

"So, when did you come in?" The sofa creaked as Logan took a spot next to her. *Not going to dash out the door, as usual?* With the exception of her interview, McKenna couldn't recall ever talking to Logan Castle one-on-one. Even then, the CEO had been in the room.

She swiveled to face him. "Got the call late yesterday. Met Amy here about half an hour later. She's actually a good friend."

"Bet that felt great. Still, long haul for you." When he stretched his legs out in front of him, the scrubs tightened around muscled thighs. *This man should never wear a lab coat again. The crisp white jacket cloaked all the good parts.*

But where was she? "A woman labors at her own speed, and I respect that. During the evaluation process, the midwives gauge the woman's potential and take her preferences into account. I don't believe in Pitocin unless it's necessary." *Good Lord, she was tossing out words like extra surgical supplies he just might need.* Her colleagues in For Women, their midwifery group, often accused her of climbing on a soapbox. Sucking in a quick breath, she shut up and went back to her coffee.

Logan's intelligent gray eyes studied her as if she'd just said something profound. Warmth that didn't come from the coffee bathed her cheeks and chest. Doggone, she hated the way her blushes could become freaking forest fires.

"When it comes to Pit, I totally agree. To my knowledge, we only use it when absolutely needed here at Montclair." Logan seemed to be turning each word over in his mind, like a rock that might hide a complete new world underneath. "I know you're in favor of more natural birthing methods, McKenna, although we've never had a chance to talk privately. What brought you to midwifery?"

"The women, the babies and…just all that." Her voice ended on a soft note. "My mother delivered all seven of us at home."

"Really?" Logan's eyes widened. "That's amazing."

"She's one tough lady."

He grinned. "Sounds like you come by that naturally."

"Thank you. I think."

His head fell onto the back of the sofa and the strong neck that suggested more football than basketball turned. "Everything's going all right in For Women? I try to touch base with all the OBs regularly. Didn't mean to ignore the midwives." He'd rolled his head toward her, as if on a pillow. They stared at each other in silence.

Her heartbeat revved. Had to remind herself that this was Logan Castle, for Pete's sake.

"Fine, ah, we're just fine. Any truth to the rumor that we might get a new LDRP at Montclair? I mean, it would be great not to shift patients around after they delivered."

With an LDRP, women labored, delivered, and recovered in one room. Like all the other mothers who delivered in the water birthing suite or the OR, Amy had been taken from one floor to another after giving birth. Not ideal and disruptive for the new family.

Leaning forward, Logan rested his arms on his knees. Darn. She missed his head on the pillow, er, sofa.

"I've heard the Foundation might shake loose some funding for OB. But I don't know if there's been any real focus outlined for those dollars. An LDRP? There may be other priorities." His sandy brows drew together.

"What would those be, Logan?" She wanted everything to be clear. No hidden agendas.

His frown deepened as he launched into a detailed description of a new ventilation system and in-suite imaging equipment for the OR that allowed immediate diagnosis during a procedure. She was afraid her eyes might roll back in her head.

Maybe it showed. "You can never be too careful when it comes to patient care, can you?" His voice dropped to a low question.

"I'm with you on that, but more equipment, huh?" McKenna rubbed her forehead with the tips of her fingers. Montclair already excelled when it came to the latest technology.

"Shouldn't we do everything possible to lower the margin of error?" Genuine concern darkened his eyes.

"Sure, but isn't giving birth a natural process? It's not like we're working with a joint that needs replacing or a broken leg. Seems to me we can help that process in natural ways." Thank God the air conditioning kicked on.

"Sometimes you can hit a bump in the road. Isn't it our job to do everything to prevent that?" Logan turned to her like he really was searching for an answer.

"Of course it is." McKenna didn't want to disagree with the head of her department. Negotiating consensus was her way of resolving differences. Discussion about the water birthing suite had gotten pretty heated in department meetings after her arrival. But Warren Mitchell, their CEO and a heck of a great guy, had insisted. Expanding the concept to a complete renovation of the OB floor might be an uphill battle with the head of the department.

"In any case, I hope the Foundation will leave it to us, the clinicians, to decide how the money would be spent." While he nursed his coffee, Logan's full lower lip stayed wet. "On *safe* options."

She jerked to attention. "Natural childbirth, hypnosis, water birthing—of course our approach is safe."

"Is it?" His eyes became a deep cauldron. "Not always, McKenna. Not for everyone."

The wind was knocked out of her by the angsting in his eyes. Whatever demons drove Logan Castle, she bet they kept him up at night.

The door blasted open. "Any yogurt in the place before I start surgery?" After flicking on the overhead lights, Griff Ramsey headed for the refrigerator.

Logan and McKenna both sat back, like they were retreating from a ledge. Griff continued to motor-mouth. "Two hips and one knee replacement in a row. Have to talk to my office about this scheduling." The orthopedic surgeon grabbed a carton of yogurt from the refrigerator, rooted around in a drawer for a spoon and then turned. "Hey, Logan. McKenna. You two have a delivery this morning?" A burly guy, Griff looked from one to the other as if they were in a huddle, deciding on the next football play.

"I had a delivery in the OR," Logan began. "And McKenna, in the water birthing suite."

"Right, right." Griff's eyes did a quick guy-sweep. Griff appreciated women, which might be why he was newly divorced. Still, he was fun and a darned good doctor. "That's a neat thingy they play over the PA." His eyes shifted to the ceiling, like the lullaby might start any moment. "What is that anyway?"

"Brahms' lullaby," McKenna supplied. "Every time a baby's born, they play it over the PA."

"They do?" Logan looked at her as if she'd just made this up.

"Yep, we made that decision at one of our section meetings," she reminded him.

Tossing his empty carton in the trash, Griff dropped the spoon in the sink with a loud clunk. "Logan, golf this Saturday? Shady Run? Duncan and Gary are on board."

"Sounds great."

So, the head of OB didn't spend each weekend going over nosocomial infection reports?

"Griff, how's that little boy of yours?" Logan asked.

Griff pivoted. "On the mend but he won't be playing any more baseball this season. Tricky, those compound fractures. You know kids, always breaking something. Thanks for asking."

"Sure. Glad to hear it." Logan's obvious concern was kind of touching. She wondered if he had kids.

As the door closed behind Dr. Ramsey, Logan and McKenna both jumped up. The long night was catching up with her. One more check on Amy and she was taking off. Maybe she could grab a few winks before her clinic appointments.

"Gotta get going. See you later, Dr. Castle," she murmured, shoving her feet back into her clogs. She set her cup in the sink, and so did Logan.

He held the door open for her. "It's Logan, McKenna," he said softly as she passed him. "Call me Logan."

"Got it."

"See you later, McKenna. And I'll give you an update on any pending improvements when I hear more." After a quick parting smile, Logan loped down the hall with the stride of a golfer on his game.

As she trotted off to check on Amy again, McKenna exhaled.

~.~

"What's up?" Selena Ruiz, another midwife at For Women, looked up when McKenna ambled into the locker room. Amy was settled in upstairs with Mallory keeping close watch. So cozy and cute.

McKenna sank onto the hard bench. "Had a talk with Logan Castle." Hands on her thighs, she stared at the green locker in front of her.

Selena's head jerked around. "Castle—our Hot Doc who doesn't know it? What about?"

Twirling the dial on her lock, McKenna struggled to recall the combination, mind still on her little chat with Logan. "Um, a new LDRP unit."

"How cool is that! Water birth included in the plan?"

"Nothing's been decided. Sure seems like Logan's in favor of new equipment instead of supporting an LDRP unit. You could say we had a difference of opinion."

"He can be strong minded, but still..."

"His patients love him. I read that all the time in our website comments. He listens to women. Sensitive guy. Still, not sure we're on the same page. He wants more equipment and high tech instead of supporting our natural methods. At least, that's how I see it."

Selena crammed her enormous orange purse into the locker. "He's a guy who doesn't like to leave anything to chance. Something sad in his background. Can't remember what, though."

McKenna batted one hand against the unyielding lock.

"Logan is doing some outstanding work with in vitro fertilization. Some new process that has to do with maturing eggs."

"Puh-lease." McKenna groaned. "Old eggs. That's the last thing I want to hear about right now."

"Not *old*. Maturing," Selena said softly, sliding over to drape one arm across McKenna's shoulders. "Look, girlfriend. You have to date more and work less. Get those eggs ready to launch."

"You're probably right." Ah, ten, twenty-one, seventeen. McKenna yanked the lock open. Her hands grabbed folders, but her mind couldn't lose hold of Logan's stormy eyes. Being a fixer, she always had a compelling urge to solve other people's problems.

After closing her locker and snapping the lock shut, McKenna pushed to her feet. "How's my handsome brother? Haven't seen him for a while. Any wedding bells on the horizon?" Selena had been dating Seth for a couple of years. No secret that McKenna would love to have Selena as a sister-in-law.

"Not yet. You know something I don't know?" Wrapping her arms around herself, Selena leaned against the lockers. She was definitely in la-la land.

"Spill, girlfriend," McKenna teased.

"Nothing to tell." Selena's lips tilted in a wickedly sensual smile.

Seth was an EMT, but this was more than a career match. Selena could enter a room, and Seth would zone in on her like a heat-seeking missile. He made it clear that Selena was always on his radar screen. At a party, McKenna's former boyfriend Nick had always worked the room. Told her she was so independent, she didn't need him on her arm.

Plunking back down, McKenna opened her locker again, stuck her material back inside and slammed it shut. "Heck, I'm not going home. I'll just head to one of the on-call rooms. One hour, that's all I need before my morning appointments."

Selena was barreling toward the door. "Don't forget the Midwives in Action meeting tonight. We're making plans for the Guatemala mission."

"Got it on my calendar." McKenna took off, grabbed the elevator to the eighth floor and slipped into a cozy, dimly lit on-call room.

Throwing herself on one of the firm cots, McKenna set her

phone alarm for one hour and texted Vanessa news about Amy's baby. Then she tried to get comfortable on the hard cot. She couldn't get Logan out of her head. He'd left her riled and she told herself it was that pained look that flickered in his gray eyes. What was his problem? Somehow she had to finagle more time with the head of her department and soon.

Patience had never been her strong suit.

Chapter 2

"Logan, come on in." Leaving his high-backed leather chair, Warren Mitchell motioned Logan toward the small conference table. Shirt sleeves rolled up, the CEO always looked ready to take on the world, although the wall of windows overlooking the lake provided plenty of distraction.

"What's on your mind?" Logan took a seat. Office hours started in thirty minutes, but he'd give Warren all the time he needed. This was the man who kept Montclair at the top of its game.

"As you probably know, the Foundation has been talking about funding another hospital improvement."

"I've heard rumors. What do they have in mind?"

Settling back, Warren rested his gaze on the sailboats below before circling back to Logan. "What do you see as the need for your department?"

After his conversation with McKenna that morning, Logan wasn't quite sure. "Updating the OR suites would be one idea." He launched into the highlights of the new technology.

"And how do your colleagues feel?"

"They may have other ideas, and I'd like to have those identified." He smiled, remembering his discussion with McKenna that morning. As his grandmother would say, the woman was quite

18

a character.

"The board meeting is at the end of the month," Warren continued. "Can you gather input and work up a rough presentation? Of course, Marketing is at your disposal."

"Sure, we can pull something together." But Warren's calculating look told Logan there was more.

"Logan, I'd like you to involve McKenna Kirkpatrick in the planning. As head of For Women, she can represent the midwives. You'll make a good team."

Suddenly, he couldn't seem to escape McKenna Kirkpatrick. "No problem. McKenna makes sense."

"She's plugged into the community and has a good read on what women want today." Warren was nodding in his patriarchal manner. "If we're going to introduce a new concept, it should be done with flair."

"Flair? Warren, this isn't a reality decorating show on TV."

The bushy eyebrows of his old family friend rose. "We need women's input. After all, they're the customer. And McKenna has that spark about her."

After that, Logan didn't hear a word.

Thinking back to his early morning encounter with McKenna, he felt a warm rush that made him change positions in the barrel chair. He hadn't felt like this in a long time and didn't know if he liked it. Since her arrival, the feisty redhead had become that "hot-headed midwife," at least for him. She disrupted meetings with questions that took them way off track.

Today she'd had him chuckling. That coffee mug? No accident.

Their conversation had left him riled and it felt damn good. But their plans for the department might put them on a collision course.

"You're frowning." Warren's eyes drilled into him.

"Just lack of sleep."

Warren didn't look convinced. "McKenna has her finger on the pulse of today's woman. Why, she keeps that water birthing suite busy every week. The women go home and write about us on one Internet forum or another."

The thought of McKenna's delicate, lightly freckled fingers on his pulse brought a warm flush. Good God. He had to snap out of it. Warren was still talking.

"McKenna is tuned in. Connected to the community. She comes from a huge West Side family, with siblings involved in the betterment of the city." Warren's eyes sparked with the fire of a man who loved his work.

"West Side?" He'd grown up in River Forest but the name Kirkpatrick wasn't familiar.

Warren shrugged. "Oak Park isn't quite River Forest, but still the kind of people your grandfather envisioned when he founded this hospital."

Ah, there it was. Warren always positioned him so Logan faced the portrait of his grandfather, Winston Montclair. The original painting resided in Grandmother Cecilia's home in River Forest. This copy hung in the CEO's office with another in the hospital foyer.

The message was clear. Logan should live up to his family

name. He checked his watch. "Fine. Sounds good. I'll contact McKenna."

"Great. Let's keep things moving." Vaulting to his feet, Warren clapped Logan on the shoulder and walked him to the door. "Seriously, how is everything, Logan?"

"Fine. Couldn't be better." His mouth felt tight. He couldn't stand pity.

With a slow nod, Warren gave him the two-handed handshake. "Glad to hear it. Now, have some fun with this project. You deserve it."

As he left the office of the CEO, Logan wasn't thinking about the project or what he "deserved," as if life were fair. No, his thoughts were on coppery red hair and a woman who'd pretty much told him to loosen up…and with a coffee cup, no less.

Now they had to work together, and she'd already made her priorities clear. She'd want more of the alternative methods that science couldn't track or measure. How could he make her see reason? He ran through some discussion points in his mind, the way he had on college debate team. Worked every time.

~.~

Tuesday night, and the Purple Frog was jammed. Logan studied his frosty mug of Amstel lager. Peanut shells crunched underfoot and the place reeked of beer tinged by smoke from ten years ago, like the bar was still exhaling. As he hunkered down, Warren's directive rang in his ears along with head banger music.

McKenna had sounded excited when he called and asked to meet about the future of the obstetrics unit. She'd picked the place for the meeting. He hadn't been in the noisy bar for a long time. Running one finger down the frosty mug, he trained his eyes on the front door. When he caught the gleam of her red hair, he stood and waved. The linen sport jacket he'd thrown on over his blue polo felt warm and out of place. Shrugging out of it, he folded it up on the wooden bench seat and sat down.

"Sorry I'm late." Sliding in across from him, McKenna pushed her hair back. A wave of fresh air rolled over him while words bubbled from her like Buckingham Fountain on Chicago's shoreline. "Had a couple of add-ons. You know how that goes. Taking patients on Tuesday can free up my Wednesdays. But then Wednesdays get busy too."

She made his head spin. "Not too long ago I didn't have hours on Wednesdays. The good old days." He sat back, enjoying the view.

"So you were one of those, huh?" She gave him a lop-sided grin. "Probably busy golfing and other fun things."

Golf and sailing were his two outlets—sometimes alone, not that he liked it. "How did you guess? But now the schedule is getting too backed up with only the three of us to handle it. We're recruiting. I have a candidate coming in next week." The recruiters better come through for him. The candidate's name had sounded familiar, like someone he'd known in prep school. "Golf's great exercise. Beats going crazy."

Tilting her head, she chuckled. "I'd like to see you go crazy."

Almost sounded like a challenge. He waved to the waiter, who headed over with a bowl of peanuts. "Are you on call?"

"Nope. Selena's got me covered. You?" McKenna wasn't wearing lipstick and somehow that appealed to him.

"Gary's on tonight. What would you like to drink?"

"I'll have a beer," she said, glancing at his lager. "Whatever you're having looks good."

"You drink beer?" Most of the women he took out ordered a Cosmo.

That cute grin flashed again. "Not in a sipping mood so bring it on. I'm parched."

"A pitcher please," he told the waiter.

Her delicate eyebrows peaked. "Whoa. A pitcher. You're upping the ante?"

"So, you play poker too, I suppose." My, she was full of surprises.

"With five brothers I had no choice."

"Warren was telling me you have a large family."

She frowned. "You were talking about me?"

He could kick himself. "Just business. Must be nice to have brothers and sisters."

"Crazy is more like it." Her smile held fond memories. The waiter returned with the pitcher and a mug for McKenna. After Logan filled it, she hoisted the frosty glass like a pro. A beer foam moustache beaded her upper lip and she quickly erased it with the tip of her tongue.

The heat that unfurled in his chest and headed lower caught him by surprise.

The music had changed from heavy metal to bluesy jazz, the

kind that mellowed him out. But no chance of that after McKenna's antics with her tongue. Muscles he hadn't used in quite a while leapt to life—like a much-needed wake-up call.

She leaned closer, as if sharing dark secrets. "It was insane, all those kids, but I wouldn't trade them for the world." Her eyes got this faraway look, like she was remembering boisterous Christmas mornings and graduations with her family cheering wildly in the audience.

Enough of that. He regrouped. "So, I suppose you have tons of nephews and nieces."

"Kirkpatricks reproduce like rabbits. Most of us, anyway." Rubbing her upper arms briskly with her hands, she shivered.

He shot to his feet. "Air conditioning's too high in here. Here, take my jacket." Shaking it out, he swung it around her delicate shoulders.

"Thanks, Logan. It was great to get your call," she continued after he'd slid back into the booth. When she tossed her head, a mischievous wave of hair fell over one eye. McKenna pushed it back but too late. That vampy image was going to stay with him and he welcomed it. No personal life, anyway. Tonight, he felt relaxed and energized. The air seemed to crackle with electricity. Crunching a fistful of peanuts, he popped one in his mouth and got back on topic.

"As I said on the phone, the rumor is true about the Foundation," he began. "They would like to fund an obstetrics project. Warren asked me for input and I mentioned both the OR renovation or your LDRP suggestion."

"That's great, Logan." But she sounded wary.

"Warren suggested we call our group together, both physicians and midwives, and arrive at consensus. Shouldn't take much, right?" Looking at her pursed lips, Logan decided that might be wishful thinking.

McKenna took a deep gulp of beer, leaving another foamy moustache. "Consensus, huh? Should be interesting." Her tongue reached out and traced her lips. His mouth went dry.

"He'd like us…ah, like us to present to the Foundation Board in a couple of weeks, so we have to get on this."

Her fingers traced the upper rim of her mug. Watching her hand, he felt a light tingle in his chest.

As if she'd touched him. As if he'd liked it. A lot.

"Gotta get moving on this one, I guess." She looked to him for agreement.

"I totally agree."

"Who should be on the committee?"

Reeling in his wandering mind, he pulled his thoughts together. When was the last time he'd felt this distracted? For a few minutes, they discussed department staff. "Once we decide on our direction, Marketing will help us tee up the presentation, but we probably won't get to that level of detail at this point. We need a basic model and some numbers to put—"

The soft coolness of McKenna's palm on his forearm silenced him. "Sorry, Logan, but I'm starving. It's been a long day and I forgot to eat lunch."

"Sorry. And here I am, blabbing away." Grabbing menus, he

handed one to her.

As she pored over the list, his jacket slipped off taking one shoulder of her deep V-neck with it. She didn't bother to tug her sweater into place. Reminded him of a robe, worn to the breakfast table before they tumbled back into bed.

The thought brought another surge of heat. Flipping open the menu, Logan scanned the list. "Good God, you could get atherosclerosis just looking at this menu."

Her robust laugh was followed by, "You are such a hoot."

Thank God their waiter arrived.

"Let's see. Think I'll have the Burger Bacado with…" She looked up and met the waiter's eyes. He seemed mesmerized by her tawny lashes. Or maybe it was the neckline of her green sweater. McKenna was generously endowed. With a smile that said you-naughty-boy, she yanked her top up. Not that the move hid much. "You have sweet potato fries, right?" There was that cute nose crinkle again.

"Yes, ma'am." The waiter lifted his eyes for one moment and then dove back into her cleavage like he was cramming for a Human Physiology exam.

"Great. I'll have the Burger Bacado and sweet potato fries." Beaming up at the waiter, she tucked the menu back behind the napkin dispenser.

With considerably less interest, the young man turned to Logan. "I'll have the veggie burger with coleslaw," he said. "Is the slaw fresh every day?'

The waiter blinked. "Yeah, sure. The bags come in every day, I guess."

Right. Logan liked his produce fresh. After the waiter left, the panting of Donna Summers cloaked their conversation. Just what he needed.

McKenna took another swig of her beer then leaned forward. "Now back to business. How should we approach this meeting? What do you want me to bring?"

"I was planning on gathering some research. You might want to do that too. You know, just the facts."

Her auburn brows had arched and he had to chuckle. His grandmother often teased him about his preoccupation with "the finer points," as she put it. "Too much detail?"

Head tilting, McKenna grew serious. Two little lines bracketed her mouth, as if straining from the weight of her luscious lips. "Your patients respect your attention to detail. Certainly you know that, Logan. And your empathy," she added.

"Attention to detail." The words felt like a prison sentence, but he managed a wry smile. "Guess that about wraps me up in a book."

Her greenish eyes softened to moss. "It's a good book."

Wasn't that the biggest turn-on he'd ever heard?

"I've been reading about your fertility clinic," McKenna continued. "You bring hope to a lot of women. That's huge."

Usually compliments sounded contrived and left him cold. Hers didn't. "We're recruiting so I can spend more time developing the clinic. You might say it's my passion."

"Everyone should have one…passion, that is." Her green eyes

burned almost blue.

Sucking in a slow breath, he was relieved to see their waiter approaching. The scent of grilled burgers reminded him that he was hungry. "Ketchup?" he asked, lifting the red container.

"Yes, please."

Lifting the top of her hamburger bun after he handed her the ketchup, McKenna swirled a red stream over her sweet potato fries and then doused the burger like she was putting out a fire. Eyes sparkling, she took a generous bite and began to chew with slow appreciation. Was that her or Donna Summers groaning?

He was toast. Logan reached for his beer.

Between fries she said, "You know, I've heard that how a person eats tells you how they make love. What do you think?" She glanced at him, all wide-eyed and innocent.

Choking, he spewed droplets of beer onto the table and grabbed a napkin. "I really haven't thought about it." Now he could think of nothing else. Had she noticed that he'd edged his coleslaw to the side of his plate? Nothing fresh about it. And how he did like fresh.

"Just hypothetical, of course, but I was talking about this with some girlfriends." Her voice had almost taken on a clinical note—like they were discussing the difference between a vaginal delivery versus a C-section. Her fingers dallied with her fries, eyes gauging his response from lowered lashes.

She was playing with him.

Time to turn the tables. "Did you come up with anything?" Why was he so mesmerized by the faint pattern of freckles on her hands? She lifted a fry to her mouth and ran it along her lips before devouring it.

He had to remind himself to chew. Chew or choke to death.

Tawny eyelashes fluttering, she gave grave consideration to swirling the next fry in her ketchup. Then she wagged it at him provocatively. For him, french fries would never be the same. "Obstetrics and gynecology have their roots in human sexuality, right? In your opinion, does our enjoyment of food indicate our enjoyment of, well, other sensual pursuits?"

He'd lost her with "human sexuality." Head swimming, he waved to the waiter. His thighs zinged as if burned by a laser gone wild.

"I really hadn't thought about it," he croaked. McKenna was grinning when the waiter arrived. "Water, please."

When had he lost control of this meeting?

Her lips closed over another fry, a small comma of ketchup escaping from one corner of her mouth. Her tongue made short work of that.

"You really are outrageous," he breathed. *Good God. Did I say that out loud?*

Smiling, she continued her sexy, mind-numbing chewing. But McKenna didn't seem to know it was sexy. At least, he didn't think she did. That in itself was a turn-on.

Finally, the waiter returned, and Logan downed the glass of cold water in three gulps.

"So, tell me about your family," she said, changing the topic. "Siblings?"

"Sadly, no." He easily slipped into words that had served him well through the years. "Only son of Isabel Montclair and William Castle. My father, an orthopedic surgeon, suffered an untimely death in a ski accident when I was only four. Six months later my mother married the first in a succession of replacements, while my grandmother took over the childrearing. Currently Mom lives in Monte Carlo with a man whose name, I believe, is Guido. Number five."

"Whoa. I am so sorry." McKenna looked stricken.

Gaze dropping, he swirled the warm beer left in the bottom of his mug. "In many ways, I've been very fortunate. My grandmother has been the backbone of our family since my grandfather's death. She lives in River Forest. In her early eighties, she still plays golf." His lovely but eccentric grandmother had spunk, kind of like McKenna.

"River Forest? We're almost neighbors."

"I like the West Side." He smiled, remembering racing his new Corvette down Division Street at two in the morning when he was a junior in high school. His grandmother had not been happy to get that call from the police.

"Sounds like you two have a great relationship." McKenna's eyes softened.

"The best. She's a great lady and I didn't always make life easy for her."

"Doesn't she still come to the opening of new units? You know, as widow of our founder?"

"You've done your homework." Not many of the staff realized

that he had Montclair blood. "Yes, my grandmother keeps up a family presence."

"And you're divorced?" McKenna continued.

"Three years ago, no children."

But he wasn't about to carve out any more personal information and was relieved when his pager went off. Just Gary about one of their patients being admitted, but the break in conversation bought him time. He texted his partner the necessary information. The return to work restored a sense of calm. Not that he didn't enjoy being rattled by McKenna. The banter took him back to college, before his life had gone south. Seconds later, he took care of the bill, although McKenna had grabbed for it.

"Business expense." He tugged it out of her fingers.

With a shrug, she slung her purse over one shoulder. They pushed through the crowd and headed for the door.

"Thursday okay? Early meeting, say seven or so?" he asked, enjoying her curves pressed against his body. "I'll have Tamara, our receptionist, check with the other staff members."

"Sure, seven is fine. I'll rally the troops." She was so close he could smell the onion from her burger. An underlying scent teased him, and he inhaled. Peaches. She smelled like onions and peaches. What a tasty combination.

The evening air bathed his face as he pushed the door open. He wanted to walk the three blocks to the lake and dive in. Since it was May, he didn't have to brace against the eye-searing wind that often sliced through the tall Chicago buildings.

The street lamp set McKenna's hair on fire as she threw her

head back. "Thanks for dinner, Dr. Cas—"

"Logan."

"Logan." She held the final "n" in his name, and his gaze clung to her lips as she slipped his jacket off and handed it to him.

"Hey, you guys. Small world, huh?" Griff Ramsey barreled toward them, his arm around a scrub nurse Logan had seen around the OR. Another hot blonde.

A question burned in Griff's eyes but Logan ignored it. "Business meeting," he threw out.

"Right, me too," Griff tossed back, grabbing the door and his date. "Have fun now, you two."

For a second, McKenna looked stunned. Then she laughed and lifted one shoulder. "Seems like we may have some explaining to do."

Obviously, she was a woman who didn't care what other people thought.

"Night, Logan." Her voice carried on the early summer air as she backed away.

"Can I walk you to your car?"

"No need. I lucked out." She pointed to an orange jeep parked at the curb. "Guy was leaving when I got here."

"Lucky break."

They waved good-bye, and he nearly walked into a parking meter when he turned. Setting off for the garage, he broke into an easy jog. By the time he reached his car on the top floor of a parking garage, their meeting had replayed in his mind at least four times.

The next day, clinic was crazy for McKenna. Since Mirandah Masterson had her twin girls two months earlier, she'd been sending her pregnant North Shore friends to For Women, not that McKenna was complaining. By the time clinic hours were wrapping up, McKenna felt exhausted. While checking her watch, she caught sight of Selena in the hall. With a quick wave, she moved into her office and Selena followed. "Busy day?" McKenna asked.

Selena stifled a yawn. "Had a late night with Andi Lewis but all went well. After two boys, their little girl is beautiful. Photo's up on the Wall of Pride." The bulletin board in their waiting area was filled with the ruddy faces of newborns cuddled by pleased parents. Those photos were McKenna's real paycheck.

She plopped into her desk chair, and Selena took the wing chair across from her. "I'll have to check it out. Had an interesting meeting with Logan Castle last night." Keeping her tone casual wasn't easy. She'd kind of pushed the envelope with the head of their department.

"Are you blushing?" Selena's eyes widened.

McKenna laughed, fanning herself with a memo from her desk. "I think Logan is trying to develop a rapport with me because we have to work together. Nothing more. Kind of cute and funny in a sweet way." She was still trying to figure him out.

"Montclair's Hot Doc—cute and funny?" Selena hooted.

"Trust me. Hot Doc can be both."

Sitting back in her chair, Selena propped her feet up on McKenna's desk. "He's over the top organized. You know that, right?"

"He's more than that. Trust me, he's not at all the aloof doctor we see in the halls." But enough of defending Logan.

Her friend's forehead was furrowed with doubt.

"He's pulling together a committee to discuss improvements to the obstetrics floor. We're not exactly together on this one." Understatement of the year. As McKenna told Selena about the meeting, her reservations came spilling out. She really did not want to back an OB project focused only on newer technology. "That's just not the way our practice works."

"All the docs at Montclair know that," Selena said with a head shake that set her curls bouncing. "Maybe Logan Castle needs reminding."

"He means well," McKenna added, maybe a little too quickly.

Legs stretched out, Selena looked lost in thought. "This is going to be tricky."

"Maybe." McKenna yawned. The thought of going head-to-head with Logan both exhausted and excited her. She glanced at the framed degrees on her wall. The elaborate scripting revealed nothing of the all-night study sessions with Selena—the pots of coffee consumed and secrets shared. Still, she held back from talking about her conflicted feelings when it came to the head of their department.

Selena checked her watch. "Why don't you go home?"

"Pretty soon." McKenna shook herself. "Mary Pat Gregory just called about some spotting. I told Lucy to have her come right in."

Hands on her knees, Selena shoved herself up. "Well, I'm heading out. See you tomorrow. Your brother and I are hosting a family NASCAR get-together Sunday. The usual drill. Bring your strawberry jello mold?"

"Got it." After Selena disappeared, McKenna shuffled through her phone messages and began her call-backs.

Two calls later, Lucy, one of their medical assistants, appeared at the door. "Mary Pat's in room four."

"Be right there." McKenna found her patient stretched out on the exam table, the hem of her gown fisted in tight hands.

Mary Pat raised puffy, bloodshot eyes. "I'm spotting."

"Happens sometimes with a new pregnancy. Why don't you tell me more? How long? And what color?" As she listened to Mary Pat's answers, McKenna did a quick exam. Because of her age, Mary Pat was a high-risk patient, and McKenna checked out every possible cause.

"Sometimes discharge carries out residue from your last period," she explained as she finished up. "I'm not saying that's what this is, but I don't see any problems right now. Cramping?"

Mary Pat shook her head. "And I don't think I spotted in the last hour or so," she added, anxiety thinning her voice.

"Excellent." McKenna helped her sit up. "Go home and relax. Have Joe order a pizza."

Exhaling, Mary Pat sent McKenna a shaky smile. "I hope you don't think I'm an alarmist."

"Not at all." Heck, McKenna would be on the phone to Selena in a second if this were her. "And don't hesitate to contact me. Give me a call tomorrow to let me know how tonight goes, okay?"

By the time Mary Pat left the office, only one lamp glowed in the waiting area. Dorothy had left for the day, and McKenna closed up. Driving home, she turned Selena's comments over in her mind.

Logan might be a real challenge.

Something she'd never been able to resist.

Chapter 3

He was looking good. Sitting at the head of the table in a blue oxford cloth shirt, red striped tie and crisp white coat, Logan could have been a cover for the *Chicago Magazine* Hot Docs issue.

But wait. He'd already done that.

"Morning, McKenna."

She felt that smile clear to her toes. "Dr. Castle. Um, Logan."

His grin tweaked up as he went back to the notes in his hands.

After a few hellos, McKenna poured a cup of coffee and took a seat at the opposite end of the table. Was this polite professional at the head of the table the real Logan Castle? Maybe the Hot Doc she'd discovered at the Purple Frog had been conjured up by a few beers and some mood music. All in her head. She tried not to notice Logan's pink cheeks, like he'd just come from a hot shower. My, her imagination was working overtime this morning. The image flooded her with heat.

Flipping open her portfolio, she wrote "LDRP Meeting" at the top of the page. She fought a smile, wondering what Logan had jotted on his notepad. Probably "New OR Equipment."

"Ready to start?" Looking up, he shot her the same delighted grin he'd worn watching her swirl sweet potato fries in ketchup. She blushed remembering how bold she'd been.

"Whenever you are." Nope, the rascal was for real.

Bethany, another midwife in their practice, plopped down next to her. "Hey, McKenna. Exciting, huh?"

"Time will tell." The thought of going head-to-head with Logan, if it came to that, sent a ribbon of anxiety through her body. Downing a slug of coffee, McKenna teared up when it singed her mouth. When would she learn to take things slow?

Eric Stone, also from Logan's practice, took the seat next to Gary. Next to them was Bob McCracken, who headed up another OB GYN group at Montclair. McKenna was glad to see Regina Drury, the Vice President of Patient Care. She reported to Regina and liked the level-headed older woman who'd been recruited from a busy urban Florida hospital. If it came to a vote, Regina would probably support the LDRP proposal. Selena hurried in and, with a quick apology, took a seat between Gary and Eric, throwing McKenna a quick wink.

At promptly seven o'clock, Logan began. "Thank you all for coming. As I told you over the phone, the Montclair Foundation Board is considering shaking loose some funding for improvements in the obstetrics department. We're here to talk about just what those upgrades might be." He cut his words off crisply, one hand playing with his striped tie.

Hard to believe this was the same guy whose troubled eyes had wrung her heart when he mentioned being an only child. Really, what was sadder than that? She wouldn't know what to do without her big, noisy family. He began to send information packets around the table.

Darn it. She'd meant to put together information about LDRP but it had slipped her mind.

Logan dove right in. "You have in your hands some background information on technological updates that could set the Montclair Obstetrics Department apart. Just one option for us to consider."

Selena arched her brows, but McKenna shook her head. She'd wait her turn to explain the one-room option. She may not have a packet of information but she was pretty good at thinking on her feet. To begin, Logan fielded questions. Gary and Eric seemed familiar with the new technology, but Bob wanted to be filled in, which gave her some time. Jotting down some points, she considered how to couch the alternative option. When Logan turned to her, she was ready. "McKenna? I believe you and your group had some suggestions?"

She sucked in a deep breath. "We sure do. That is, I think I speak for the midwives." Bethany and Selena both nodded. "We were hoping for a total reconfiguration of the floor." The heads of the physicians came up. Forging ahead, McKenna described the concept of the labor delivery recovery and post partum unit, beginning with the multi-functional bed and concluding with the home-like furniture and hidden high-tech equipment. She would have killed for a tidy packet like the one Logan had brought but that wasn't going to stop her. "Often times, each room has a birthing pool that can double as a jacuzzi," she added. No sense in dancing around that detail.

"Like the birthing suite you have now?" Gary asked.

"Exactly, only this time the birthing pool would be a part of a much larger concept."

McKenna often talked with her hands. Once or twice she found Logan following her flitting fingers, but when she mentioned the birthing pool, he tented his own hands against his lips before asking, "Would you really need one in every room?"

Taking a deep breath, McKenna nodded. "Usage is growing."

Logan didn't look convinced. She wanted to wave a sweet potato fry in his face again. But all she had was a mug of cold coffee. Her mouth was dry, and she took a sip.

Regina Drury leaned forward. "Let's talk about space. The old neurology area on the eighth floor is empty now that renovation of the fourth floor has been completed. Neuro moved down to four last week. If we go ahead with this idea, the OB unit on six could continue as usual while we renovate the eighth floor. Warren might be open to that."

McKenna could've kissed her. "What a great view of the city for our moms."

Regina nodded. "No other OB unit in the city has that benefit."

Logan's flush had paled. "But that's not patient care. It's window dressing."

McKenna bit back her frustration. How could she help him see this in a different light? "Isn't anything that improves the patient experience considered patient care?"

The other doctors kept silent. Selena and Beth exchanged glances. What was McKenna missing here? The air felt charged. Out in the hall, pages came over the PA system. The hospital was gearing up for another day. They had to wrap up the meeting.

"Where do we would go from here?" Regina glanced from Logan to McKenna.

Although McKenna knew this might be the time to draw back and give Logan time to digest the information, her words came rushing out. "Although I think new technology is important, isn't it just one piece of the birth experience?"

The only sound in the room was the low hum of the air conditioning.

"Our patients have similar needs, McKenna." Thank goodness Gary finally spoke up. "Sure, the patients would probably like to be in one room and their families would enjoy the convenience." Eric nodded and the two physicians looked to Logan for agreement. Two spots of color had appeared on his cheeks.

"Do we really want to tear everything up and start over?" Logan asked with a puzzled frown.

"We're building, not tearing anything up. Sometimes it's good to begin again." How McKenna wished she could smooth that frown from Logan's forehead.

"For a lot of people, it's not that simple, McKenna." Logan's gray eyes had turned to slate. He dealt with some difficult cases. She realized that.

Regina was sending her a message with raised eyebrows, but McKenna wasn't going to back down. Let the silence settle. She didn't care how uncomfortable it became. Her brothers had often coached her with "The first person who speaks in a negotiation loses."

Oh, how she'd spoken up with Nick. Pressed him for answers. And she'd totally lost. She never wanted to feel that rejection again.

"Well, let's pick up on this discussion next week," Logan finally suggested. The whole room exhaled but consensus felt a long way off.

"Do you mind if I contact Jack Frazier in Marketing?" McKenna asked, slipping her pen into her portfolio. "Maybe he can find a model unit somewhere else in the country. Give us input on how an LDRP looks and functions."

"Great idea." Logan began stacking his notes

"What exactly does Warren need from us?" Regina asked.

"A proposal for the Board. First of all, he'd like the group to come to some agreement." Logan checked his watch. "Looks like we're out of time. Can we meet again next Tuesday? My office will send out an agenda. We have to move this along."

Heads nodded. Gary's pager went off and he stepped out into the hallway. Bob and Eric picked up their packets and followed him. Draining the last drop of cold coffee from her cup, McKenna was determined not to wrangle about this in front of the committee. Somehow she had to connect with the fun-loving guy she'd laughed with at the Purple Frog.

Just for business purposes, of course.

As she was leaving the conference room, her phone went off. It was Brody Lightcap, one of the ER docs. "McKenna, one of your patients was just admitted. Mary Pat Gregory. Heavy bleeding."

"On my way. And Brody, I'll need the ultrasound equipment."

"You got it." Clutching her phone after she ended the call, she hesitated. Gary usually provided backup for any surgical needs, but he'd been called away. The other docs were gone. Only Logan was still here, scrolling through messages. "Logan, can you come with me to check out a patient in the ER?"

"Of course." Sliding his phone neatly into his upper pocket, he matched her stride as they headed for the elevator. On the way down to the ground floor and the ER, she filled him in on Mary Pat's medical history. When they reached the Emergency Room, Logan quickly pulled up the electronic medical record and began scrolling through it.

All hell broke loose when the outside doors crashed open. Ambulance personnel pushed two gurneys into the department, rattling off information to waiting ER staff. From the look of the casualties, these were crash victims. One flash of reddish hair and she knew her brother Seth was part of the Emergency Medical Transport team. Before dashing back outside, he turned and gave her a quick wave.

"Friend of yours?" Logan asked.

"Brother. One of the many."

"Right. The Kirkpatrick clan." He closed out of the document. While the ER staff assigned the patients to the glass cubicles that lined the hall, McKenna and Logan made their way to number four.

Mary Pat lay with eyes closed, hands folded over her chest. A nurse had started an IV and Brody had just brought in the ultrasound machine. McKenna's heart twisted as she bent over the bed. This never got easier. "Mary Pat?"

When her patient's eyes fluttered open, they were dark with apprehension. "Am I losing the baby?"

"Let's see what's going on," McKenna reassured her, snapping on her gloves and smoothing gel on Mary Pat's tummy. While Logan hovered at the end of the bed, McKenna grabbed the wand from Brody "Dr. Castle is here with me in case we need him."

But as she guided the wand over Mary Pat's abdomen, McKenna's heart sank. No heartbeat. No movement.

"McKenna? Is it bad?"

She turned. "I'm sorry, Mary Pat. So sorry."

"Oh, God." Flinging one arm over her eyes, Mary Pat began to sob. Because of her age, she'd been wildly excited on her first appointment. McKenna knew how much this baby meant. Putting the equipment aside, McKenna squeezed Mary Pat's hand. Every loss like this felt so personal, as if she'd lost her own baby.

After a quick exam, McKenna moved back to the head of the bed. "Mary Pat, we have to get to the OR."

"Joe? Has he gotten here yet from work?"

"I'll check. You're almost fully dilated, Mary Pat, and you're losing a lot of blood. We have to move."

"Okay, fine. Joe is going to kill me. He didn't want me to go running, but I've always run. It relaxes me."

Running? McKenna's mind flew back to her final instructions the day before. What exactly had she said? *Go home and relax.* Guilt swept her stomach in a sickening wave. Clinically, she knew that sometimes bleeding just happened. The running may have not been a factor.

McKenna's mind raced while Logan asked Mary Pat a few questions. He had a great bedside manner, almost as if he were dealing with a family member. "We're going to get you ready, Mary Pat. Let me know if you have questions."

After Logan left to call the OR, McKenna tried her best to calm Mary Pat. Without giving her the old "You can always have more children," she wanted her to go into the procedure with some hope in her heart. When Brody came back in the room with a nurse who would handle the transport, McKenna stepped into the hall. She pulled up the medical record and reviewed the notes Logan had just written. The heavy bleeding probably indicated a ruptured placenta.

Sometimes placentas healed if the tear was slight and early in the pregnancy. Not in this case. The rupture might have happened before or after the fetus lost viability. McKenna's own heart tore a little as she closed out of the document. A nurse appeared with Joe Gregory in tow, pale skin stretched tight across his cheekbones.

"Mary Pat's experiencing some heavy bleeding. She's fine but we have to get her to the OR."

Joe's face contorted. "But we're past the three month mark. We're safe now, right?"

She guided him into one of the consult rooms and closed the door. "I'm afraid the baby's gone, Joe."

Joe's disbelief turned to horror. "What?"

"I'm so sorry." She remembered how thrilled he'd been at the first clinic appointment. So proud to finally be a father. "How can that be?"

She took him through the clinical facts she always gave a spouse in a case like this. When she finished, Joe still stared at her with empty eyes. "We should go up now," she said. Logan would be scrubbing down and she wanted to join him.

After taking Joe to the waiting room, McKenna met up with Logan in surgery. Leaning against the cold stainless steel sink in the scrub room, she said, "Okay if I scrub in?" Gary Rice never had a problem with it, but she'd never worked with Logan.

"Of course. She's your patient." As Logan pulled up his face mask, his eyes softened. "Sorry, McKenna."

"Part of the job, isn't it?"

His jaw hardened. "Not the part we enjoy."

"You got that right." As she suited up and scrubbed down, McKenna sucked in deep breaths, trying to ease the heaviness in her heart. She'd become a midwife for the sheer joy of helping build healthy families. Working with a couple to heal this type of hurt was part of her profession. The part she always had trouble with.

In the OR Logan worked with calm certainty. As she assisted, McKenna had to continually remind herself that Mary Pat and Joe would have another chance to have the family they'd always envisioned. But there were no guarantees. Her own siblings were proof of that. Her older brother Connor and his wife Amanda were having a terrible time conceiving.

The case was moving like clockwork until the chatter of the monitors alerted them to Mary Pat's diving blood pressure. McKenna's head snapped up. She couldn't even think about facing

Joe Gregory with two losses.

Lips set, Logan guided the team until Mary Pat stabilized. His calm certainty soothed McKenna's own anxiety. No wonder the nurses admired him. The monitors regained their steady rhythmic beeping. The tension in McKenna's throat eased. But at the end, when Logan lifted his head, McKenna could swear the eyes behind his goggles were damp.

After Mary Pat had been taken to the post-op area, McKenna and Logan stripped off their gloves and yanked down their masks in the surgery locker room. Not even noon and she felt totally drained.

"You did a great job, Logan. We could have lost Mary Pat too." Unfortunately she'd seen that happen once during her training. Totally horrifying.

Tossing his mask into the trash, Logan shook his head with disgust. "Not if I can help it. Let's go talk to the husband. I asked one of the nurses to bring him to a consult room."

When they pushed open the door, Joe Gregory sat rigid on the edge of the chair. The bright blue poster on the wall about having hope seemed to mock them. He sprang to his feet.

"Your wife lost a lot of blood," Logan began, his voice low, "but she's fine."

Sagging back into the chair, Joe closed his eyes and dropped his head into his hands. "We tried to have this baby for so long."

Logan never lost a beat. "Joe, your wife is fine. No reason not to expect a full recovery but she'll need comforting."

Slipping into the chair beside Joe, McKenna wished she could

47

siphon off the young husband's pain. "She needs you now, Joe. More than ever. When you're ready, I'll take you to see her."

Joe wiped his eyes and pulled himself to his feet. "I'm ready."

Leaving the consultation room with Joe, McKenna glanced back. Logan still stood there, arms folded and eyes focused on the empty chair as if a brokenhearted man still sat there.

The day didn't get any better. With any miscarriage, McKenna always gave herself a hard time. What could she have done differently? Self doubt pestered her that afternoon like a cloud of gnats. Slowly the daily routine returned her to reason. Placenta tears and abruptions were not uncommon. Still, she couldn't dispel the sadness.

Just like she couldn't shake the feeling that beneath Logan's compassion lay a deep hurt.

Snap out of it. Vanessa and Amy would give her a hard time. They'd both tell her she was putting on her fix-it gloves. Maybe. McKenna had to make several trips to her top right drawer that day—the drawer that held the foil wrapped bits of dark chocolate that called to her in times of stress. Closing her door, she'd unwrap a piece and revel in its scent before nibbling off small bits that melted on her tongue.

Logan's intelligent gray eyes came to mind more than once. Totally ridiculous.

She stayed late, checking research regarding ruptured placentas for answers she already knew weren't there. The arrival of Myra, their cleaning lady, and the lemon scent of her spray shook McKenna from thoughts that were getting her nowhere.

"You finished in here, Miss Kirkpatrick?" Myra stuck her head in.

"Getting out of your way right now." Slipping into her jacket and grabbing her purse, McKenna left the office.

The halls were deserted as she took the overpass to the garage and rode the elevator to the top level. She loved to park up here. Lights were blinking on, dotting the cityscape from downtown Chicago to the Near North Side. Down below, a few boats drifted into Munroe Harbor. Nightfall bruised the summer sky. Her hair felt heavy on her neck and she lifted it, grateful for the cooling breeze from the lake.

"Beautiful, isn't it?"

She turned. Logan always parked his Porsche up here. With his casual long-legged stride, he drew closer, hair whipped about by the breeze and eyes unreadable. Before, he'd been just one of the preoccupied docs who rushed past her with a polite nod.

Not anymore.

"Thanks for today."

"It's our job." His eyes were an empty cup. "And some days our job really sucks."

"I feel so guilty, Logan. Mary Pat came in last night with spotting. Maybe there was something I could have picked up."

"Sometimes there's just nothing you can do, McKenna."

"But I'll never know that. Makes me crazy. Why is this always so hard?"

Was she going to cry right in front of Logan? But as she jabbed at her eyes with the sleeve of her khaki jacket, Logan didn't look horrified or disgusted. Moving closer, he slipped his arms around her, like this was the most natural thing in the world. God help her, she leaned into him, his navy windbreaker cool against her cheek. This could have been one of her brothers comforting her.

Except he wasn't. The scent of his woodsy aftershave, the scratch of his whiskers on her forehead...so not her brother.

"McKenna, don't," he murmured into her hair. "We're trained to do the best we can. But we're not superhuman. Babies are so fragile..."

His voice broke, and she was right there with him.

Looking up, she ran her palm down his cheek. She loved the roughness of the stubble. He tightened his hold. This was so wrong but felt so right. Her reservations were swallowed in the first kiss. Logan's lips were warm and searching, opening with a groan she felt vibrate to the soles of her feet. Her tongue swept in, a shameless invitation. Whatever he was offering, right now she needed it. Nestled in a cove behind the elevator bank, they pressed into each other. Hands cupping his head, she welcomed heated kisses that salved the hurt.

Thank God for the warning vibration of the wall behind them. The elevator was coming.

Stunned, McKenna pushed back, fingers pressed against her lips. "Sorry, Logan. Don't know how that happened."

Logan dropped his arms and backed away. "Not your fault."

This day was totally out of control. Her lips throbbed along with a few other parts of her body. She tasted the cool breeze from the lake, but she wanted to dive back into Logan's heat.

Wordlessly, they stared at each other. Eyes burning, Logan bit his lower lip, the lip she still tasted on her tongue. The elevator bell tinged before the doors slid open. Two nurses exited and headed in the opposite direction, their loud chatter breaking the still night air.

"Want to come sailing with me Sunday?" His words sounded dazed. Maybe they'd both lost their minds.

"You have a boat?" A day alone on a boat with Logan?

How delicious. Delicious and dangerous.

Cripes, she had to bring this collegial friendship back in line.

"I keep a sailboat here in town. Just a thirty-footer."

"*Just?* Sounds impressive to me." Then she remembered. "I'm going to my brother's Sunday. Seth's having a family thing."

"Sure, well, maybe another time." He looked disappointed. Here was an only child and she was prattling on about family. Sanity returned, along with her usual urge to make things better.

"Why don't you come too?" Had she really said that?

Logan's face brightened. "Sure. Love to."

After a few directions, they both headed for their cars, almost as if they'd never had that steamy session. Her pulse still thrummed. What had she done? Two minutes later, she was leaving the garage and phoning Vanessa. Amy would be busy with her new baby, so Vanessa had to handle this. McKenna needed help.

"Got time for some ice cream? I'll drive out. Think I need an intervention, Vanessa," McKenna groaned. Navigating the heavy traffic on Lake Shore Drive, she told her friend about the loss of the baby that day, but she didn't mention Logan or the kiss that still pulsated on her lips. At least, not until they were seated across from each other in Petersen's Ice Cream Parlor in Oak Park. The familiar retro atmosphere connected her to deep roots. Since grade school, McKenna, Amy and Vanessa had shared more than a few heartbreaks at one of these small marble-topped tables. The place held their history.

"God, Vanessa, what a day."

"So sorry about the baby, McKenna." Vanessa's eyes filled. She was probably thinking of her own little boy at home. "That poor couple."

"Exactly. Maybe I'm not cut out for this work."

Vanessa's head jerked. "Wait a minute. You're a great midwife. Couples love you. Besides, I want you to deliver my next baby."

"Is this an announcement?" McKenna yelped.

With one of her secret smiles, Vanessa nodded. "Three months."

McKenna almost advised Vanessa not to tell anyone, but she bit back the words. Most babies came to term. Mary Pat had just been unlucky. "So, Alex is excited?"

"Over the moon. A planned baby? Who would have thought it."

McKenna's two close friends were good at unplanned pregnancies.

When the waitress arrived, Vanessa ordered her usual hot fudge sundae. Her jaw dropped when McKenna asked for a banana split. "This is my dinner," she explained.

"We could have met someplace else for real food."

McKenna shook her head. "This works for me. Vanessa, there's more. I invited one of the docs to Seth's place for a Nascar party Sunday." Goodness sakes, this felt like the confessional. She could almost smell the dusty privacy curtain.

Vanessa's eyes brightened. "Wow. Guess I'm out of the loop. Tell me more."

The waitress arrived with their sundaes and the friends picked up their spoons. "Logan's just a friend, the head of my department. Always good to have more friends at work. I barely know him. That is, I work with him but I'm just starting to know him. I really like him."

Her friend stared at her, chocolate sauce dripping from the spoon halfway to her mouth.

McKenna was on a roll, turning that friendship idea over in her mind. She wasn't much good at relationships. But a buddy? Her brothers were living proof of that talent. "I think I like Logan the way I like my brothers. That's probably it."

Vanessa didn't look convinced as she swallowed. "Don't kid yourself. That fire in your cheeks? This kind of excitement doesn't come from a friend. Besides, you already tried that friendship thing with Nick. He wasn't too pleased, as I recall."

"There were a lot of things Nick wasn't pleased with. He called me the 'fixer.'" Her stomach sank to the size of the cherry on her sundae.

"You can intimidate men. Maybe a doctor would be good for you. Aren't some known for their egos?"

Not this one. But how did she know? "It's too soon and he's too close. I work with this guy, Vanessa. Sure he was voted a Chicago

Hot Doc, but he's so sweet and serious. I think he just needs more fun. I'm the one to help him with that." She let that idea settle in, ignoring the crazy kiss in the parking garage. She just couldn't go there although her body apparently didn't agree. The metal chair squeaked as McKenna squirmed.

"He's not a problem, McKenna. He's a man, with all his complexities."

McKenna took a breath. "Better to just be buddies."

"Don't start that again," Vanessa warned her.

"Start what?"

"That buddy thing you do." Vanessa was scraping the chocolate from the bottom of the sundae glass. "Amy and I decided it's just a protective measure with you. Being a buddy keeps guys at a distance. You'd probably take in stray dogs if you didn't own the highest maintenance cat on the North Shore."

They moved on to other things, like when they were going to visit Amy and the new baby. Hard to say goodnight and head to the Eisenhower Expressway. Sometimes McKenna wished she still lived out here.

Bud-dy, bud-dy. She thumped her steering wheel in time to her new mantra all the back downtown, the ice cream curdling in her stomach while her lips pulsated.

The taste on her lips wasn't ice cream.

Chapter 4

On the drive to McKenna's apartment Sunday afternoon, Logan felt uncomfortable. What was he doing going to a family party with a woman he barely knew? It was hard to say no to McKenna. What had gotten into him in the parking lot? She seemed so sad that day, so defeated. He knew that feeling.

Never in his life had he known a woman like McKenna Kirkpatrick. With her gutsy appeal, he didn't quite know how to take her. Very sexy and maybe a little unnerving. The past three years stretched behind him like a barren desert. He was determined not to overthink this. Maneuvering the Porsche into a parking space, he grinned, knowing that his Grandmother Cecile would agree.

When McKenna opened her door Sunday afternoon, Logan wasn't at all surprised by the Cubs' hat. With a ponytail poked through the back, she looked darned cute and motioned him in like they did this every day. "Should warn you, I'm on call."

"Not a problem. I lucked out. Gary is covering for our group." Her apartment was done in pale green and orange. Was that the smell of peaches again? Probably her perfume or soap. Sun spilled through a bay window onto a mass of plants. Bright orange and pink pillows were piled on the sofa and magazines formed piles on the coffee table. The place felt homey. Maybe he should rethink his Lake Shore Drive condo. Seemed kind of stuffy compared to this.

Jamming his hands into his pockets, he watched her lock up, giving him a chance to admire her legs in those khaki shorts. No disappointment there, from her shapely calves to her sandaled feet. Felt like he was back at Harvard, lusting after some sorority girl he'd made out with for ten minutes at a frat party. He'd told himself a million times the kiss in the parking garage was a mistake. Still, here he was, and she was acting as if nothing had happened. His shoulders loosened.

Bustling about her small apartment, McKenna dashed down a hallway into what looked like a kitchen to say good-bye to a huge white cat sitting in a window. "See you later, Sasha." After grabbing a plate wrapped in foil and her purse from the kitchen table, she came back with a bounce in her walk that kept her ponytail bobbing. "All set."

"Here, let me take that." Foil-covered platter in one hand, he led the way to his car and opened the passenger door. He tried not to stare as she folded those long legs into the front seat. Popping the trunk, he slid the platter in the back and whistled as he climbed in next to her. Going to be a good day. Birds chirped in the trees overhead and it was starting to smell like summer.

"Hot car." She ran one hand over the dash.

"I have my weaknesses."

"You? A weakness?"

Her mock surprise made him smile. "I just don't have many chances to indulge them."

"Let me know when the urge strikes." She sent him a wicked grin that brought the parking lot roaring back. Then the smile disappeared and she became all prim and proper, tugging at the hem of her shorts. "Glad you decided to hang out with us today."

Hang out? Almost sounded like he'd invited himself.

She adjusted the brim of her Cubs' hat. "I mean, since you have that boat and everything."

Why did he feel she was pushing him away? "I'm looking forward to meeting all those siblings you mentioned. Large families fascinate me."

"Don't let them give you a hard time."

"Trust me, I'm a big boy. Think I can handle it." They'd reached the Eisenhower Expressway. Not much traffic yet and he jammed the gearshift into third and then fourth.

On their way to Oak Park, McKenna launched into stories about her family, which seemed to be mainly guys, except for a younger sister. He doubted he'd remember any names but enjoyed the stories. With McKenna every incident was an event, hands fluttering to make a point. Hard to keep his mind on traffic.

"When my younger brother Malcolm heads up the food drive for Christmas, we almost have to hire a bus to take in our family's donations." McKenna's robust chuckle filled the car.

"Your family sounds generous. I'll enjoy meeting them."

With a sigh, she settled back, almost as if she'd given up...on something. "Like your music."

"Billie Holiday on Sundays mellows me out."

"Me too. Jazz is so sensual, don't you think?" Humming along, she began to move. He'd never seen anyone dance sitting down, and her body movements weren't relaxing. At least, not for him.

Only early June, but he turned up the air conditioning.

McKenna's brother lived on the edge of Oak Park, home for a lot of politicians, firemen and police. The tidy brick houses with postage stamp lawns were vintage Chicago, so different from the stately mansions of adjacent River Forest, where he grew up. You could live two miles from someone in this area and never know each other. Sometimes he thought all those private schools had kept him isolated.

When Seth opened his front door, serious party noises spilled out. McKenna's brother had the same copper-colored hair, cut short on the side and long in the back. "About time," Seth said with a crooked smile, pulling his sister into a warm hug before extending a hand to Logan. "Welcome."

"Logan Castle," McKenna quickly supplied. "Dr. Castle, my friend from work."

So she had to define their relationship? "Just Logan. Nice to meet you, Seth." He reached around McKenna to shake Seth's hand. "Think I've seen you around the hospital once or twice."

"Seth is an EMT," she told Logan.

"And Selena's main squeeze. My number one function in life. Just ask her," Seth added with a grin.

They all laughed. Logan liked McKenna's brother immediately.

"Can I get you a beer?" Seth waved them in.

"Sounds great. Thank you."

"Coke for me, Seth," McKenna told him. "I'm on call."

As Seth led them toward the back of the house, Selena joined them, slipping her arm around her boyfriend's waist.

Seth gave her shoulder a hug. "So you probably know McKenna's friend, Logan?"

Selena smiled. "Sure do."

"Buddy," McKenna threw in.

Selena looked as annoyed as Logan felt. Her sigh was audible as she reached out for the plate. "What's that you got in your hands, *buddy?*"

"My strawberry jello mold," McKenna said, pink staining her cheeks.

Selena whisked it from his hands. He almost laughed out loud at the appraising look she gave his shorts.

The kitchen buzzed with activity. Selena put Seth to work stirring a pot. When she opened the oven door, a rich aroma curled Logan's way.

Logan sniffed. "Baked beans?"

"My brothers love them."

His stomach gurgled. "Guess I forgot to eat breakfast again."

"Again?" McKenna whipped around.

He managed a sheepish grin. "Some mornings I just go out for my run and then have a power drink."

She was looking at him like he'd lost his mind. "Not gonna happen on my watch," she said with a shake of one finger.

Logan trailed her into a back room that ran the width of the house, McKenna's family filled a brown U-shaped sofa and two black lounge chairs. Some sprawled on the floor with sofa pillows jammed beneath their heads, staring at one of the biggest screens he'd ever seen. Definitely a man cave.

Bowls of popcorn were set on any available surface along with pretzels, salsa and chips. Serving platters crowded a table against one wall. McKenna maneuvered her plate onto the table and pulled off the foil. On the big screen TV, stock cars roared around a track while the group cheered, booed and hissed so loud no one could hear the commentators. Almost everyone in the room wore a hat or T-shirt with a different logo or number. No consensus here and they weren't shy about showing it.

"Hey, McKenna. Over here." Another auburn-haired guy waved a muscled arm. McKenna tugged Logan along behind her. "Sit," the man said with a smile, patting the sofa. "I've gotta check on the kids."

"This is Mark. His wife, Janie, is in the kitchen." Rising on tiptoes—the stretch made her legs even more attractive— McKenna moved to the plate glass window and peered out at a play area. "Their boys are quite a handful. Randy and James." Her eyes softened as she watched the two little guys argue over an inner tube that swung from a large maple tree.

After Seth brought the beverages, McKenna and Logan settled onto the sofa. Introductions were handled during commercials while everyone refueled, loading paper plates with potato salad and beans. Outside, Connor, the oldest of the clan, manned the grill. Platters of sizzling bratwursts, burgers and hot dogs kept coming through a sliding glass door. Keeping names straight became impossible. In the end, Logan just concentrated on the food.

He hadn't eaten homemade potato salad in a long time, and the hint of mustard and pickles filled him with contentment. Myrtle, one of his grandmother's housekeepers, had prepared potato salad just like this. The brats were hot and seasoned just right. Sitting with the group crammed on the wraparound sofa felt strangely comfortable. How amazing to have this group around every day growing up. His family's River Forest mansion seemed almost museum-like in comparison.

The lack of space kept McKenna close. After whacking him once with the bill of her hat, she took it off and pulled the band from her ponytail. Red-gold waves fell softly to her shoulders and he inhaled that tantalizing smell of peaches. Just when they decided to grab more food, another brother arrived, ushering in three little kids and a flustered wife.

"Malcolm and Dana," McKenna explained, handing Logan a plate. "And their three kids—Darby, Amy and Nick."

Malcolm was the brother who worked for the food bank, McKenna explained. So Warren had been right. The Kirkpatricks were all involved in work benefiting the city.

When Mark returned from the backyard, he had in tow the two little boys who'd been arguing outside earlier.

"Aunt McKenna!" They dove for her.

"Are you two behaving?" McKenna asked after sloppy kisses that didn't seem to bother her a bit. The shamefaced look on their faces told the story. Randy had a scrape just above his eye and James had dirt all over his red T-shirt.

Sometimes Logan wondered when he'd get over this awful

squeeze in his heart every time he saw a little boy. Maybe never. Coming here might have been a bad idea, but he couldn't avoid children for the rest of his life.

"Last time you said you would play animal dominoes with us," James was pleading with McKenna.

Slapping her hands on her thighs, she jumped to her feet. "I am a woman of my word." She glanced down at him. "Can you spare me for fifteen minutes?"

"Not a problem." She'd be taking the little guys with her. Maybe his appetite would return.

But after a few minutes, Logan missed her. Dumping his empty plate in the trash, he grabbed a beer and wandered outside. In the backyard McKenna held court at a picnic table, slapping down cards with James and Randy.

He felt the familiar squeeze in his chest and took deep breaths until the tightness eased. Babies didn't bother him, just the boys who were about *that age*. A therapist had once suggested desensitization. Maybe this was an opportunity. After a deep breath, Logan took a swig of his beer.

"Almost over." She glanced up, pushing her hair behind one shoulder. Cute as the dickens, James was wearing his aunt's cap.

Logan settled next to McKenna at the picnic table. Some kind of yellow bushes rimmed the rectangular yard. Reminded him of the house where his family had lived before his parents got divorced and he was shuffled off to his grandparents. This yard took him back to a life when he'd been like one of these little guys and thought life was uncomplicated. Only it wasn't.

~.~

McKenna had never seen Logan so relaxed, long legs stretched out under the picnic table. At first she'd been horrified about her last-minute invitation. What was she thinking? But Vanessa had talked her off the ledge. "Enjoy the day." After all, with her family, you didn't have to do much talking. Lately, her parents often stayed home when "the kids" got together, although her dad might drive over for a beer. All her siblings were present and accounted for, with the exception of Harper. Sometimes she wished her younger sister didn't live in Savannah.

Logan seemed fine with the chaos, sipping his beer at the picnic table in his shorts and blue polo.

The casual outfit made Hot Doc even hotter.

The heat spiraling through her body cooled when she yanked her mind back to "friend," a concept she still had to explain to Selena.

"I'm out, Aunt McKenna!" James's freckled face brightened when he slapped his last elephant card down. "I won!"

"Man, oh, man. You two get better every time we play." She fanned her remaining gorilla, zebra and giraffe cards while Randy grumbled. Next time she'd make sure that Randy won.

While her nephews charged into the house to tell their parents, she noticed her brother Connor and his wife Amanda sitting under the wisteria arbor. Amanda was wiping her eyes, looking miserable. McKenna's heart twisted. But she didn't want Logan to see the couple.

"Ready for dessert?" she asked him.

"Absolutely." When Logan smiled, she could forget their differences. This casual side of him was attractive, maybe too attractive. When she started seeing Nick, they'd gotten along great. Took time for the nitpicking to begin. At the end, Nick left the room every time she began to tell a story. Thought she was too aggressive, too self-assured. Kidded her about being "the fixer," only it wasn't funny.

One kiss does not a relationship make.

Buddy. She felt the nervous flutter in her stomach settle.

Smiling, she nodded toward the house. "Come and get it."

Inside, Randy and James were at the serving table, along with Malcolm's kids. Probably thinking no one was watching, James poked one finger through the strawberry jello and plunked the loaded finger into his mouth.

"James, I'm telling Mom," his brother whined.

"You stinker, James," McKenna admonished her nephew. One stern look and the little guy crumbled, burying his face between her legs, his sticky hands clutching the backs of her knees. "I'm sorry, Aunt McKenna. I just wanted to taste it."

"Aw, I know, honey." Crouching, she gave him a quick kiss. "But use the spoon. Now, both of you go wash up, okay?"

Looking up, she caught Logan watching them march off. "Cute, aren't they?"

"Very. You're lucky."

He'd probably make a great father. Kids really seemed to affect him.

When James and Randy returned with clean hands, she scooped

out bowls of jello topped with a generous scoop of whipped topping.

Turning, she waved the spoon in Logan's direction. "Want some?"

His head jerked, eyes still on the boys. "Sorry, McKenna. What was that?"

The plundered jello mold didn't look very appetizing. "Maybe you'd rather have some carrot cake in the kitchen? That's my favorite." Putting the spoon down, she led the way.

Set on the kitchen counter, the cake was still covered. Carrot cake was Dana's specialty. Pulling back the foil, McKenna cut neat squares and placed two on paper plates.

"Here you go." She handed Logan a plate, but something was off. Some guys just didn't like sweets, and she thought back to the plain doughnut that morning in the doctors lounge.

Selena had wandered into the kitchen and, to McKenna's embarrassment, began to fill Logan's ears about the benefits of an LDRP unit. He listened politely as he nibbled at the carrot cake, but McKenna fumed. She didn't want Logan to think she'd had an ulterior motive in inviting him here. Although she tried to catch Selena's attention, her friend steadfastly avoided her eyes.

Hating to leave Logan in Selena's clutches, McKenna saw Amanda disappear into a back bathroom. Quietly following her sister-in-law down the hallway lined with pictures of nieces and nephews, McKenna waited outside the closed door.

"Hey, how's it going?" she asked when Amanda reappeared. Her brother and sister-in-law wanted a baby so bad. The last five years had been heartbreaking.

Her sister-in-law's lips trembled and her eyes filled.

"Not good?" McKenna asked, gently rubbing one hand across Amanda's rounded shoulders.

"Oh, McKenna, is this ever going to happen? Are we ever going to have a baby? And now we've started to argue. I hate this."

"Oh, sweetie. I am so sorry." She hugged her sister-in-law closer.

"And it's so expensive," Amanda continued, trying to keep her voice down while her tears flowed. "On a fireman's salary, we can't afford this. The doctor's saying something might be wrong with my ovaries…or maybe it's the stress from teaching high school. Do you think I need another opinion?"

That's when it hit her. "Do you know Logan has a fertility clinic at Montclair?"

Amanda blinked. "No, I didn't realize that."

"Why don't you call him? Want me to speak to Logan?"

Amanda nodded, dabbing at her red nose with a tissue. "Sure. Why not?"

Her resignation broke McKenna's heart. Maybe someday she'd be in Amanda's spot. Giving her another squeeze, McKenna led her back to the kitchen. The small room felt warm from all the cooking.

"We've got another recruit for Guatemala," Selena announced, her voice jubilant.

"Really?" McKenna scanned the room. The midwife training group didn't need firemen or cops, even though they sometimes did deliver babies.

"Logan's signed on." Selena trumpeted. "I told him Guatemala's gorgeous in July. Mosquitoes as big as your fist."

McKenna's stomach sank. She never should have left Logan here with Selena. When it came to Midwives in Action, her friend was a recruiting machine. "Sure, with smelly latrines and more rain than you've ever seen." McKenna stared at Selena. Was she kidding?

Logan looked up from studying his Nikes. "Actually, I said I'd consider it. Sounds like a worthwhile venture. According to Selena, sometimes a doctor is needed."

He'd been put on the spot and McKenna wanted to strangle her friend. "Well, I…you know, I think that's exciting." But she could barely get the words out. Logan in Guatemala? Was Selena crazy? The man was a technology freak. How comfortable would he be in a country where women pounded dried corn on rocks for supper? But there was plenty of time for him to change his mind. She'd make that clear on the way home.

In the family room, a cheer went up. The race was over. Her family began packing up. "Be right back," she told Logan. "Could you grab my serving plate?"

"Sure." He turned toward the table of empty platters.

Dashing outside, she found Seth pushing James on the tree swing and said a fast good-bye. "Thanks so much. We're ready to take off."

"Hey, I like this guy a lot better than Nick," Seth said with a wry smile.

"Just a friend. We work together," McKenna emphasized. "I just wanted him to have some fun."

Seth frowned. "What does that mean? Logan can't plan his own activities?"

She gave him a peck on the cheek. "Just don't start planning the wedding, okay?"

"Right." Eyes narrowing, Seth cocked his head to one side. "Someday we have to talk about this buddy thing you have going with guys. Not a turn-on."

"You're just trying to marry me off. See you later." What was wrong with being a man's friend?

On the drive back to North Side, McKenna relaxed, cupped in the leather seat. Daylight was slowly draining from the sky. Logan's smooth jazz filled the car, but McKenna's mind was still on Seth's last comment. *Friend. Buddy.* Did the words cocoon her from possible disappointment?

"Did you have a good time?" She swiveled toward Logan in the butter soft leather seat.

"I had a *great* time," he emphasized with a convincing smile.

"You did? Really?" Hot Doc had a great profile, and she loved the lock of hair that never stayed put.

"It's been a long time since I've been with one big happy family." His words held a reflective note.

"You were a good sport. It can get kind of crazy."

"Sometimes crazy is good. Thanks for inviting me."

Sunday evening and everyone in Chicago was coming back from somewhere. Took a while to negotiate the Eisenhower, but

Logan managed. Gunning the engine and shifting like crazy, Logan whipped from lane to lane. The man had a crazy streak. What else about Logan would surprise her?

He pulled up in front of the apartment, engine idling. Should she ask him in? Wouldn't a friend do that?

The memory of their parking lot kiss held her back from suggesting coffee. She clamped her lips shut. But her body gave a reluctant tug. Felt like her feelings and her mind were at war. When he opened the car door, she led the way up the stone steps, shoved her key into the lock and pushed the door open.

"Glad you had a good time today." Turning, she held the empty platter in front of her like a breast shield.

His attention fell to the plate, a smile teasing his lips. "You have a great family. Thanks for inviting me."

"Isn't this what friends are for? Share families...and stuff." God, this was awkward. She wanted to hurl the plate into the bushes and grab him.

Logan's brows rose as his glance lifted. "So you want to meet my grandmother.?"

"Absolutely not." Meet his family? Heat flooded her neck and cheeks. "That's not that I meant."

With a chuckle, he began backing away. "When you decide what you *do* mean, let me know."

Seconds later she watched the tail lights of the Porsche until he turned the corner.

Shoot. She lowered the plate. This friendship thing was getting complicated.

Chapter 5

McKenna's head had barely hit the pillow when her phone went off.

"Damn." Struggling to sit up, she peered at the number—Sarah Lewis, who was pregnant with twins. With one click, she answered. "Hey, Sarah, what's up?"

Five minutes later, she was headed for the door, car keys in hand. The complexities of this case ran through her mind as she drove through the darkness to the hospital. Delivering twins through water birth could become tricky, especially identical twins since they share a placenta. The first one usually arrived easily but the second birth could be more difficult. Yet Sarah had been adamant about wanting natural childbirth in the water birthing suite. McKenna had assured her they'd take that route if it seemed appropriate.

They were about to find out, and her heartbeat revved up a little as she drove through the dark streets. When she pulled into the parking garage, she called Gary, Logan's partner, who'd already been prepped about Sarah's case. Then she got in touch with Bethany.

"On my way," Bethany told her, excitement vibrating in her voice. "Can't wait." When it came to twins, two midwives were common protocol, but McKenna would also need physician backup in case they needed a C-section.

A short time after McKenna reached the hospital, Sarah arrived with Dan, her husband. She was panting through a contraction as a nurse wheeled her into the birthing suite.

"Now, are we on the same page about this? Water birth if everything goes without a hitch?" McKenna asked. She did not want Sarah to be disappointed.

"Right. Absolutely." Nodding, Sarah looked to her husband for agreement.

"We don't want to risk anything," Dan said. Shirt half buttoned, he'd obviously dressed in a hurry. So often the father was the nervous one. The couple had a little girl at home who had been delivered through water birth, so this wasn't a first for them.

"Let's see where we are." McKenna helped Sarah from the wheelchair. "Dr. Rice will be here, just for backup in case we decide to take another route."

After a quick check, McKenna and Dan helped Sarah into the water. With contractions coming regularly, Sarah was ready to settle in and prepare. Dan had brought their music and soon the pulsing strains of Enya filled the suite.

McKenna attached the monitoring equipment, the rise and fall of the music pleasant in her ears. "A sassy girl and a rambunctious boy. Sure you're ready for this pair?" she joked, checking the screen.

"You bet." Sarah's eyes glistened.

The couple had chosen aromatherapy as part of their birth plan, and the crisp scent of eucalyptus soothed McKenna's sinuses. Letting her head fall back, Sarah inhaled deeply and closed her eyes. The air brimmed with guarded anticipation.

With Dan coaching his wife, labor progressed quickly, and McKenna was glad Sarah had called when she did. When Bethany arrived, McKenna updated her in the hallway. "Dan and Sarah have things under control. We're good to go," she concluded. "So far, the twins are both head down."

"I've never delivered twins in the birthing pool." Excitement rippled in Bethany's voice.

McKenna smiled. "You never know with twins. We have to be prepared for anything. Gary will be here in case we have to move to the OR for a C-section."

But it was Gary's partner who was on her mind as McKenna entered notes in the laptop. Their Sunday together had felt so natural. Easy to see that her family liked him. Away from the hospital, Logan seemed to drop the reserve that she dealt with in the department.

Wanting to give the young couple as much privacy as possible, McKenna and Bethany took turns in the birthing suite. Mary Beth and Simone, the two neonatal nurses, peeked in from time to time. They would be ready when the babies arrived. With the monitoring equipment in place, all systems were go.

McKenna enjoyed working with Bethany. Dimples flashing, the younger girl reminded McKenna of her sister. Harper had gone to school in Savannah, eventually settling in the historic city. The entire Kirkpatrick clan had been dismayed to have Harper so far away, but they sure enjoyed visiting her. The two sisters remained close and each had her own dating adventures to share.

Bethany helped fill the hole left by Harper's absence. For Women was the only practice where the younger midwife had applied—at least that's what she told McKenna during her interview. Recently, she'd gotten engaged. Everything was falling into place for her.

Leaving Bethany in charge, McKenna dashed to the nurses' station to drop off some papers. Her clogs squeaked against the shiny tile floor. Sunday evening, and visiting hours were over. TVs blared from the rooms, along with the low murmur of voices as meds were dispensed. If an LDRP unit was approved, families would be allowed to come and go when they pleased. No more limiting family visitation hours.

But first she had to convince Logan that the new unit was a good idea.

More meetings loomed on the horizon—not her favorite thing. She cringed when she remembered the last planning meeting. Regina had caught her in the hall and asked if there were any problems with Dr. Castle. McKenna had assured the VP of Nursing that everything was fine. "My practice champions the natural route," she'd emphasized and Regina's eyes had softened with understanding. "More diagnostic equipment and a new ventilation system in the OR…Montclair already has more than most of the area hospitals."

Thoughts of a possible disagreement with Logan brought acidic twinges to McKenna's stomach. For now, she had to concentrate on the Lewis twins, gearing up to enter the world.

About three hours later, Sarah was ready to deliver, calmly panting through the contractions that had fully dilated her cervix. Gary had arrived but stayed in the shadows.

"Next contraction, Sarah, use those pelvic muscles," McKenna coached. "Nothing else." McKenna glanced at the monitor. So far, so good. The solemnly hopeful sounds of Enya pulsed in the background and Sarah grunted in concert with the music.

"Here we go, Sarah. First one crowning." All seemed well as the dark-haired top of one head appeared. When Mary Beth, the neonatal nurse, looked in, Bethany motioned to her. Simone, the second nurse for the babies, slipped in behind her.

Approaching the next contraction, Sarah's gaze sought her husband, who nodded encouragement. "Again, Sarah. You're doing great." His voice caught in his throat as Sarah pushed and his daughter came into the world.

"Ladies first," McKenna exclaimed, scooping the female infant from the warm water. The infant blinked and frowned when she opened her eyes.

"Oh, honey." Dan was beside himself, bending over his new daughter. "She's so beautiful. Looks just like you."

"Hello, Kristen." Sarah beamed when McKenna placed the baby in her arms. After cutting the cord, there was still work to be done. The baby was transferred to Mary Beth and Sarah got ready for round two.

Eyes on the screen, McKenna ran the doppler wand over Sarah's taut stomach. "Jason's an active little guy. Typical man."

The second baby was now in the transverse position and she cut her eyes to Gary. The game plan had changed. Sarah and Dan must have seen that in her face.

"McKenna, what's going on?" Sarah asked.

"Everything's fine, but I think we're headed for the OR." McKenna kept her voice matter-of-fact and reassuring. "Jason's been having a good old time since his sister left. He's not in a position to come out anytime soon."

"Is anything wrong?" Sarah's face constricted.

"Absolutely not. Heartbeat's strong, but the OR is the best place to welcome this little guy into the world."

"Not totally unexpected, Sarah," Gary added, stepping up. "I'll do a C-section and McKenna will be there." As he talked, the worry dissolved from the parents' faces.

"Can I be in the room?" Dan asked.

Gary nodded. "Absolutely." The couple relaxed a little, Sarah clinging to Dan's hand.

A nurse arrived to take Sarah to the third floor operating rooms while Mary Beth took charge of the new baby girl. "Kristen will be waiting for you on the obstetrics floor," McKenna told Dan, who was beginning to look frazzled.

~.~

Ninety minutes later, McKenna was relaxing in the staff lounge. Sarah had been transferred to her room on the obstetrics floor while her husband fussed over the twins. Everything had gone smoothly. The couple did not seem at all disappointed that the delivery plan had to be changed.

After pouring a cup of coffee, McKenna stood at the window studying the nightscape. She'd heard that Logan lived in one of the high rises. Behind her, the door opened, and Gary came in, stripping his surgery cap from his head and heading for the coffee.

"Thanks for your help tonight," she said. As she got to know Logan's partner better, she liked the low-key doctor a lot.

"Don't mention it." Then he shrugged and grinned, brown eyes glinting gold. "Okay, mention it."

Gary was dating Mindy Muenich, a neonatal nurse, and they made a cute couple. "I was kind of surprised that you called that C-section so quickly," he said, pouring himself a cup of coffee.

"Water birth is a great option. But I never take any chances."

"I agree." Stirring some creamer into his cup, Gary looked at her like a man with something on his mind. "Since you came a year ago, you've brought some welcome changes to this hospital, McKenna. I want you to know that. New ideas. New ways of doing things. Good for us all."

"Montclair was attractive to me because the administration welcomes innovation." Pleased, she collapsed into a chair. Time to plant some seeds. "Gary, I appreciate your support of the LDRP. Hope it comes to pass. I'm not sure everyone sees it that way."

Gary's jaw shifted as he slid into the barrel chair across from her and plunked his feet on the coffee table. "You have to take Logan with a grain of salt. Sometimes he needs time to process things. Trust me, there's a lot more to him than meets the eye."

"And you're telling me this because..."

"The last few days Logan's been a different man. Don't know

what you two are doing." He held up one hand. "Don't want to know."

Really? A pleased flush warmed her cheeks. "Logan and I have been working closer together lately. That's about it. I invited him to hang out with my family. We're... friends." That mind-blowing kiss flitted through her mind and the heat in her cheeks ratcheted up.

"Whatever. I'm just saying we all need a personal life. And he hasn't had one since..." Gary stopped, as if he'd said too much.

"Since his divorce?" she offered softly, lifting her head.

"Yeah, but that's not all, McKenna." Gary bit on the tip of his stir stick before blowing out a sigh. "Look, Logan keeps his life pretty personal. I respect that. But I think you should know what you're dealing with. Logan had a son—a baby that died shortly after birth. Problematic delivery with a midwife who probably didn't make the right decisions."

McKenna set her coffee down on the table so fast it slopped over the side. "I had no idea."

"Logan keeps his personal life private." Gary's face tightened. "I'd appreciate it if you didn't mention this until he tells you."

"Understood. But he may never bring it up."

"Somehow, I think he will."

"Is that what ruined his marriage?"

Gary shrugged. "Maybe. Logan and Rebecca were never a great couple. You have to realize, when we're residents, we only meet nurses or other doctors. We don't have time for anyone else. So we marry them, for better or for worse. As I recall, Rebecca was someone he'd known from his past, but later, they just didn't have what it takes to stay together. She chose midwifery for the birth and, as I heard it, insisted on staying the course when it was time to make a different decision. Logan couldn't be there and in the end, they both regretted it. Deeply."

~.~

McKenna muddled through that Monday, Gary's words replaying in her mind. She'd grabbed some sleep in one of the on-call rooms, but time alone made her restless. She ached for Logan and his terrible loss.

As the day wore on at a glacial pace, she retreated to her desk drawer several times for some serious chocolate relief. Thank goodness her natural childbirth classes didn't start until Wednesday.

Selena grabbed her when she came in later that morning. "Hey, I may have been wrong about Logan. Hate to admit it, but he didn't seem half bad Sunday."

"Glad you decided to give the guy a chance," McKenna teased before growing serious. "He seemed to have a good time with my crazy brothers, Seth included. It was fun hanging out with him."

"Hanging out." Selena laid each word down like a brick.

"Exactly. He's an only child. You know how much fun my family can be." A storm cloud was building on Selena's brow and McKenna rushed on. "Still, let's not get crazy. Maybe you should hold back on the Guatemala trip until he has a chance to understand what it's all about. Up to you."

Selena's forehead smoothed. "Why not bring him to one of our Midwives in Action meetings?"

"I'll see what he thinks." My, she sounded so proprietary. "I mean, why don't you ask him about coming to the meeting?"

Selena gave her a long, silent look. "Maybe I'll just do that."

Later in the afternoon, McKenna decided to switch her fix from chocolate to Dr. Pepper. The pop machine in the Medical Office Building was out, so she headed over to the main building around three o'clock. Logan stood at the end of the walkway with a striking blonde. McKenna had never seen her before. This was a woman she'd remember.

As she approached, Logan turned. "McKenna, want you to meet Priscilla Preston. Think I mentioned our recruitment efforts. Priscilla is interviewing. We're finding out if we'd make a good fit."

With a wide smile that didn't touch her eyes, Priscilla extended one French-manicured hand. Suddenly McKenna felt grungy. She wasn't wearing makeup, her hair was in a sloppy ponytail and she was in serious need of sleep. Priscilla's shoulder-length hair was probably sprayed to last all day. The dainty pearls in her ears suited her subtle makeup.

The woman was perfect. Dazzling and perfect.

"So pleased to meet you, McKenna." Priscilla's slender hand was delicate but strong.

"Welcome to Montclair. Hope we're making a good impression."

Priscilla's cool blue eyes did a dismissive sweep from McKenna's messy hair to her worn white clogs. "Why, everything's almost perfect."

McKenna pulled her lab coat tighter around her rumpled blue

scrubs.

When Priscilla turned to Logan, her smile revved up a notch. "And Logan, ah, Dr. Castle has so much to teach."

"Priscilla and I knew each other in grade school," he said. Was he blushing? "Long time ago." The two of them laughed, Priscilla a little louder.

"So, you're from Chicago then?"

When Priscilla nodded, not a hair on her head moved. "Yes, my two little girls are so happy to be back near their grandparents."

"I was just telling Priscilla about our plans for obstetrics," Logan continued, looking very pleased. "Might be a good idea to have her attend our committee meeting this week. Give you an idea of where we might be headed. That is, if you have time, Priscilla."

"Well, of course." Priscilla's smile widened.

McKenna could almost see the silver spoon in Priscilla's mouth. In so many ways, this woman might be perfect for Logan. At first, the thought leveled McKenna. A welcome wave of relief followed. Yesterday with Hot Doc had felt totally out of control. She didn't like it one bit. Was she just setting herself up for another heartbreak? When McKenna pictured him with Priscilla, the anxiety in her chest eased, like she'd just escaped a train wreck before impact.

"Since I'm a single mother, my life is really busy," Priscilla continued. "My parents are glad to have their grandchildren closer and happy to help out." Then her eyes swung to Logan. "But I'm being presumptuous. I mean, if the practice is a good fit for everyone."

From the look on Logan's face, there was no *if* about it. He'd mentioned needing another physician onboard, but McKenna sure hadn't pictured anyone like Priscilla. Was this jealousy snaking up inside her?

When it came to Logan, she was seriously screwed up.

"So nice meeting you, Priscilla. I'll let you two continue your tour. Off to a meeting." With a pert nod, McKenna marched toward the elevator that would take her to the cafeteria and the vending machines. How pathetic was it that she had to make up a meeting? Was she trying to make herself look important? She hated managers who pulled that trump card. While the elevator doors closed behind her, McKenna's mind worked overtime. Conflicted feelings about Hot Doc sent a wave of jitters through her stomach.

When had she ever felt so wildly attracted to a man? All the advice she gave her friends so freely clamored in her head. But this was her life and her risk. These early feelings for Logan dropped the floor right out from under her feet. Could she take another heartbreak so soon after Nick? On top of that, she liked it here at Montclair. Dating a colleague posed risks. She wanted to stay at Montclair for a long time.

Only when a woman entered with a small child did McKenna realize the elevator had arrived at her floor. "Excuse me. Sorry." She darted out just before the doors whooshed closed.

Close call. The best thing, the safest thing might be to steer Logan in the direction of another woman.

Chapter 6

That evening McKenna drove to Oak Park and met Vanessa for a visit with Amy. Time to see how that sweet little Gianna was doing. Mallory met them at the door. So cute how he chattered about the baby's feeding schedule in that smooth-as-butter southern accent as they followed him upstairs to the nursery. The baby's room was wallpapered with silly monkeys and smiling giraffes. Amy sat in a white wicker chair nursing Gianna.

"Almost finished." She kissed her baby's head. The air was filled with the scent of powder and baby.

"Y'all probably have a lot of catching up to do," Mallory said from the doorway, clearly doting on his new daughter. "I'll leave you to it."

"Scoot, now." Amy waved him away. After a reluctant last glance, he disappeared

"You've never looked better," McKenna told her. Was this the same girl who'd once been so stressed out because she thought she couldn't have a baby? Cuddling Gianna, Amy positively glowed.

"Thanks, McKenna." Amy settled Gianna onto her side in the bassinet. "Don't know when I've felt happier."

"A present from Petersen's." Vanessa held up a white paper bag before setting it on the dresser.

With a pleased grin, Amy reached for the treat. "Oh, yum. I don't even have to look inside. Thank you!"

While the new mother enjoyed the hot fudge sundae, Vanessa and McKenna plopped down on a daybed in the corner. Vanessa asked Amy questions another mother would ask. "Sleeping through the night yet?"

"Are you kidding me?" Amy clucked. "I swear, Mallory wakes her up just to play with her."

"I swear, you are picking up your husband's Savannah accent," McKenna teased.

"Do tell. But what about you? Tell me about your doctor friend—the hot doc Vanessa mentioned over the phone," Amy said between mouthfuls.

"Hope you don't mind, McKenna." Vanessa shot her an embarrassed look. "I kind of brought Amy up to speed about Logan."

McKenna began to jiggle one foot. "Nothing to tell. We work together. Logan's a nice guy, who needs more fun in his life, so I invited him to Seth's last Sunday."

Amy tipped her head to one side. "Really? Took him to a family gathering, huh?"

"He's a new friend and I thought he'd have fun. End of story."

"That story is *so* not over." Vanessa exchanged a look with Amy, who rolled her eyes. "I am ready to shake you, McKenna Kirkpatrick."

"Sometimes a guy makes a better friend than a, a..."

"Husband candidate?" Vanessa challenged her.

"There you go! Now you understand."

But their frowns told her they obviously didn't.

"You just want to feel safe after what happened with Nick. That's not you." Vanessa was ticked, pouting with arms crossed. "You're the woman who encouraged us to be risk-takers."

"Exactly," Amy chimed in, setting the empty ice cream cup on the dresser. "Sounds like you're making this way too complicated."

The truth pulsed behind McKenna's lips. "Okay, here it is. Nick told me I was too much...too showy, too boisterous. He was always asking me to tone it down." Embarrassed her to admit it. The memories stung. "Maybe I make a better friend than a, well, girlfriend."

Both friends hooted.

"Oh, sure. Nick chased you because you were hot and tried to suck the blood right out of you!" Amy howled.

"Honey, don't let a man make you less than what you are. Isn't that what you've always told us?" Vanessa reached over to squeeze her hand. "Be yourself. If he doesn't like it, move on."

McKenna stared at her sandaled feet. They were right. But it didn't make Nick's ultimate rejection feel any better. She could never forget his exasperated looks when she'd laugh too loud or too long. "I know you're right. I just want to be...careful."

Priscilla Preston was a lady from the top of her blonde hair to the bottom of her soft leather shoes. Maybe that's the kind of woman who could go the mile with Logan.

Next to her in the bassinet, Gianna slept, delicate eyelids twitching while she dreamed.

If only adult life were that simple. The air in the room had turned contentious. McKenna leapt to her feet. "Look, I should really head out. Early meeting tomorrow."

McKenna and Vanessa kissed Amy good-bye, promising to return soon. McKenna took one last look at the baby she'd helped bring into the world. Gianna was so very precious. Vanessa had driven herself over to Amy's so they went their separate ways. When she hugged McKenna good-bye, she whispered, "Taking a chance is so worth it. You're the one who taught me that."

McKenna pushed away, raking one hand through her hair. "I don't know, Vanessa. The timing's not good. But as a friend? Logan will be terrific."

Vanessa threw up her hands and got into her car.

Doubts bombarded McKenna on the way home. Sure she'd been the one urging Amy to "be a babe" while she traveled Italy with Mallory. And yes, she'd urged Vanessa to let Alex into her life. Still, the end of McKenna's last relationship had sure taken the wind out of her sails.

By the time she left the Eisenhower and turned onto Michigan Avenue, McKenna had racked up plenty of reasons why she should keep Logan at a distance.

~.~

Sitting at the conference table the following morning, McKenna sipped her hazelnut coffee. She'd made rounds early, and seeing Sarah nursing tiny Kristen while twin Jason slept in the bassinette just about turned her inside out. Her own breasts tingled and she had to give a hurried good-bye.

The last few days had made her overly emotional, and she wanted no part of it. That jittery feeling in her stomach? Time to settle down.

When she'd arrived for the meeting, the physicians were looking over some rough sketches. Jack Frazier from Marketing had contacted the architectural firm that had worked on the neuro floor, and they'd produced some impressive sketches. Excitement replaced the trepidation in her chest as she studied the comfortable rooms, wide hallways and, yes, water birthing pools that could transform the OB floor. Also on the table were photos of the OR equipment Logan had suggested. Her excitement chilled just looking at the cold metal.

Most of the group had arrived and she was chatting quietly with Regina Drury when Logan swept in with Priscilla promptly at seven o'clock. Today, the Blonde Bombshell was wearing a trim blue suit that accented her eyes.

Eyes widening, Selena caught McKenna's attention. Sure, she'd casually mentioned Priscilla but a mere description didn't do Dr. Preston justice.

"Good morning. Let's get started." The color was high in Logan's cheeks and, darn it, the flush made him even more handsome. *Friend. Colleague.* The words pulsed in her mind like a warning sign. "Let me introduce—" and somehow she knew what was coming before Logan said it "—my new associate."

"That's great. Welcome." Surprise lifted Bob McCracken's voice, perhaps relieved that his practice would no longer have to cover for Logan and his doctors.

"We're thrilled to have Priscilla on board," added Eric Driver while Gary nodded.

"Dr. Priscilla Preston will be joining Castle and Associates as soon as she can find living arrangements," Logan explained, rocking back in his chair with a satisfied smile. "Since Dr. Preston comes from a market in San Francisco, she may have interesting input on this project."

As a mother, Priscilla might be an ally. At least, McKenna sure hoped so.

Jack Frazier practically leapt across the table. "No kidding. The model unit we found is just outside San Francisco." He named a facility Priscilla seemed to recognize.

"I have colleagues who are on staff at that hospital." Priscilla's smile became more confident with each word. Then her gaze slid to Logan. "That is, if the new unit is the direction you decide on."

Oh, puh-lease. Was Priscilla going to defer to Logan? McKenna's skin prickled with irritation.

Logan picked up his pen. "Should we get to work?"

Quickly they went over the points touched in the last meeting. "We were discussing whether or not each room should be equipped with a water birthing pool. That is, if we decide to pursue the LDRP project and present it to the Board."

"Who'll be making that decision, Logan?" McKenna wanted clarification.

"Um, the group, I guess." His glance swept the table.

A lively discussion ensued, with Regina weighing in on the side of the midwives. Logan's hesitation was evident in the questions he posed concerning infections and mortality rates. McKenna took notes. He brought up good points, and she'd get her office on this today. This type of unit would not be popular in other markets if it were unsafe. Gary, Eric and Bob seemed to hold back. Did they hesitate to disagree with Logan? Since they'd all been at Montclair for a while, they probably knew about Logan's past and were familiar with the secret sorrow he harbored.

Undeterred, McKenna continued to list the benefits. "This is all about delivering in a comfortable and safe environment. Adjustable beds, big screen TVs. Sound systems. Birthing pools. The latest technology concealed in attractive cupboards."

Okay, maybe she was going overboard. Logan began clicking his pen. "Sounds expensive."

"But we're fund raising, right? And we have the support of the Foundation." She was not backing down.

"My question would be," Logan continued, "does every woman want to give birth in a pool of warm water?" The words came slowly as if Logan were feeling his way through a sensitive topic.

"Well, my goodness." Priscilla gasped. "I don't think so. That's just from my own experience, and I've only had two children."

Oh, good grief. McKenna bit back a groan.

"Although I realize some hospitals are using this capability, *I* wouldn't have wanted to climb into a pool to give birth to my little girls." Priscilla's voice rose, as if she were championing the rights of all decent, childbearing women. "But that's just my experience. What do you think, McKenna?" Her limpid blue eyes widened in innocent appeal.

McKenna sucked in a deep breath. "I wouldn't know from a personal standpoint, but my patients come to Montclair because we offer water birthing. Before you flew out to Chicago to interview, you probably became familiar with our website and blog."

Priscilla's vacant expression was priceless. She hadn't even checked out their website? A shuffle of papers filled the room. Bob glanced at the clock.

"We have a blog?" Logan's forehead wrinkled. With the exception of Gary, the other docs seemed equally surprised.

McKenna's mouth opened, but thank goodness Jack Frazier got there first. "Dr. Castle, we've had the blog for about six months." He glanced in McKenna's direction. "When For Women came on board, McKenna suggested it. Marketing keeps up the website, as you probably know, but the midwives contribute a substantial portion of the OB blog. We'd be happy to have physicians participate."

"The patients would love that, Dr. Castle." Turning to Priscilla, McKenna added, "A female physician's perspective would certainly be welcome."

"Sounds great. I'd love to pull something together." Priscilla picked up her pen, as if she would begin right this moment.

The meeting continued. Logan had brought further information about the radiology equipment and other technology for a renovated OR.

"Wouldn't Orthopedics benefit from this renovation as well?" McKenna asked.

"Why, yes. Good point." Logan's smile took her back to Seth's. When Hot Doc relaxed, he became the endearing guy who sat at the picnic table with her nephews.

"The Foundation Board meeting is at the end of the month," Logan finally reminded them. "Will we be able to come to some consensus on this?"

McKenna's stomach tightened. If Logan called a vote, she'd lose all hope. She might even question her decision to join Montclair. How she wished Warren were here.

"Why not let the Board decide," Regina offered with her usual pragmatic approach.

"Great idea," Gary Rice agreed and the other physicians nodded. "Present both suggestions and see which one they feel is appropriate for Montclair."

The group agreed unanimously.

"Great idea. I don't think Warren will have a problem with this," Logan said, sitting back. "McKenna and I will make the presentation." The group murmured agreement.

They were in this together. An air of collegiality followed McKenna back to the office. She really didn't want to be in an adversarial position with Logan, but she'd take him on about this renovation, if it came to that.

Take him on. Took some effort to rein in her imagination.

This buddy thing might be harder than she'd expected.

"Dorothy, when you have time today, could you search for some information?" She briefly outlined the questions that had been raised at the meeting, while her receptionist jotted notes.

If Logan wanted information, why, she would give him information.

~.~

The patient load at For Women continued to build. McKenna felt the demands on her time increase. In addition to seeing patients, she had a blog to write that week about the complications involved in delivering twins in the birthing pool. Although Sarah's experience had been positive, McKenna wanted expectant parents to realize certain factors might rule out that option. Since twins were becoming way more common, they needed to put more information out there.

By the time she made it to her natural childbirth class Wednesday night, she'd heard nothing from Logan. Fine with her. Felt safe and right now, maybe she might need some distance. After her debacle with Nick, she didn't need to sprint into a relationship that might go south.

Nick Hanes had been the roadblock she didn't see coming. Used to throwing herself into projects with fierce abandon, she'd approached Nick that same way. From the start, they got along like gangbusters. An attractive contractor, the two had met when he put an addition on the clinic where she was working at the time. Instant chemistry. She'd never trust that quick, crazy heat again. Sure, she could urge her friends to "be a babe," but the truth was, that approach hadn't worked out for her. At least, not with Nick.

After more than a year together, he decided her family was "stifling." She actually began to avoid the frequent family gatherings. Although she enjoyed Nick's keen interest in cars and enjoyed swap meets, she began to wonder if his boy toys might come before family. And then there was that attitude, which she saw as rejection.

At first she closed her eyes. And then she opened them wide.

Following the end of her relationship, she'd eagerly accepted Warren's offer to accommodate For Women at Montclair. For her, the clinic represented failure, but they'd all wished her well when she left.

Now here she was. McKenna planned to build a career at Montclair. Dating a co-worker was never a smart idea. If only she could take back that crazy kiss. For now, if working longer hours kept her away from the Hot Doc, she was grateful.

That evening the couples in her natural childbirth class filed into one of the hospital meeting rooms, all excitement and plump bellies. The chairs were pushed back against the wall. "Grab a mat from the back of the room and get comfortable," she called out over their nervous chatter.

Everyone laughed. Pregnant women are never comfortable.

Husbands and other labor partners grabbed a blue padded mat and wrestled it onto the floor. Friends and even mothers sometimes served as labor partners. A couple of the women had come alone and they looked kind of lost. She paired them up for tonight. Later she'd get their stories. No one went through this class alone. She made sure of that.

"Good evening and greetings. I'm McKenna Kirkpatrick, nurse practitioner and certified midwife." The session began. As she looked around, McKenna was filled with something bordering on awe. By the time these women delivered, she would know them very well. And they would trust her—or Bethany or Selena—implicitly. That piece was huge.

Ninety minutes later, she was turning out the lights and yawning. One of the women lagged behind. Skinny with unkempt dark hair, the girl looked way too young to be having a baby.

"Did you have a question?" McKenna asked. Sometimes, women had concerns they hesitated to ask in a group.

Hollowed out eyes stared at McKenna as the girl pushed a lank strand behind one ear. "Do you need a partner for this class?" the new student asked. A cold sore bloomed on her lower lip.

"It's a big help to have someone with you in labor, but no, you don't need a partner for the class." McKenna tried to read the girl who looked ready to beat a quick retreat.

"Well, that's good cuz Melissa, the woman I was partners with tonight, her husband will be here next time. But I've got...nobody."

"No mother? No sister?"

Looking away, the girl shook her head.

"Not a problem. And your name is..." McKenna glanced down the class list.

"Angie. Angie Dowd."

Giving her shoulder a soft squeeze, McKenna walked with her. "Going to the parking garage?" she asked when the elevator doors opened.

Like a ragdoll, Angie jerked away toward the stairwell. "No. I got other transportation."

This didn't feel right. "Okay, see you next time, Angie."

Shoulders sloped, the girl took off. Such a skinny thing. From the back, Angie didn't even look pregnant. McKenna would have to check the name with Bethany or Selena since she'd never had an office appointment with this girl.

Preoccupied, McKenna exited the elevator. The warm summer evening greeted her. Below on Lake Shore Drive, headlights beamed through the darkness. The city hummed. That's when she saw him. Eyes focused on the lake, Logan lounged against her car. Her heart leapt, steps slowing when he swung his gaze her way.

"Hey, kind of late. Still here?" She ignored the warm rush that banished her exhaustion. Here he was, just when she'd worked so hard to push him to the back of her mind.

In the semi-darkness his eyes were unreadable. "Waiting for you."

Amazing that her body could perk up like this. Every pore was sending her a text alert. Logan stepped away from her car, and she clicked her car door open while he watched her with those brooding eyes, now bluish gray.

"I enjoyed meeting your new partner." McKenna tried to fill the silence that hummed like an exposed electric wire. The darkness closed around them, intimate and seductive. "She'll be a good addition to your practice."

"Yeah, sure looks that way." When Logan ducked his head, she wanted to rumple that slicked back hair with both hands. "I wondered if you want to go sailing on Sunday. Thought I'd give this one more try."

"Oh, well." She had to shut this down fast. "Sorry but I already have plans."

"Family stuff again?" She took his obvious disappointment as a compliment and wished she didn't feel so pleased.

"Um, no. Not really." They were so close that she could inhale the salty scent of a man after a long day. It would be easy to step into his muscular arms. But a bold move like that would take her right down the slippery slope. His mention of her family reminded her of Amanda. Good grief, how could she have forgotten?

"Logan, I hate to ask you for a professional favor..."

"Not a problem." No hesitation there.

"It's for Amanda...my sister-in-law."

He nodded, and gosh, she loved that scruff on his chin. Longed to feel it against her palm. "Right, the girl who was crying at Seth's party."

So he'd noticed? "She's been trying to get pregnant for a long time, and I mentioned you had a fertility clinic...."

The concern that turned his gray eyes to soft suede almost made her change her mind about Sunday. But she had to stick to her plan. One good moment does not make a relationship. "Have her call the office. I'll leave a note with Tamara."

"Great. Thank you." After tossing her purse into the car, she turned to face him. Standing with hands crammed in his khaki pants, he looked as awkward as she felt.

"And thanks for the invitation, Logan. Wish I could make it." Her regret felt so real, but she had to shut this down. "Maybe Priscilla would like to go."

His head snapped up. "What? You're suggesting another woman?"

She swallowed. "You know, since she's new here. Might make her feel more at home."

But Logan didn't look pleased. "Nice of you, but I can take care of myself, McKenna."

"Just thought I'd make a suggestion." Had she made him angry?

"I'm a guy who likes to make my own choices." Logan's voice had dropped so low, it barely carried on the night breeze as he stepped closer. She backed away, hating the confusion on his face.

"See you later, McKenna." Pivoting, he closed the short distance to his car with long strides.

"Later," she echoed, disappointment battling relief in her stomach. When she slid inside her jeep, the car was still warm from a day in the sun. The onslaught of heat must have caused the sick taste in her mouth. She couldn't look back as she stepped on the gas and headed for the exit ramp.

~.~

Watching her drive away, Logan wished he'd kissed her silly. But maybe that's not what she wanted. Sure didn't seem that way earlier. Why was she pushing him away now? Public displays of affection had never been his thing, but lately he'd changed his mind.

Now he wanted to be that reckless guy who'd pull a hot redhead into his arms just to taste her plump peach lips again. He didn't give a damn what anyone thought. So what if his grandfather had founded Montclair. Impulses he'd kept in the neat box of his past were roaring to life. Disturbing but inviting too.

When he slid into his Porsche, he blasted the air. Damn, his thoughts were making him sweat like he'd just finished a seven-hour surgery.

Dating again wasn't easy. Sunday had been fun with McKenna's family, and he'd had a good time. He'd hung out with guys in college but he'd never run into a family like hers. He wanted to spend more time with her. Was she being cautious because they worked together? He had to respect her for that. Separating their personal lives from their professional positions might be a good idea. But the heat searing his thighs at the thought of her long red hair didn't agree. Steering wheel warm in his hands, he circled the almost deserted upper level of the parking lot and took the ramp down. He drove slowly to allow McKenna to clear the exit.

She wanted him to see other women? He didn't know her game but he was perfectly willing to play.

For a while, anyway.

Chapter 7

The weekend dragged. Taking the trash out Sunday morning, McKenna lingered in the warm breeze. Good grief, and she'd turned down a day on the lake? But she would have been in deep water with Logan. And she wasn't talking about the wet kind.

Although she was on call, her darn phone didn't ring. Any of her siblings would have welcomed her call, but then her brothers would ask questions about Logan. McKenna didn't want to go there. She called her sister Harper and they caught up. Harper's life in Savannah was always interesting. McKenna loved to hear Harper's stories and her hearty laugh. After they ended the call, McKenna drifted outside to garden.

Breathing in the sweet scent of soil, she spent the afternoon planting zinnias and geraniums in the postage stamp back yard. Then she filled her multiple bird feeders while the robins and cardinals twittered with approval from the branches of a tall oak.

Cripes, it was hot in the apartment when she went back inside. Her T-shirt felt glued to her back and she splashed her face with cool water. Then she turned her air conditioning up, thoughts drifting back to Logan. Had he invited Priscilla on his boat? McKenna's chest constricted at the thought of the Blonde Bombshell's hair blowing in the breezes of Lake Michigan. Maybe she was wearing a small blue bikini. Maybe Logan was helping her apply sun lotion. Maybe McKenna needed to have her head examined.

An imagination can sure make a girl miserable.

She hauled out her waffle maker.

Thank goodness she'd picked up strawberries on Saturday. Five o'clock was not too early for dinner in her book. Not after a long day full of self reproach. Crisp on the outside and buttermilk soft inside, her waffles turned out perfect. She drizzled warm maple syrup over pads of butter and heaped the sliced berries on top. Still not satisfied, McKenna nuked a jar of her favorite chocolate sauce and added it to her concoction. You can never have too much of a good thing.

Watching "Downton Abbey" re-runs that night, she reminded herself that this boring weekend had been the safest course. Hadn't she worked this all out in her mind? She reached for her reasoning.

Truth was, she had a short memory when it came to Logan.

When Monday morning came, she rolled out of bed, sleepless and ornery as heck. At the office, the lights on the main phone were blinking like crazy. Luckily, Dorothy had it all under control. Hot weather brought on dehydration that could cause expectant mothers all kinds of problems. McKenna swept through the waiting room and plodded back to her office at the end of the hall.

By noon, she'd fielded her third call from a patient complaining of dizziness. "How many times do we tell them to drink more fluids when the temperature spikes?" McKenna fretted to Selena.

"They're tired of peeing all the time," Selena commented while she charted. "I totally get that."

"Can't Marketing print up something for the education packets and add the information to the website?" McKenna combed one hand through her hair. The office was closed for lunch. Bethany, Lucy and Dorothy were eating in the break room, their giggles traveling down the hallway.

"How was your weekend?" Selena asked, closing out of the document. "Any action with your Hot Doc?"

Head down, McKenna kept leafing through her phone messages. "Had a great time. I, ah, gardened and straightened up my kitchen."

Selena shoved her chair back from the desk and it crashed into the file cabinets behind them. "Are you kidding me? After the way that man looked at you that Sunday?"

"I told him no."

"To what?"

"Sailing on his boat." McKenna stashed the pink phone slips into the pocket of her lab coat. "What do I know about sailing?"

"Are you out of your mind? Why did you say no?" Blowing out a breath, Selena looked ready to commit McKenna to their psych ward.

Sliding the glass window aside, McKenna stuck her head out and checked the waiting area. Empty. She closed the glass. "I'm putting some distance between us."

"What are you talking about?"

"I'm talking about my sanity. After Nick I'd like to go slow. Friends first, all that stuff."

Selena was seething. "Let's get some lunch. Obviously, your brain needs food."

Minutes later, they were headed for the overpass connecting the Medical Office Building to the main hospital. Below them, a siren shrieked, red lights flashing as the ambulance barreled toward the ER.

"Look, Marketing's new campaign." Selena stopped to admire the giant size posters displayed along the walkway. "*Let Our Team be Your Team.* Not bad."

"Wouldn't you know." McKenna came to a halt and balled her hands on her hips. One of the posters featured OB and Logan. Leaning against his desk with a disarming smile, Logan looked hot as all get out.

Impressively professional.

Devastatingly handsome.

The knot in McKenna's stomach cinched tighter.

Turning to McKenna, Selena pointed. "Take a good look at the guy you blew off."

"Button it up, girlfriend. Not backing down on this." With a shrug, McKenna resumed her walk, Selena galloping to catch up with her.

Conversation bubbled through the open doors when they neared the cafeteria. After grabbing trays and utensils, they headed to the salad bar. At one end of the long narrow eating area, volunteers were clustered in their pink jackets, silver heads bobbing as they visited with each other. TV sets with closed captioning were mounted strategically, giving employees access to the news or pro sports. Administrators were scattered among the tables of employees. The policy at Montclair was to mingle and stay in touch with the employees. Most visiting families chose to eat in the Atrium Café on the first floor.

Warren was seated with some of the Imaging Department staff, nodding as he listened. McKenna wondered what the radiologists thought about bringing more imaging equipment into the OR. This group could be pretty territorial. Logan had been here long enough to be aware of hospital politics. Still, he might be the type who forged ahead, no matter what people thought. She had to admire him for that.

When they passed his table Warren glanced up. "McKenna, how's that OB committee coming?"

"Great. We should be ready for the Board Meeting." She wasn't about to mention that they hadn't reached consensus. Let Logan be the bearer of that news.

When they sat down at an empty table, Selena glanced over at McKenna's plate and sputtered. "That's not lunch. That's a food tasting."

"I'm not that hungry. Must be the heat." Two tablespoons of broccoli salad, four grapes and some big chunks of watermelon were about all she could stomach. "Besides, I'm trying to lose weight."

"So, what's on your schedule?" Selena asked. "I mean, after you shake off whatever's bothering you."

"Preparing for my childbirth class after I finish clinic." She thought back to last Wednesday's class. "Selena, do you know a patient named Angie Dowd?"

"Sure do. Came through the Healthy Start Program." Montclair
had a partnership with Chicago's Healthy Start Program for
mothers without insurance or other resources.

"And?" McKenna pressed her.

"Got a funny feeling about that girl. Okay, she's young to have
a baby, eighteen or nineteen, but that's not unusual with Healthy
Start. Probably has a job in some store on Halsted Street. Just
getting by or living with her folks. But most moms are happy, even
when they're strapped for cash. Not Angie. Why are you asking?"

McKenna shrugged. "It's just that she didn't have a partner
when she came to the first class, not even a relative or friend. And
I agree, she seems kind of sad."

Dangling her fork in one hand, Selena nodded. "Yeah, well, you
always seem to have a sixth sense about people. Let's keep an eye
on her."

For a few seconds, they ate in silence. Then, eyes sparkling,
Selena leaned across the table. "Back to Hot Doc. Is he going with
us to Guatemala? Or is he too damn picky?"

"Haven't got a clue. You'll have to talk to him, but go easy."
McKenna's cheeks were probably as pink as the watermelon she'd
just eaten. After asking Logan to help Amanda, she wasn't going to
badger him about Midwives in Action.

Spearing a piece of pineapple, Selena gave her a cheeky grin.
"We could use a doc on that trip. Gary and Eric both have family
commitments on one of the weekends, so they have to stay local."

McKenna huffed out an impatient sigh. "Isn't there anyone

else? I'm not crazy about having Hot Doc in the hammock next to me, although we need a physician. We could run into trouble like last year."

Selena nodded. "Amazing how far some of the women walk to get to us. Kills me to send them home without resolving their problem."

"Remember Sarita last year? We were lucky to get her into a hospital in time but that was…" Then she saw them. Logan escorting Priscilla Preston into the physicians' cafeteria, totally engrossed.

"What are you staring at?"

"Hot Doc. And I am not staring." She dropped her eyes.

Selena glanced over her shoulder. "Girl, you have to stake your claim."

"Not going to happen. I'm all aboard the buddy train, remember?"

Selena snorted.

Just then Jack Frazier stopped at their table. "Glad I ran into you, McKenna. The blog on delivering twins brought in a lot of traffic to the website. What's your suggestion for this week?"

"Oh, Jack. I'm so sorry, but I'm slammed." She pitched her fork onto her empty plate.

"You mind if I take this one?" Selena asked Jack. "Women need to read about hydrating during hot weather."

"We warn them, but they're just not getting the message," McKenna agreed.

"Sounds like a winner. Thanks, Selena." With a wave, Jack went on his way.

McKenna eyed the closed door of the physicians' inner sanctum. She shouldn't feel like body checking Priscilla every time she saw her with Logan. Had to work on this.

~.~

As the week unfolded, McKenna didn't bump into Logan—not in the parking garage, not in the medical building. Relieved? Definitely. Frustrated? That too. The OB committee continued to piece together a presentation for the Board. Throughout the meeting, Logan was crisp and efficient, Priscilla at his elbow, leaning close as if she could not hear him unless they were breathing the same air.

Friend. Colleague. McKenna tried to keep those words front and center while she watched the two. Wasn't easy.

When the meeting wrapped up and people scattered, McKenna hoofed it toward the cafeteria, desperate for a cup of mocha coffee sold in the coffee machine. While she was inhaling the frothy liquid filling the styrofoam cup, she looked up to find Priscilla bearing down on her.

"Hey, how it going?" McKenna lifted the cup to her lips and yelped when she burned her tongue.

"You okay?" Priscilla's lips curled, like she was almost enjoying this.

"Fine, just fine." McKenna blew onto the surface of the coffee while her tongue throbbed. "So you're settling in?"

"Sure are. Thanks for asking." Priscilla looked tired this morning, eyes shadowed as she pondered the selections. Must be difficult to be a single mother and McKenna wondered what her story was.

"Bet your parents are happy to have their granddaughters around."

"Thrilled, although it's temporary until I find my own place." Priscilla fingered a wisp of hair behind her ear. "So much has changed since I lived here years ago. Guess it will take time."

"Logan can probably help with that." McKenna could almost hear Selena, Vanessa and Amy hissing at her.

Priscilla's head did a slow swivel. "You think? I hate to impose on him."

Ah, hah. So he hadn't taken Priscilla sailing. Yet.

McKenna battled the surge of relief into submission and cleared her throat. "No really. He has a boat and golfs, or so I've heard. Probably be thrilled to show you around." She could tell the idea was getting some traction with Priscilla.

"From what my parents tell me, he might need to get out more," Priscilla said slowly, her voice gaining assurance. "After all, our families are old friends. What would make more sense, right?"

Done. "Yep, exactly."

Priscilla's eyes flicked over. "So kind of you to call that to my attention, McKenna. Thank you."

"Don't mention it. Gotta run." Sprinting toward the door, McKenna left Priscilla standing at the coffee machine, studying her own reflection in the stainless steel surface. As she hoofed it back to her office, her clogs were whisper soft on the tiles, unlike her chattering mind.

She thought she'd feel better about this.

~.~

On Wednesday night, McKenna's natural childbirth class focused on deep breathing. Once again, Angie Dowd showed up alone. Her big plaid shirt might hide her growing tummy but her legs and arms were stick-thin. How could Angie stand that heavy shirt in this heat? At the end of the girl's spindly legs were worn tennis shoes with laces not tied—a real safety hazard for an expectant mother and one of McKenna's pet peeves. As it turned out, Angie was the only one without a partner that night.

"Remember, coaches. Mom is going to have a lot on her mind when she goes into labor," McKenna emphasized before they started the drill. "You're the one who has to encourage her to take a deep cleansing breath when she needs it."

Angie looked lost, and McKenna sidled over to her. "Want me to be your partner tonight?"

"Sure. Why not?"

McKenna slid down behind her. The girl felt like she was made of matchsticks.

"Draw in that air," she coached Angie and the class. "Picture yourself pulling oxygen right down to your tummy."

The entire room inhaled—except for Angie. Her shallow breaths barely raised her shoulders.

"You okay?" Peeking around Angie's shoulder, McKenna got a glimpse of one cheek. She froze. The unkempt shanks of Angie's hair didn't quite cover the purple bruise.

She couldn't let Angie know anything was wrong. "A little

deeper, Angie. Picture drawing the air into the bottom of your stomach." While Angie sucked in a mouthful of air, McKenna's eyes blurred. Squeezing the girl's shoulders, she leapt up to circle the room, coaching the couples on the floor and trying to control her anger.

No way was she going to ignore this. Later, she'd talk to Angie. But what would she say?

When the lesson ended, the coaches dragged the mats to the pile in the corner. Clutching the latest handouts, women shuffled out the door with that wide pregnant gait. Angie lagged behind, the last one at the back door.

"Angie, could I talk to you for a minute?" The girl's brown eyes darkened to stone as McKenna approached. "Everything okay? You're kind of quiet tonight."

"I'm fine." Shifting from one foot to the other, Angie rolled her handouts into a tight cylinder. "I'm only coming here because it's free, you know, so I can do this on my own."

"Do this on your own? I don't follow you."

"Hospitals and doctors and stuff—they all cost money, right? Don't got none."

"So, you're thinking you'll do…what on your own? Not sure I understand."

Hands on hips, Angie faced her. "Have the baby." The choked words negated her bold stance.

McKenna's heart squeezed. She wanted to take Angie home, give her a bath and a good meal. "Do you mean that you plan to have your baby at home?"

"Maybe."

"That's always an option. In fact, my mother had all seven of us at home."

Angie's face brightened, making her almost pretty. "She did that all alone?"

McKenna nodded. "Sure did, but a midwife helped her."

The girl swallowed hard. "Maybe she didn't have any other way to do it. Some people don't, you know."

"Do you plan to keep the baby, Angie?" she asked gently.

The girl's face deflated like a pricked balloon. "Haven't decided. Not yet, anyway."

"We have social workers on staff. Would you like to talk to one?" Each word felt like walking across a mine field.

Angie edged toward the door. "No reason for that."

"It's free." She could not lose this girl.

The conversation had turned into a stare-down.

Sometimes McKenna just could not let things go. "Angie, how'd you get that bruise on your cheek?" she asked softly.

The girl jerked back, distrust curling one lip. Then she pulled a hunk of hair over the purple stain. "Ran into a kitchen cupboard. I'm so clumsy. A clumsy girl. My...mother always says so. Gotta go."

She took off down the hall, shoe laces slapping the tile floor. Worry tied a knot in McKenna's stomach as she watched her go.

That night when she went to bed, McKenna wasn't thinking about Logan. Angie Dowd occupied her thoughts. Curled up at her feet on the green and orange quilt, Sasha regarded her with wise blue eyes.

"Some women are fools when it comes to men," she told her cat. Sasha blinked as if she totally agreed.

Chapter 8

The next day, Amanda called, an excited lilt in her voice.

"McKenna, I've got an appointment with Dr. Castle. Thanks so much for your help."

"Don't mention it. There are probably a lot of factors involved." McKenna chose her words carefully. Her sister-in-law had already been through so much, and she didn't want to dangle false hopes. "Logan's not a miracle worker. But he is a darn good physician, and he's kind. You'll be in good hands."

"I'm just saying I feel hopeful, McKenna. That's all," Amanda said quietly.

McKenna wanted to kick herself. "Don't mean to dampen your hopes. Let me know how it goes."

"Absolutely."

As McKenna stood in the hall of the Medical Office Building, tapping her phone against her palm, Logan appeared at the end of the corridor. No mistaking that posture. He carried himself well, lab coat shining like fine table linen. Walking with him, Priscilla had two darling little girls in tow. In matching blue dresses with bows at the waistline, they were clones of their mother—a striking family. As they walked toward her, the children were laughing over something Logan said. The four of them looked perfect together.

"McKenna, so glad we ran into you!" Face glowing, Priscilla nudged the girls in front of her. "I want you to meet my daughters."

"We're giving the girls a tour." Logan seemed fascinated.

"Meredith is seven, and Ashley's five. Girls, I'd like you to meet McKenna Kirkpatrick. She's a nurse…" Priscilla stressed that last word. "…who helps women have babies."

"Like you, Mom?" Ashley piped up.

Priscilla gave her head a little shake. Of course her hair stayed in place. "Not exactly, but pretty close."

Surprise left McKenna breathless. Was that a smack down, especially after their helpful girl-to-girl chat yesterday? Priscilla was putting her in her place…and apparently enjoying it.

Still considering Priscilla's girls with barely concealed wonder, Logan didn't seem to notice the slight.

"McKenna, do you mind showing the girls your office? We're packed with patients this afternoon and have to get back." Priscilla glanced over at Logan for confirmation.

Okay, then. Now I'm a baby-sitter. "Not a problem. I'll be happy to have your daughters tag along. I'm finished with my patients for the day, but I can show them around." McKenna kept her voice bright. If she was irritated with anyone, it was herself.

"Are you sure you have time? We can find someone else…" Logan began.

McKenna waved his concerns away. "Trust me, we'll have fun. Dorothy, our receptionist, keeps special lollipops in her desk drawer." She smiled at the girls, but only Ashley returned the favor.

Meredith glared.

"Oh, we don't eat sugar before dinner," Priscilla said in a Disneyland voice.

At that, Meredith groaned. "Not the point, Mom. A lollipop? You think we're going to eat those?" All of seven and she was kicking her mother to the curb.

Obviously Priscilla was used to it. "Children. Just wait." She lifted her brows at McKenna.

Right. A direct stab to the heart. McKenna pulled her lab coat closer around her.

Priscilla consulted her Rolex watch. "Grandpa will pick you up in thirty minutes at the front of the Outpatient Rotunda. McKenna, You don't mind, do you?" She didn't even bother to look up.

"Not at all." By that point, McKenna was feeling sorry for these kids. Something told her they got shuffled around a lot.

"Thank you, McKenna," Logan said. "And it was great meeting you, ladies." With a parting smile, he turned to leave, Priscilla trotting after him in peep-toe patent leather heels. McKenna's feet hurt just looking at them.

"Bye, Dr. Castle," Ashley called after him.

Logan turned, looking startled and pleased, like she'd just called him Daddy. "Bye, Ashley. See you soon, honey. Meredith." He gave the older girl a brisk nod, Meredith wasn't buying it. No smile. Just daggers for her mother.

"Come on, girls. Time for a tour." McKenna herded them toward the For Women office.

"What do we have here?" Dorothy asked when they pushed

open the glass-paneled door into the waiting room.

"I'd like you to meet Dr. Preston's daughters." McKenna introduced them.

"Well, well. And aren't you just the cutest things?" Gray hair bobbing, Dorothy reached into her top drawer.

Meredith snorted. "Cute?"

Dorothy's eyes widened, hand still in the candy drawer.

"These girls are so smart. They never eat sugar before dinner," she said for Dorothy's benefit. Meredith glowered while her younger sister looked crestfallen.

McKenna squeezed Ashley's shoulder. "But we'll pick up something later in the Gift Shop for after dinner. Are Bethany and Selena in with patients?"

"Actually Bethany's got a delivery," Dorothy told her. "Got the call right after you left." Selena's with the patient in room five, and Lucy is straightening up the education room."

Two very pregnant patients were flipping through magazines in the waiting room. They smiled at Ashley and Meredith with the blissful hope of expectant mothers.

By that time, the Wall of Fame had caught the children's attention. The two of them spent at least five minutes scrutinizing the baby pictures. "This is what my mom does too," Meredith said with obvious pride. "She delivers babies, just like McKenna."

Suddenly McKenna had come up in Meredith's eyes.

The rest of the tour didn't take long. When they reached McKenna's office, Meredith criticized everything from the brown carpet—her mother's office always had an Oriental rug—to the messy desk. Never had thirty minutes seemed so long. By the time McKenna walked them down to the rotunda, she was in bad need of a sugar fix. After introducing the girls to Phyllis, who ran the Gift Shop, McKenna picked out three bars of dark chocolate with caramel inside, handing one to each girl. Broad smiles indicated she'd hit the jackpot.

"Do you have your own little girl?" Ashley asked, blue eyes wide.

"Nope. Not yet." Leading them outside, they took a seat on one of the metal benches, munching and waiting for their grandfather. The summer sun beat down and McKenna was wishing she'd brought sunglasses when a silver-haired man pulled up in a black Lincoln. She immediately pegged him as Priscilla's father. Dressed in a green polo, he looked as if he'd just come from the golf course as he circled the front of the car.

"How are my girls?" When he opened his arms, Ashley bounded toward him with Meredith trailing behind.

McKenna stepped up to shake his hand. "Mr. Preston, I'm McKenna Kirkpatrick, a midwife at the hospital. I, ah, work with Priscilla. Just had a delightful thirty minutes with your granddaughters."

"Oh, thank you. But my goodness, I'm sure you have better things to do."

In a heartbeat McKenna knew Mr. Preston realized the kids had been dumped on her. Probably happened a lot, from the expression on his face.

"Girls, thank McKenna for taking time out of her busy day."

He waited while the girls thanked her. With a set smile, he took both girls by the hand and walked them to the car.

Watching the black car circle the drive and leave, McKenna felt sad for the whole family. This certainly wasn't the happily-ever-after life any of them had pictured.

Once inside the air-conditioned lobby, McKenna shifted her thoughts to the Board Meeting. Was she about to go head-to-head with Logan for donor dollars?

~.~

Wasn't like her to feel this nervous. McKenna's black and white spectators clicked on the brown laminate floor as she made her way to the Board Room, presentation materials under one arm. Felt weird to wear heels in the hospital instead of her trusty clogs, but tonight she was pulling out all the big guns. She'd even swept her hair into a sleek knot and wore the pearl earrings her parents had given her when she earned her nursing practitioner certification.

What a relief that this project had been pulled together so quickly. Jack Frazier had given her the architectural drawings and Logan would bring the OR presentation. She'd made a quick run home to change into a white linen summer suit with a peach silk blouse. Palms damp, she pushed open the door.

"Good to see you, McKenna." Always warm and welcoming, Warren greeted her. "Logan tells me you have some great ideas to present tonight."

Hmm. And had Logan favored one idea over the other? "Sure do."

"Want me to put these boards someplace for you?"

"Thanks, Warren." Although she glanced around, Logan wasn't here yet.

Warren beckoned to his assistant Melanie, who took the sketches up to the front of the room.

The door opened behind them.

"Logan," Warren greeted him.

Oh, my. Logan was looking very Jay Gatsby in a navy pinstriped suit. The man was heart-stoppingly handsome. She could almost feel the silk blouse flutter over her heart.

"McKenna." Nodding, Logan brushed one hand over his red and white tie.

"Logan." She could barely get his name out.

Warren steered them toward the front of the room. Board members clustered around a table where a white-coated waiter dispensed drinks. McKenna took something icy that looked like fruit punch but definitely had a kick. Bring it on. Tonight she might need it.

"Glad to hear you have another physician on board," Warren commented, nodding at Logan. "Priscilla, is it?"

McKenna took another slug of her drink.

"Right, Priscilla Preston. Gary and I are relieved. Good thing for our practice," Logan said with his characteristic certainty.

Warren turned to her. "Will it be helpful to have a female doctor working with your group, McKenna?"

Time to play the team player card. "Probably won't make much difference," she said carefully, not wanting to offend Logan. "But it might help to have a woman's perspective."

Warren introduced her to the board members. Dennis Heckman was CEO of one of the larger banks and she'd seen his picture in the *Chicago Tribune*. Mark Winston chaired the Health Care Services Department at the University of Chicago. The introductions and the names kept coming. Everyone seemed to know Logan and some asked polite questions about his grandmother. Among the group of ten select members, Fay Shriver was the only woman. A well-known attorney, she often championed women's rights.

"Delighted to meet you, Fay." McKenna offered her hand.

Fay's eyes lit up. "Warren was telling me you travel to Guatemala every summer to teach."

"Right. I'm part of Midwives in Action, a group that works with villages that have little access to care. We train other women to step into the midwife role. They also help families with general health issues."

"Impressive." Fay nodded her well-coiffed silver hair.

Standing near them with Warren, Logan seemed to be listening but said nothing, just sipped his drink. Selena might have some convincing to do to persuade Hot Doc to join them on their trip south.

Although the board room was impressive with its mahogany wainscoting and rich brown and black striped wallpaper, her attention was drawn to the pictures of former chairmen of the board. A portrait of Logan's grandfather also hung in a place of honor. Just looking at the stately gentleman with the kind smile, McKenna knew what Logan would look like in his old age.

He might have to work on those laugh lines.

"What is it?" Logan asked when he caught her staring.

"Just admiring your grandfather. You look like him."

"My grandmother misses him." Sadness echoed in his voice.

"I would imagine so." Although she wanted to ask more questions about his family, two servers had pushed carts into the room, trailing delightful aromas. The board members took their seats at the large oval table. Warren sat near Logan and beckoned to her to sit between them. Dinner was served. Seemed like chicken had become a staple in every meeting, this time with wild rice and fresh green beans. The cucumber salad smelled of summer, sprinkled with dill and some kind of creamy dressing.

As she nibbled, McKenna keyed into a conversation across the table. Fay was talking about a new women's shelter that helped abused women. "The volunteers prepare women to reenter the workforce with clothes suitable for the office. The closet is always open for donations."

"What a terrific effort." McKenna had some suits she hardly ever wore.

On Logan's left sat Mark Winston and they chatted while she updated Warren on the LDRP committee meetings. At one point, she looked up and Logan was staring at her plate, a grin tilting one corner of his lips.

Startled, she glanced down. "What, you want my beans?"

Logan shook his head. "Just thinking about our conversation at the Purple Frog," he murmured with a naughty tweak of one eyebrow.

That provocative conversation seemed like eons ago.

Her cheeks warmed. "Sometimes words can come back to haunt you."

"Really? I kind of enjoyed that meeting," he whispered in a voice meant for only her ears.

"You have a little bit of dressing in the corner of your mouth."

He didn't blink. When his tongue darted out to remedy the problem, she almost lost it. Cripes, she was mangling the napkin in her lap. Just when she had relegated Logan Castle to "buddy" and had pushed Priscilla into his path, McKenna's body roared to life and betrayed her.

Grabbing her ice water, she drained the glass.

By the time the strawberry cheesecake was served, a hunger for more than food had carved a hollow in McKenna's body. She twitched at the first slight pressure of Logan's thigh against hers. Must be accidental. He was talking to Mark.

The second time? Two could play at this game, and she aligned her thigh with his, a gentle but persistent pressure. Logan's muscles felt firm and powerful.

Was he flexing them? She was toast.

"Enjoying the evening?" When Logan finally turned from Mark, mischief danced in his eyes. My, he could be such a surprise, her Hot Doc.

"Absolutely." Savoring her final bite, she swallowed and then slowly licked the spoon of strawberry gel, hoping to heck no one was watching. Her hunger for sugar had been insatiable lately.

"Too damn hot in here," Logan muttered, tugging on his collar.

"If you can't take the heat..."

His eyes pinned her. "Oh, I can take it. Trust me."

Grabbing the program she began to fan herself.

And he wasn't finished. Those delicious lips were serving up more. "I understand from Priscilla that you two had an interesting conversation yesterday."

Although McKenna didn't think it possible, her stomach plunged as the heat rose. "We did?" she managed to squeak out.

His eyes bored holes into hers. "Something about you suggesting me as a tour guide."

"I, ah, just thought..."

"I'm capable of filling my own time, McKenna. You may have missed that, but I know my own mind. And right now, my mind is..."

Good Lord, she was actually leaning toward Hot Doc to catch that last word when Mark asked him a question. Logan turned away. Butterflies were doing a mating dance in her stomach. Why was she pushing him in Priscilla's direction? Every assertive cell in her body stood up to be counted.

But memories seared her, burning away that fluttery feeling. When she first met Nick, he'd been fun. Sometimes it took time for the real person to be revealed. McKenna passed on coffee when the waiter circled the table. She had enough acid in her stomach to last all night.

Finally, Dennis Heckman took the floor, and the meeting began. While staff from Food Services cleared the table and served more coffee, Dennis began introductions. "With us tonight are obstetrician Dr. Logan Castle and midwife McKenna Kirkpatrick to present, from what Warren's told me, some exciting ideas for the future of the Obstetrics Department."

Logan stood and took command of the room. The board members gave him their full attention. After all, his grandfather had founded this hospital. "We have two projects for you to consider tonight," he began. "The one I'm most familiar with is an opportunity to optimize the operating suites by adding radiology equipment for on-the-spot diagnosis to handle emergencies that can crop up."

Melanie, the board secretary, began to distribute Logan's packets. When he'd finished walking them through the proposed updates, he fielded some questions. The room became warm and perspiration prickled around her hairline. McKenna slipped off her jacket, just as Logan introduced her. "And now McKenna will take you through an equally exciting project to renovate the unit itself."

Taking a deep breath, she pushed up from her chair and walked to the front of the table where the sketches were displayed. As she explained the all-in-one room concept, excitement kicked up in the room. Montclair was known for cutting edge service delivery, and the Board's interest was clear. Her spirits rose.

"Water birthing suites?" Fay Shriver's face was a question mark. This was only her second board meeting.

Quickly McKenna filled her in. "We hope to familiarize more women with the benefits of giving birth in warm water. The Jacuzzis can also be used to soothe labor during a traditional delivery."

"And of course we follow proper sanitation protocols," Logan interjected.

This time, Logan's obvious caution didn't annoy her. She thought back to what Gary had told her. Tragedy could make a man cautious. How could she help Logan through this?

After twenty minutes of discussion, Dennis said, "And what do you need from us?" He winked at Warren.

"Well, Dennis, I think you know what we need," Warren said with one of his magnanimous smiles. He'd won the support of this Board over his tenure, and they trusted his judgment. "The question is, how much would you pony up? And is it enough for both projects?"

Wow, the breath left her body. McKenna couldn't even look at Logan, although he'd become very still. Would the Board back both initiatives?

"Of course we're willing to dig into the coffers," Dennis began, glancing around the table. "Montclair is known as a leader in healthcare innovation. If it makes sense to do both, well, then, that's what we should do." The other Board members seemed to agree. No objections were voiced. "But it's customary to also raise funds. When donors are excited about a project, the Board feels more sure that we're heading in the right direction."

Logan leaned forward. "We're happy to be involved in any fundraising effort."

Dennis inclined his head. "With your family history, Logan, we would expect nothing less."

A muscle twitched in Logan's jaw. Probably wasn't easy to work in a place where you continually had to live up to your family name.

"I'll second that." McKenna jumped in to draw attention from Logan's obvious discomfort. "Our committee will be involved as well."

"That'll be great, McKenna," Dennis said while Fay smiled her way.

Granted, McKenna's experience with fundraising was a lot more informal than what the Board was considering. Someone in her family was always having a potluck for a neighbor down on their luck or a bingo night for a hospitalized fireman. Still, might be fun to work on the outing.

Dennis nodded. "Just occurred to me that we have our golf outing in August. Haven't designated a specific beneficiary for those dollars. Might it be possible to rev up that initiative for the new OB projects?"

A rustle of approval filtered through the group and they took a show of hands. McKenna felt heady with relief as she walked to the parking garage fifteen minutes later. The Board's support for both projects helped her side step any open confrontation with Logan. Still, she wanted him to feel more comfortable with the whole concept.

The breeze blew cool on her bare neck and arms. Clouds scudded across the night sky. Not many cars left on the upper level, and she hurried, not wanting to run into Logan. His mischievous teasing under the table left her heady and breathless.

Tossing her jacket and purse onto the passenger seat of the

jeep, she slid inside. In her rear view mirror she saw Logan's red Porsche in a distant corner. He was always so careful.

Before starting the engine, she rested one hand on her thigh.

Tonight he'd been reckless.

And she wasn't one bit sorry.

~.~

When Logan reached the top level, McKenna's car was gone. Damn. Warren had grabbed him on the way out with questions.

Now Logan ripped off his tie, undid his top shirt button and whipped off his jacket. Summer was settling on Chicago like a blasted suit of armor. He'd hoped to corner McKenna up here with some pretty direct questions. Heck with being polite. He was going to have to make his point, and he didn't intend to be subtle. The independent redhead might call for a more direct approach.

Chapter 9

Anytime McKenna saw Logan later in the week, Priscilla was always with him.

Hanging on his every word.

Tuning into him with soulful nods.

McKenna should have felt relieved instead of downright annoyed. At herself.

As the week wound down, McKenna's elation following the Board meeting eased. The weekend loomed and no word from Logan. Her relief held a hint of disappointment she hoped would dissipate with time. She just wasn't ready. The timing was off.

Usually girlfriends were safer, but not right now. They'd ask too many questions. When her younger sister Harper called from Savannah, they had a long chat. Harper always needed advice, and McKenna felt flattered that her younger sister turned to her for suggestions.

McKenna gave no indication that she was struggling herself.

That weekend, she chilled out. Had one patient in labor and she thoroughly enjoyed the process. Lily Green and her boyfriend Ralph were as unconventional as they come. Lily was the kind of woman who milled her own corn meal and made yogurt all the time. No need to talk to Lily about watching her sodium or sugar.

When Petunia Green was born, Ralph just about turned inside out. Lily had been a trooper throughout the labor and birth. By that time, it was late Saturday night and McKenna told herself she was glad she didn't have any plans. Sunday was a recoup day—time to sip her hazelnut coffee and read the paper, feet up on the hassock where Sasha slept, sprawled in the sunlight.

Then Seth called and invited her over for pizza. "Whole family coming?" she asked.

"Nope, just Selena."

"I'll be there."

The casual meal quickly turned into an interrogation.

"Did you see Logan last night?" Selena asked as they split the last piece of Santa Fe pizza.

"Nope," McKenna managed around a mouthful.

Selena groaned and rolled her eyes, cheeks bulging while she chewed.

"Okay, I'm out of here. This is turning into girl talk," Seth mumbled, pushing up from the table.

"That's right. Run away," McKenna teased. "We're going to talk about feelings."

Seth disappeared into the family room.

"So what's this about no plans? I tell you, that man is into you. He can hardly look at you without blushing in those meetings!" Selena's protest ended on an outraged uptick.

"You know, I don't think I'm ready for this. After, you know, my last relationship." McKenna pushed her plate away.

"Girl, you are the woman who is ready for anything, no matter what the day or time," Selena sputtered.

"Maybe Logan needs a different type of woman," McKenna said quietly.

Selena snorted. "I think you should let that man decide who he does or does not want."

"Don't want to end up investing another two years in the wrong guy." Might as well put it out there. But she wasn't about to share the information about Logan's son. Was he even ready to have a relationship, especially one that might lead to children?

Her mind took a huge leap that left her breathless.

Selena's brow furrowed. "But you don't really know him yet. I'm talking to him tomorrow about the Midwives in Action meeting Thursday night."

"Don't get your hopes up." Logan in the mountains of Guatemala? Two weeks ago, McKenna couldn't picture it. Now? She wasn't sure.

"We'll see." Selena smiled mysteriously as she began to clean up. "How about some rocky road ice cream?"

"Chocolate with marshmallows? You're on and make it a double."

The following day, McKenna's morning was filled with patient appointments. By noon she'd seen six women including three new patients, all interested in water birthing. It was amazing. In fact, she'd had a call from the *Chicago Tribune*, asking for an interview. But she needed to talk to Selena and Bethany before she called the writer back. Her one fear was that any article might sweep in more business than they could comfortably handle.

She kept herself busy and left the office late, glad to see that Logan's car was gone. When she got home, she went out for a run. Physical exhaustion helped her sleep and staved away the memory of a warm thigh or a laughing pair of gray eyes.

~.~

"My goodness, Ashley just can't stop talking about you," Priscilla told her at the next OB meeting. She looked a little miffed, and McKenna almost laughed.

"Your daughters are really special," McKenna told her, opening her portfolio and taking out a pen. One was especially bratty and the other, especially sweet.

"Aren't they something?" But Priscilla looked a little unnerved instead of blissed out.

Logan began the meeting. The architects were hard at work on plans for the new unit. Designers were completing several sample boards with swatches of paint, fabric and flooring. Oh, how McKenna wished it were eighteen months from now. Lost in her eager anticipation, she almost missed Logan's comment.

"…and so of course we'll have birthing pools in half the rooms," he threw out. "That should take care of it."

"Oh, I would certainly think so," Priscilla quickly agreed.

Stunned, McKenna glanced up to find Regina's eyes on her.

"Do you think that will be adequate, McKenna?" the VP of Nursing asked.

McKenna blinked, struggling to pull her mind back from la la land. "Ideally, I'd like to see every woman have an opportunity to use water birth, if that's what she chooses."

Logan tilted his head as if he were trying to get his mind around that concept. "You really think that's a possibility, McKenna?"

"I definitely think it's a possibility." The room fell silent. There they were, nose to nose again. The clock on the wall ticked loudly.

Priscilla was staring holes in McKenna. She had begun to shadow Logan in the OR, and the word was that she was exacting—like him. Logan's face cleared and he leaned toward her. "Mind if I stop in some time, McKenna, to learn more about water birthing? Do you know if your group anticipates any cases today?"

"Hard to know but I'll text you if we do, how about that?"

Really? Truth was, it was about time. She knew he was insanely busy, but still, it would be good for him to see what really went on in that room. The meeting was just wrapping up when Logan mentioned that the vendor who carried the special beds for the proposed unit would be coming soon.

"Why not have some fun with that?" McKenna suggested, her mind leaping ahead.

Logan's brow wrinkled. "Fun? How?"

McKenna glanced around the table, ideas forming in her mind. "We could ask vendors to bring samples to create a model labor, delivery, recovery and postpartum room. Everything from the bed to the bassinet to the big screen TV. Let's get the entire hospital involved in the excitement. Employees can tour the model room, enter a drawing, and fill out a suggestion card." Her mind kept flashing ideas with strobe light intensity.

Enthusiasm sparked in the room while they brainstormed to make A Day in the LDRP fun and memorable. The adrenaline rush carried McKenna through the first part of the morning. When she returned to her office following the meeting, patients crowded the waiting room. Dorothy was busy answering phones at the front desk while Lucy dashed from room to room, taking urine samples and vitals.

"Where's Bethany?" McKenna asked Lucy. Selena had just disappeared into an exam room.

"In the birthing suite," Lucy told her. "Sandy Johnson went into labor early this morning."

Taking out her phone, McKenna texted Logan. Of course she'd get patient approval before bringing Logan in to observe, but Sandy was the type of girl who wouldn't mind if her birthing experience became a teaching moment.

"So, I guess you got to him?" Selena commented when they passed in the hallway a few minutes later.

Puzzled, she turned. "Who are you talking about?"

"Logan," Selena murmured. "He's coming to the meeting of Midwives in Action Thursday night."

"Really?" The man was full of surprises. "We can always use more docs, right?"

"You bet." Snatching her next chart from the wall, Selena disappeared.

McKenna was giving Trish Carter a pep talk on cutting down on the salt when a knock came on the door. Lucy poked her head in. "Got a minute, McKenna?"

"Be back in a second," she told Trish. "And you can get dressed."

"Bethany's having some trouble with Sandy Johnson," Lucy told her in a low whisper once McKenna had stepped out and closed the door behind her. "Shoulder dystocia. She said to call you."

McKenna was already rushing down the hall, binding her hair back with a scrunchie. "Ask Selena to finish up with Trish, could you?"

The warm air of the birthing suite swallowed her as McKenna slipped inside and the door whooshed closed behind her. Despite the soothing guitar music, tension wired the room. Quickly she scrubbed down, grabbed a mask and snapped on her gloves. Face flushed, Sandy was hard at work in the birthing pool, supported by her husband. Jason's face was tight with concern.

The downy head turtled in and out with each contraction. The baby was stuck.

A reassuring smile stayed on McKenna's face as she turned to Bethany. The younger woman had been through this situation before and McKenna trusted her. God bless her, Bethany's voice was cool and measured as she gave the instructions they'd used the last time. "Now, Sandy, for the next contraction, I want you to hold back. Let's just give the baby a minute to turn."

"No pushing?" Sandy's blood shot eyes bulged with frustration.

"Not yet, okay?" Bethany told her.

Jason's lips tightened. Like most guys, he wanted to help but didn't know how. McKenna knew him from the natural childbirth class. "We've got time," she assured them both. Any additional stress now could make Sandy tense her muscles. "Just nice and easy. No pushing. Just pant."

McKenna had some experience with this problem, which had come up a couple of times in her practice. The baby's shoulders could get hooked on the mother's pubic bone. For one delivery, Bethany had been with McKenna. Sure helped to have another midwife in the room because things could get tricky.

"With a little patience, the baby will often eventually find the right position," Bethany assured the parents, echoing McKenna's words from their similar delivery. She'd come a long way during her months with their practice.

McKenna and Bethany settled in. Another contraction came and went. Sandy's face paled with disappointment when her baby didn't budge. The little guy's shoulder was probably still lodged tight. Frustrated tears trickled down the laboring mother's cheeks.

"Honey, you can do this," Jason assured his wife. Stress sharpened his usual jovial features.

"Time to change positions." McKenna barely heard the door open behind her. "Sandy, let's get you on your feet. Jason, can you help with this?"

Soothing his wife with soft words, Jason coaxed her from her crouched position. She leaned against him and he blotted her face with a towel.

"Now, let's just put one foot on the edge of the pool," McKenna suggested as Jason held Sandy steady. "Picture your body opening to give the little guy room. Bet you've already picked out a name."

"Shaun," Sandy whispered. "Shaun Jason. Oh, God. Here it

comes." Below her pink sports bra, her tummy grew shiny hard.

"Pant, no pushing," Bethany reminded her. "Pant."

As Sandy panted, her face turned red from holding back the muscular push that just seemed so right at this stage. The baby needed time to move.

"The head is rotating." A small measure of relief rippled through McKenna as she watched the furry top of a tiny head turn just a bit. When the contraction eased, they all relaxed. A little movement might release that tiny shoulder.

"We're making progress," McKenna told the parents.

"Gosh, I sure hope so," Sandy sobbed.

Jason kissed the top of his wife's head and she clutched his arm tighter.

"Oh, so soon?" Sandy squeaked, as the next contraction caught her.

"Everything's fine." Bethany kept her voice low and calm. "Pant and keep your muscles relaxed. I know that's hard, but settle into it."

Sandy panted, her husband gently swiping back the blonde hair that had escaped her topknot. These moments could seem so long—for both the parents and the midwives. As the contraction eased and Sandy's features relaxed, McKenna's heart lifted. "I'm seeing more baby now. A couple more might do it."

Jason gave his wife a concerned smile.

At the end of the next two contractions, the baby had made some progress and was rotating. "Next time, push," she told Sandy.

But even after pushing during the next contraction, the baby's head was still turtling.

Still caught. Damn it.

Sandy's hopeless sob broke in the silence. Jason's head dropped.

"That's okay." Angling her position, McKenna crouched in front of the laboring mother. "When the next one comes, I'm going to slip my fingers up inside. You'll barely feel them. I'm just going to help him out."

"Anything. Anything." Sandy's voice held a note of desperation.

The next contraction came, and Sandy gave it her all. When the baby's delicate head bobbed out this time, McKenna slipped her fingers into the birth canal on either side, like one of those devices for stubborn wine corks. Rotating the baby's body just a bit, she eased one slippery shoulder past Sandy's pelvic bone. The baby sprang free.

Thank God. Sandy laughed and cried when her son gave a hearty wail as Bethany lifted him from the water. McKenna rested on her heels and called the time of birth while Bethany settled the newborn into his mother's arms. The pediatric nurse who'd been waiting in the shadows stepped forward, taking the infant to the bassinet while Bethany worked with Sandy to deliver the placenta. McKenna got to her feet.

"Nice job." Logan's voice startled her as she was stripping off her gloves.

"Have you been here long?" She'd forgotten she'd texted him.

"Long enough to see exceptional work." His smile held admiration.

Her exhaustion fell away. Bethany could handle it from here, and she waved good-bye. She welcomed the cool air when they pushed through the door into the hall.

"Thanks for that compliment, Logan." Her chuckle clutched in her throat. "Heck, I feel like I'm the one who just had that baby."

"You handled it well. Got a minute to come with me to the unit?"

"Sure." Pleased that he wanted to do rounds with her, she felt the heat rise in her face.

Maybe now Logan would understand the water birthing process better. They'd have a minute to chat, one professional to the other. Too bad her thoughts were anything but professional as they walked onto the OB floor, nodding briskly to staff in the nurses' station.

"Good morning, Dr. Castle. McKenna," two of the nurses greeted them. Instead of continuing on to the unit, he pulled her inside the office he had on this floor and closed the door.

So, no rounds?

Alone. With Logan.

Sunlight poured through the blinds. Heat poured through McKenna.

"McKenna, I can't tell you. Until I saw this today...I wasn't a believer."

"Really?" She hoped she didn't look smug. She also wished her body would stop humming like a well-tuned guitar.

Raking one hand through his sandy hair, Logan began to pace. "No, I admit it. Let's just say I'm cautious. Please don't take offense."

Took everything she had to settle for a silent smile.

Logan plunked down in his chair, long legs extended and hands steepled while he continued to verbally process. She almost laughed as she perched on his desk and crossed her legs. This was the Logan she was starting to know.

Her friend, she reminded herself. Colleague and buddy.

"Birth is such a natural process, isn't it, Logan? And water birthing is safe, especially with the resources we have here at Montclair."

His eyes fell to her legs.

Being this close in the small office was probably not a good idea.

When he pushed up from his chair, Logan's eyes were molten steel. "McKenna?"

Way too easy to slide off that desk and into his arms. No written invitation needed. No remorse either. Snug against his chest, she took a heady whiff of clean linen, soap and Logan.

"God, McKenna. I miss you," he murmured.

Cripes. Of course she kissed him.

Forget her earlier intentions. The kiss was just that good.

A couple more and he reached over with one long arm and locked the door. A shiver cart-wheeled down her spine. His arms closed around her like a steel band. Suddenly a bold bad boy, Logan nudged her lips open with a tongue tasting of coffee. She moaned and matched him stroke for stroke. His hands skimmed down her sides, thumbs grazing the sides of her breasts until they anchored at her hips and tugged.

Like he couldn't get enough of her.

Oh, goodness. She moaned and then bit her lip, remembering where they were.

Having a confidential meeting on the OB unit?

Oh, this was confidential all right. When she pressed into him, Logan groaned. She anchored herself to his shoulders with both hands.

When his hands went to the drawstring of her blue pants and tugged, reason returned. "Hold on. What are we doing here?" She laid one hand on his.

Hissing in a tight breath, Logan pulled back. Giving his head a jerk, he looked around the pristine office as if wondering how he got here. "Thank God I locked the door."

"You got that right." Part of her wanted him now, here, on a desk that looked like he never used it. So hard to put the brakes on, but McKenna groped for the lever in her mind.

One hand cupping a grin, Logan rocked back on his heels and stared at the tops of his loafers. "Well, McKenna. I wanted to ask you…if you wanted to go golfing Sunday."

"Ah…"

"Priscilla can't go."

"What?" she squawked.

He chuckled. "Not really. But you deserved that."

She did and released a shuddery breath. "Sure."

"We could tune up our games."

"I'd say our game is just fine."

Reaching out, he ran one finger down her cheek. "I meant for the golf outing."

"Oh, right. *That* game. Sounds good."

He looked delighted. "Great. Terrific." When he removed his hand, she missed it.

After sweeping her hair back, she tied it up with a scrunchie. Her neck felt damp and warm. Criminy, her entire body had turned liquid. She backed toward the door. "So, golf? Sunday?"

Logan nodded. "You're on."

He sure was. Maybe later she'd regret this.

But not now. Her body sang.

Outside, trees branches bent in the breeze. McKenna felt the hot, dry air before remembering she was in air conditioning. She had to get out of here. Stepping to the door, she gave him a cool nod, as if they were passing in the hall. "Dr. Castle."

"Ms. Kirkpatrick." His bemused smile quirked up.

Unlocking the door, she escaped and closed the door behind her. For a second, she leaned against the cool, firm wood. Sanity returned. Out on the unit, the world seemed normal. Food Service was delivering trays, and the smell of spaghetti and warm rolls filled the air. At the end of the hall, Leonard from Facility Maintenance mopped a floor with slow, rhythmic strokes.

Sucking in a cleansing breath, McKenna headed to the elevator. Time to give Vanessa an SOS call. Her best friend golfed and McKenna needed help before Sunday. As she passed the nurses' station, Maggie McCree looked up. "Good day, McKenna?"

"Great. Thank you." Eyes straight ahead, she marched toward

the elevator. After punching the button, she happened to glance down. The drawstring of her pants was still undone. Wrapping her white coat tight around her, McKenna was glad no one was around to hear her laughing. She had to get a grip.

~.~

Logan fell back into his chair, folding his hands behind his head. What the hell was that? Right here, in his office? He chuckled. McKenna was crazy and she made *him* crazy. What was happening to him? Life with his grandmother had been pretty structured. His marriage had run along the same lines. Maybe a routine life was a recipe for disaster.

Now the warmth stirring in his gut felt good. How sick was it that watching McKenna work had been a turn-on? His admiration for her clinical skill in the birthing suite had converted quickly to roaring lust.

A woman passionate about her work was sexier than hell.

So why was she fighting him? Granted, this whole thing surprised him. Not what he planned. His conversation with Priscilla had been a total surprise and maybe added some insight. McKenna was such a gutsy girl. But underneath? Maybe not. Logan let his spine curve into the back of the chair. On Sunday they'd have time to take it easy. Measured play on the golf course. Today had been so impetuous.

This desk? He'd never look at it the same again.

Since he didn't want to look suspicious, Logan gave McKenna a five minute lead before exiting his office. Head up, he surveyed the area. The OB unit seemed to be running smoothly. Dishes clattered as the staff served a meal. His stomach growled as he passed the nurses' station, nodding to Maggie. "Good evening, Maggie."

She grinned. "Hi, Dr. Castle."

Wasn't until he was waiting for the elevator that he realized it was noon, not evening. Taking one thumb, he jammed it against the button.

He'd caught McKenna with her guard down, and he wanted to keep it that way. No more talk about other women. Ignoring the tiny voice in the back of his mind that asked if he was ready for this, he hit the button again.

Suddenly he felt impatient for a lot of things.

Chapter 10

McKenna took a few practice shots at Logan's private club that Sunday while he picked up a golf cart. Moist air from the lake drifted over the city and hung heavy under low clouds. After adjusting her visor, she placed her yellow ball on the tee, took her position and swung. "Rats." She totally missed the ball.

Golf was just a game. That's all.

Today it felt more like a proving ground.

She was hanging out with Logan today, determined to prove they could spend time together without getting crazy. Thank goodness she'd been able to play nine holes with Vanessa the day before. But her good friend had wanted details.

"You're not leveling with me," Vanessa had protested.

"Logan often golfs with people he works with, and he asked if I wanted to play."

Vanessa's lips twitched. "He did, huh? Said he wanted to play? Really?"

"Golf. You can just wipe that evil smile off your face, missy," McKenna had huffed. They were pitching onto the green, but she whacked the ball so hard, it rocketed over the hole and into the woods behind.

Vanessa watched the arc of McKenna's shot with a knowing

smile. "Anything you say."

Today McKenna had to concentrate on golf when she played with Logan. The golf outing wasn't that far away—just a couple weeks after the group returned from Guatemala. She hadn't played much since last fall, and her game showed it.

As she stared out glumly over the driving range, Logan drove up and parked the cart right behind her. Neither one of them was on call that weekend so the day felt free. Instead of cleaning her apartment or heading over to Connor's for a barbecue, she was golfing. With Logan.

"All set?" His gaze swept her white shorts and moss green polo.

Holy hellfire. One of his looks, and her whole body sizzled.

"You bet." Grabbing her clubs, she headed for the cart.

"Looks like you know what you're doing," he said with satisfaction as he belted her clubs to the back of the cart.

"Looks can be deceiving."

After she'd slotted her clubs back into her bag, she jumped into the cart and they were off. At the first hole, she hit a decent drive. Of course, Logan whacked his ball a lot farther. No surprise to her after years of golfing with her brothers. Men had those broad shoulders, and Logan was no exception.

In his case, those shoulders tapered to slim hips. Hard to look at him in his fitted blue polo shirt and not remember how his chest had felt against her during the heated session in his office.

Thinking about it brought a hot flush. Stepping up to the tee, McKenna took a deep breath and tried to center herself as she went into her swing. She smiled at the satisfying crack when her driver made contact with the ball.

"Great shot. You're on the fairway," Logan said, jostling her back to the present. "You're good at a lot of things, McKenna. A talented lady."

Might be overcast today, but his eyes? Blazing with approval.

"Have you spoken to your grandmother about the Foundation golf outing?" she asked as they putted the second hole a little while later.

"I did. She sounded kind of excited." His hand rested on his thigh and she had to pull her eyes away. "She enjoys being part of things that recognize my grandfather and my dad, of course."

"Sounds as if you're close."

They were headed for the next hole. Obviously comfortable on this elite course, Logan steered the cart down a path that wound through stands of mature oaks. "She's all I…" Logan began before pressing his lips together tightly and looking down at the scorecard. "Looks like this is a par five."

His words hung in the air. Was his grandmother all he had? Her heart turned over. He was so quiet about his background. McKenna liked the fact that he didn't make a point of his family connection to the hospital. Some physicians wielded their name like a weapon. Not Logan.

"I think you're up," he said.

She hopped out. Just as she swung, thunder broke the air with a rumble she felt in her toes. Fat drops of rain plopped onto her visor.

"I don't like the looks of this." Logan glanced at the sky. They both hustled back to the cart.

Five minutes later she was sliding into the Porsche, Logan's windshield wipers working frantically. Huddled in the front seat, they were caught in a downpour. "Do you mind if we just wait out this worst part?" he asked. "I hate to drive on the Dan Ryan during a storm."

"Protecting your prize car?"

"Protecting my prize passenger."

McKenna could hardly hear the pounding rain above the beat of her heart. Logan's front seat smelled like leather and his spicy aftershave.

She was learning all these personal details about Hot Doc. And she liked them way too much. Made it so hard to distance him.

"A penny for your thoughts." His fingers played with her hair.

"Just thinking about how crazy this is."

"I'm beginning to like crazy." With a mischievous smile, he pulled her toward him.

Not that it took much effort. She was already into a serious lean, so why not go there? Sure, she should have stopped it right there. All things considered, that would have been the reasonable thing to do.

Now she welcomed the slight scratch of his chin, the bump of his nose. The kiss wasn't a first-time kiss. Not after his office. The curves of Logan's lips felt warm and familiar.

What was a girl to do? Restraint was useless.

Water coursed over the parking lot. Didn't take long for the windows to fog up. In no time at all she'd bridged those bucket seats and was cuddled in his lap, arms around his neck. Sometimes she was just too darn bold for her own good. "This is insane."

"Maybe we should commit you to the psych ward." He whispered kisses onto her neck.

"My friends might agree."

The laugh deep in his chest reverberated in her breasts. They responded. In fact, every pore in her body reacted to him. When his lips circled back to hers with a lot of tongue, she almost went through the roof.

Could. Not. Get. Enough.

And that was dangerous.

They didn't notice when the rain stopped. Suddenly the only sound was their breathless panting. The silence brought her back to her senses. Catching his face between her two hands, she dropped a kiss on the tip of his nose. She slid back over into the passenger seat and straightened her polo. "Enough for now."

He lifted one brow. "You can be very bossy."

"Not the first time I've been told that." But he didn't seem to mind. Now.

What was she going to do? Her stomach growled.

"Did you have breakfast?" he asked, starting the car.

"If you can call a bagel breakfast, then, yes." But her tummy gurgled again.

With a knowing smile, he shoved the car into gear. "I make a mean omelet. And I'm famished."

"In that case, I'm hungry." Food might help her stop trembling, She may have had "just hanging out" in her mind, but her body didn't agree. Slipping off her golf shoes, she slid on her flip flops.

When they reached his condo, he got to work in a kitchen that was all gleaming white and stainless steel with black accents. "Look around if you like," he said after he handed her a mimosa. Couldn't pass up that invitation. Taking the flute in one hand, she wandered. Tall bookcases reached the ceiling of the main room and floor-to-ceiling windows offered an expansive view of the lake. Every book, every lamp seemed placed with precision, the black alternating with gray in the furnishings. Her stomach dropped.

Could this man handle one week in Guatemala?

Deep in thought, she returned to the kitchen. The glass panels of the white cabinets gave a glimpse of neat stacks of plates. Cups all faced the same direction. She was relieved when he pulled open a drawer crammed with towels and pulled out an apron. The drawer was a jumble. *Hallelujah.* After donning the apron, he popped English muffins in the toaster and began slicing red peppers and onions with the same precision she'd seen in the OR.

He looked up. "What?"

"Like the apron."

Logan looked so darn cute standing there with "Hot Doc" scrolled in white across the black apron. "The magazine gave it to me." He almost sounded apologetic.

"I think it's spot on."

"If you say so." Grabbing a whisk, he started to beat the heck out of the eggs with a practiced hand. Soon onions sizzled in the skillet. Leaning against the black granite counter, she enjoyed watching him cook. Her brothers liked to mess around in the kitchen. A weight lifter, Nick had thought it was woman's work. She could just imagine her former boyfriend's comments about the apron.

Perching on a tall stool at the black marble counter, she peered over into the pan. "Let's see, so far I've seen you throw in peppers, crabmeat and shrimp."

"And don't forget the kalamata olives. Bam!" He whirled his spatula in the air, imitating TV chef Emeril Lagasse.

"You never cease to amaze me. So much more fun than I imagined."

A frown creased his forehead.

"That's a good thing, Logan."

His sculpted lips twisted. "Maybe I'm too serious for my own good. Except with you, McKenna. With you, everything is fun."

Such an open admission. She swallowed hard.

"Thank you. I think." She was relieved when Logan returned to his cooking. Hadn't she heard these compliments before? But this was different. Logan was a guy in an apron.

Strong men wore aprons.

Two minutes later, he nudged an omelet onto each of two black-rimmed plates and she picked up her fork. "Enjoy." He took the stool next to hers.

"This is fabulous," she groaned after her first bite. Oh, my God. Logan's omelet was coming in a close second to waffles. He'd pulled croissants from his freezer and nuked them in the microwave. The flakiness broke in her hands when she wielded a butter knife with cinnamon brown sugar butter that made the croissant a delight. For the next few minutes they concentrated on food. But she couldn't keep quiet for long. "Do you mind if I ask some questions?"

His eyes turned wary. "Fine as long as I have the same opportunity."

"Understood." She had to choose her words carefully. "When a man is divorced, of course you wonder about what happened to that marriage."

Elbows on the counter, he seemed to consider the question. "Sure, I guess so. Rebecca was a nurse interested in midwifery. We came from similar backgrounds, so we knew each other."

What did that mean? West Side and wealthy?

"What brought you together?"

"We made a common mistake." His expression turned reflective. That happened a lot with Logan. "We assumed that because we were alike in a lot of ways, we would make a good couple. We'd gone to the same prep school, had some of the same friends, But that wasn't the case."

"Why didn't it work out? What were your differences?"

Logan jumped to his feet and jerked open the refrigerator door. "How about some seafood sauce? I think this omelet calls for a little something more."

As he dabbed the sauce on his eggs, Logan launched into a complicated explanation of the various sauces available and which one was best on eggs. The information was about as interesting as watching paint dry. Maybe time to fall back. Obviously he didn't want to say anymore about his ex-wife. The good thing was, he didn't press her for her story. She definitely didn't want to talk about Nick. The closed door felt comfortable. For now.

After clearing the plates, Logan brought out a small gold box of pricey chocolates. She sighed with contentment as he led her into the living room that overlooked the rainy city. What could be cozier than curling up on a leather loveseat, nibbling chocolates?

One or two things came to mind.

For now, she'd stick with the chocolates. After whisking off the gold cover, Logan offered her the box. The sinfully rich scent of dark chocolate teased her. He smiled when she took her time choosing.

"Mocha chocolate. Yum. I can't resist." The dark shell cracked under her teeth, releasing the thick, rich interior.

"Why even try?" A strawberry cream in hand, he hesitated. After taking a bite, he kissed her. The strawberry taste curled around her mocha chocolate.

Great combination. Great kiss.

She should have stopped it right there.

Instead she breathed him in, linking her hands around his neck. When it came to pheromones, they had it in spades. Pretty soon, the chocolates were forgotten, the box left open on his glass-topped coffee table. When his hands wandered, she didn't stop him. McKenna ached to be touched. Her breasts tingled when he cupped them, hummed when he stroked a thumb over their aching peaks. Arching her back, she leaned into him, winding her arms tighter around his neck.

It would have been so easy to get totally crazy. But something stopped her. Thoughts about their working relationship and pain down the road made her plant both hands flat on his chest and push away. Cripes, this vacillation was going to give her whiplash.

"What?" He opened lazy eyes, heart thundering under her palms.

My word, he was gorgeous.

"Maybe I should be getting home."

"Really?" Lips swollen, he traced her eyebrows with his fingertips. "Right."

When he drew away, she told herself this was a good thing. He drove her home in silence and gave her a perfunctory kiss at the door. McKenna's golf bag felt heavy on her shoulder when she lugged it inside.

~.~

The following week was so busy that she almost didn't have time to obsess about Sunday with her Hot Doc. She was just grateful that they'd called a halt. She needed time to think.

Still, it was difficult to concentrate on work. According to Jack Frazier, their blog had become increasingly popular. The article on hydration brought a strong response, along with Bethany's entry about shoulder dystocia.

But as McKenna dealt with each day, her thoughts returned to Logan. The golf date had been a game changer. Oh, he hadn't dragged her into his office again. That was way too embarrassing. She could hardly see Maggie McCree in the hallway without blushing. He was a lot more subtle than that.

Hot Doc had turned to texting. His messages weren't anything mundane like, "thinking of you." Instead, she'd find the words "dark chocolate" or "tasty" pop up on her phone. One or two words and she'd be a whimpering puddle. She began consuming the chocolates hidden in her desk like popcorn. Her stash needed replenishing almost daily.

Took some effort to tear her thoughts from Logan. So many other concerns clamored for her attention. For one thing, she was really worried about Angie. What if she didn't come this Wednesday? How would she ever forgive herself if Angie Dowd slipped through the cracks like a lot of other abused women?

In her gut, McKenna knew Angie was being mistreated. Maybe it was her dark, slippery eyes or the slumped shoulders. Something was wrong.

On Wednesday around five o'clock, she found Cindy Hamilton, the OB unit social worker, in her office. Shoving folders into a satchel, Cindy looked like she was packing up for the day. McKenna almost felt guilty when Cindy turned to her with her warm hazel eyes. "Hey McKenna."

"Heading home? I can come back tomorrow." McKenna paused in the doorway.

"Absolutely not, McKenna. Haven't seen you in a while." Shoving her briefcase aside, Cindy motioned her in and plopped her stocky body in her office chair. With her unassuming style, Cindy related well to everyone.

"Thanks." Exhausted after an especially long labor, McKenna collapsed into a chair so hard her tailbone hurt. "I need your help."

Pushing a bowl of chocolate kisses toward McKenna, Cindy

smiled. "Figured as much. You're not someone who wanders over to chew the fat. You never have time."

"So you noticed." McKenna slowly peeled the silver paper from a kiss and brought Cindy up to speed. "I don't want to frighten Angie away," she concluded. "As it is, she didn't show up last Wednesday."

"Why don't I stop in tonight?" Cindy offered without batting an eye.

"On such short notice?" Semi-sweet chocolate melting in her mouth, McKenna nodded toward the briefcase.

"If I'm not home, my husband will appreciate my miserable dinners more. You can introduce me to the class as a possible resource. The Social Work Department always likes free PR. Or I can wait until most of the class has left and hope that we can corral Angie."

Relief eased the tension in McKenna's chest, and the dark chocolate slid easily down her throat. "Thanks so much. I'll be interested to get your take on this girl. Maybe it's nothing, but..."

"That's why your patients all love you. You really care."

Embarrassed, McKenna jumped to her feet. "Great, see you later."

That evening after the For Women office had emptied out, McKenna sat in her office going over the agenda for the class. She was covering breast feeding, comfort measures and second-stage labor techniques. Defining the coach's role was also on the list, which would give her an opportunity to be closer to Angie. Maybe tonight the young woman would bring a mother or a sister. Maybe all this worry would have been for nothing. Hope lifted the heavy weight from McKenna's chest.

"So, what's happening with you, girl?" Selena leaned against the doorframe, car keys dangling from one hand.

"Going over my notes for tonight."

"I'm talking about your glow, not your class."

"Glow, huh?" Tucking her hair behind one ear, McKenna grinned. She'd just gotten another text from Logan.

"There it is!" Selena wagged one finger. "That secret smile is *exactly* what I'm talking about."

Lips locked, McKenna sat back.

"Okay, okay," Selena said with frustration. "Then I'm not even going to mention that Dr. Castle left a message saying he's coming to the Midwives in Action meeting."

"He is?" Surprise yanked McKenna upright in her chair.

Lips curling into her Cheshire cat smile, Selena looked pleased. "Chalk it up to my expert salesmanship." She buffed the nails of one hand on her chest.

"You get a gold star for this one." McKenna's mind raced ahead. Having Logan on the trip could be a test. She almost didn't want to know the result.

"And I have a very special task for him once we get there. Short timeline, for sure. One week." Selena's dark eyes sparkled. "He'll find that a lot of ladies are waiting for him."

Suspicion tickled the back of McKenna's neck. "What are you talking about? Tubal ligations? C-section training?"

Selena shook her head. "He's needed in a far more interesting manner by women who will be very, very appreciative." Drawing closer, she said, "Here's the plan ..."

As her best friend detailed Logan's mission in Guatemala, McKenna's ballpoint slipped from her hand. This could be a deal-breaker. The trip might take Logan far outside his comfort zone.

The nagging fear in her chest told her she expected the worst. Sometimes disappointment can leave you cynical, and McKenna was afraid that's where she was right now. Clicking on his latest message, she read it for about the fifteenth time.

Man, oh, man, he could be naughty.

Right now she was enjoying Logan...his secret smiles when they passed in the halls, his provocative texts. They were in what Vanessa always called the "luminescence." In the beginning, you imagine the person you're dating is perfect. But when he doesn't measure up, or vice versa, why, it can be devastating. She pocketed her phone.

Two hours later she was still thinking of Selena's unusual proposition for Logan when she began the natural childbirth class. She'd invited Terry Lincoln from La Leche to speak about breast feeding. As Terry began her short talk, McKenna fought disappointment as her eyes swept the room. No Angie.

But just when Terry was wrapping up, Angie slipped into the room, grabbed a mat and plopped down in the very back. Terry left and McKenna continued. "You'll...you'll be happy to know that massage is a big help during labor..." she continued. As McKenna talked about the role of massage, lollipops, oils and other comfort measures, she made a point of making eye contact with Angie. The girl didn't blink. Just sat back on her haunches, staring straight ahead.

After taking the group through pushing techniques, McKenna moved on to the coach's role. Out of the corner of her eye, she saw Cindy Hamilton slip in and take one of the seats pushed back against the wall. The social worker gave McKenna a small wave.

She nodded back. "I'd like you to meet Cindy Hamilton, the social worker for our obstetrics unit. Cindy is the woman you go to with all your questions and all your complaints, I might add."

Everyone laughed as Cindy moved to the front of the room. Angie seemed to be listening, head tipped to one side, her eyes smudged with dark circles. Even though it was eighty degrees outside, she was wearing another one of her gigantic shirts that reached almost to the knees of her black tights. Her tennis shoes were untied, of course.

"Cindy will be around after class if you have any questions," McKenna added at the end. She prayed silently that Angie wouldn't leave before she had a chance to get to her.

Oddly enough, Angie lingered as the others filed out at the end of class. Cindy was studying notices posted on a bulletin board. Not at all suspicious.

"Hey, we missed you last week, Angie." McKenna approached the girl.

"I had to... work."

By that time, Cindy had peeled away from the bulletin board and hovered in the background. "Great job, Cindy." McKenna angled her body to include the social worker. "Did you have any questions?" she asked Angie. Good chance that Angie had no clue social workers could help people with a whole bucket load of problems.

Biting her bottom lip, Angie shook her head.

"Well, if anything ever comes up, Angie," Cindy said in her disarmingly casual way, "I'll be glad to steer you toward any resources you might need."

Angie blinked. Yep, she didn't have a clue.

As the girl backed toward the door, it was all McKenna could do to stop herself from lunging and dragging her back by the arm. That approach totally wouldn't work.

Cindy offered Angie a card. "Here's my office phone. I brought a bunch of these cards with me tonight to pass out and forgot."

Angie looked at the white business card in her hand and closed her fist around it. "Nice talking to you. Gotta run." And she was gone.

McKenna and Cindy looked at each other in silence. "Guess I really blew that one," McKenna muttered, moving out into the hall.

"Small victories. That's what it's all about." Mouth tightening, Cindy watched Angie push open the door leading to the stairs. "And if it makes you feel any better, I think you're probably right about her. Let's keep at it."

Chapter 11

Midwives in Action was in full swing when Logan arrived. High-pitched female voices filled the hospital conference room. He was definitely outnumbered. After ripping off his tie, he tucked it in a pants pocket and took a seat. Usually he was in charge of the meetings he attended in this room. Tonight it felt good to sit in the back.

Up since three that morning, he pressed his aching back into the curved wooden seat. First baby for Monica and Pete Meyers, so this had been a long labor and long day, punctuated by trips back to his office. He needed coffee. Jumping up, he followed the dark, rich scent to a side table. After grabbing an oatmeal cookie and coffee, he nodded at the nurses and ambled back to his seat.

Around him, the women were chattering—and probably not about midwifery. Outside the long narrow windows it had been another hot day in Chicago and darkness fell begrudgingly. Thank God the air conditioning was on full blast.

Up front, McKenna was talking to Selena, who was setting up her PowerPoint. He enjoyed looking at McKenna. The overhead lighting carved deep copper hollows in her wavy hair that felt like silk. He curled his hand tighter around the coffee cup. Nothing seemed to slow this woman down, and her hands fluttered like a bird's wings. Excitement flushed McKenna's porcelain skin and her green eyes flashed. For all he knew, she could be talking about the weather. McKenna Kirkpatrick found the world fascinating—a big turn-on.

But he felt her reserve. Irritating but he had to respect that. He thoroughly understood the dangers of developing a relationship with someone at work. Careers were important, and he loved his life at Montclair. If things fell apart, the career could suffer. No one wanted that.

Sometimes Logan asked himself if he knew what he was doing. Since his divorce, he'd avoided any kind of commitment. Good God, it took him a year to even ask a woman out for dinner. Then his grandmother tried to fix him up with a friend's granddaughter. That did it. He was jolted into action and had to start dating.

But he was careful. Although there might be a second date, rarely was there a third. Logan was a red-blooded American male, but he didn't want any jabber about the future. No clothes left in a woman's home. He wouldn't be another Griff, mowing through the nursing ranks. The hurt in the last woman's voice when she called to ask why she hadn't heard from him brought a stop to what he thought was considerate behavior.

He didn't want to be that man.

Then he got to know McKenna. She was an intriguing woman. But she didn't know he was damaged goods. And he couldn't bring himself to tell her.

Logan took a slow sip of coffee and then went back for cream. Selena was setting up and a colored map of Guatemala flashed

onto the whiteboard up front. Although he'd taken Spanish in high
school and some in college, he knew absolutely nothing about the
country except that it was in Central America. After stirring the
cream into his coffee, he tossed the stir stick into the trash and sat
back down.

"Did you grab something to eat?" McKenna asked as she
plopped down next to him.

That seductive peach smell teased him as he turned toward her.
Nodding, he inhaled the coffee in defense. "Got a salad in the
cafeteria. Oh, and an oatmeal cookie."

"No truffles?" Her green eyes danced.

Sputtering, he choked. That box of chocolates was enshrined in
his refrigerator, hoping for her return. "Not tonight."

"Why are you staring at me like that?" McKenna's auburn
lashes fluttered innocently.

"Trust me, you don't want to know."

The laughter faded from her eyes. "Now, remember, you don't
have to do this if you don't want to."

"Are we talking about Guatemala or something else?"

McKenna wrinkled her nose. "What? Guatemala, of course."

"I never do things I don't want to do. Are you trying to talk me
out of one week in a foreign country with you?"

She chuckled, one of those rolling, throaty laughs that made the
other women glance around. "Dr. Castle, this is hardly a romantic
getaway."

"Ms. Kirkpatrick, I realize that. I came tonight for
information." Not quite true. He'd pretty much made up his mind

about this trip. "I'm just glad that with Priscilla on board, I have this option."

"How is Priscilla working out?"

"It's great to have another OB on staff, I can tell you that much." Relaxing back in the chair, he stretched out his legs. "Sure, Bob McCracken's group provided coverage for us, but I should've expanded earlier. And Priscilla's sharp. The women like her. What?"

Her forehead smoothed. "Nothing. Just glad that…the women like Priscilla." Were those questions marks she was doodling on her pad?

Women. He'd never understand them. Despite the caffeine fix, the long day rolled over him and he glanced at his watch. Seven o'clock.

"Could I have your attention please?" Selena stepped up to the podium and began to introduce the group by name. Most of them were midwives—some from other hospitals—along with a nutritionist.

"Beans, corn and rice are the staples in Guatemala," Selena explained. "When they have them. Sherry Barry, one of our nutritionists, is coming to teach them to help themselves."

Sherry waved a hand and the group clapped.

Selena's next comment made him shrink in his chair. "Many of you know Dr. Logan Castle. I'm hoping we can convince him to join our group." A polite patter of applause followed with some neck craning. He was relieved when Selena moved on. "We leave two weeks from this Saturday. We'll be landing in Guatemala City and then travel into the highlands, where people have difficulty accessing care."

They all nodded. Seemed to be a group who knew the expectations. He liked what he saw.

"Although Montclair Specialty Hospital is officially sponsoring us, several other hospitals—your employers—have generously donated equipment and pharmaceuticals hard to come by in Guatemala. Those who've volunteered before for Midwives in Action know that the people speak Spanish as well as several indigenous languages. If you can't speak Spanish, don't worry. Some of us can translate."

He'd have to brush up. Was McKenna multilingual? He glanced over. She was the type of woman who was good at everything.

"We've got our work cut out for us, and a big role is bolstering the spirits and expanding the knowledge base of Guatemalan midwives. Following the Peace Accords of 1996, the government insists on sending patients to hospitals, where midwives are not allowed," Selena continued. The group shifted in their seats. "Hospital care in Guatemala is not necessarily top-notch. They have a very high C-section rate in the hospitals, which worries the midwives. On top of that, if anything goes wrong, the midwives are blamed for their early involvement."

The room fell silent. Laughter from a group passing in the hallway was a sharp contrast to Selena's grim expression. "We hope to fortify those practitioners as well as train newbies in ways to handle some of the emergencies they may run into. They need to know when a transfer to a hospital might be the only hope."

For a second, the only sound was the hum of the air conditioner.

"What about the food?" Sherry asked, breaking the tension. "We bring our own stuff?"

Selena nodded and a list appeared on the screen. "Of course, basic food is supplied, but it's simple. If you drink tea, bring it. Gluten free products? Pack them in your duffle bag. Also, you might want to bring a small umbrella or poncho. Still the rainy season down there. Reading light or small flashlight. Backpack to keep organized. Never hurts to have some mace handy, not that we expect any problems. Insect repellant is also a good idea."

McKenna was jotting things on her pad while Logan took a few notes on his phone.

A hand went up to the side. "What about family photos? Didn't we take those last year?"

Selena nodded. "Sure, bring family pictures. Pictures help break the ice. Even if you can't speak their language, the pictures do."

He'd take a pass on that.

Slides continued to flip on the screen. "Here is a little background about Guatemala." As Selena ran through data on a country struggling in the aftermath of a thirty-six year civil war, Logan was amazed and humbled. Talk about resilience. Although he'd always known his life had been privileged, the information on the screen served as a stark reminder. To spend the summer golfing and sailing in his free time almost seemed criminal in the face of need like this.

And the children. They looked hungry. The taste of the oatmeal cookie lingered on his tongue, criminally rich. The dark-haired kids with wide smiles and hollow cheeks, sitting on hard-packed dirt with sticks for toys did it. He made his decision right then.

Haiti? The Philippines? He'd felt helpless in the face of those two enormous disasters. Now that he had this opportunity in Guatemala, he was taking it.

"There's a desperate need for family planning education," Selena continued. "Our base station this year will be El Limar, a village in the highlands northeast of Guatemala City. Once people from other villages hear we're there, they come, usually on foot."

McKenna stopped writing and focused on the photos fading in and out on the screen. He saw his own sadness in McKenna's face.

Any homes pictured were mere sheds or huts. Then the pictures took a different turn. In contrast to the disturbing poverty, the location looked jaw-droppingly beautiful. And unlike a lot of European countries, its lush tropical vegetation, soaring mountains and crystal streams hadn't been spoiled. Not yet.

But you can't eat scenery.

"So what did you think?" McKenna asked when Selena brought her talk to a close.

"About what? Bringing my special tea?"

McKenna swatted him playfully with her notebook. "Not quite. Is this something that interests you?"

"Is this a pass or fail test?" What did this project mean to McKenna? Funny, but he didn't want to disappoint her.

Her presentation completed, Selena had taken the chair on his other side. "So, Dr. Castle, can we count on you?"

"Selena, you should work for the Foundation. Of course I'd like to help," he said slowly, trying to fill in the blanks. "What do you see as my role?"

Never breaking eye contact, Selena leaned closer. "Some of the women need your surgical skill."

Was he imagining that McKenna tensed next to him?

"Tubal ligations? What are we talking about here?"

His apprehension deepened when McKenna and Selena exchanged a glance. "Restoring vaginal integrity," Selena finally said in an undertone.

"What?" Okay, that came out louder than he'd intended. Logan sucked in a breath when Sherry Barry glanced their way. "That sounds more like a Congressional bill than a medical service."

McKenna had fallen silent, hands twisted tight in her lap. "Guatemala is a conservative country," Selena said, keeping her voice low. "To be respected, women must marry with their hymen intact. But for some, that isn't possible."

"They have little or no knowledge of effective contraception, Logan," McKenna added. "So far the government has not been proactive. Women have few choices." A delicate line appeared between her brows as the two of them described what was probably the case in many underserved countries—few rights for women and punishment if they broke the rules.

Hypocrisy at its worst and he hated it.

"Teresa, the midwife organizing our visit, has told us that women will travel a long distance for this service. Don't worry, this is not an epidemic, but it happens. Although some unscrupulous physicians are offering the surgery, the price is high and there have been many problems," McKenna concluded with a disgusted shake of her head. The intensity of her conviction stirred something deep inside.

What they were describing was far from his antiseptic operating room where well-heeled women delivered babies into lives of baby formula and doting grandparents. Of course, even in the best environment, mistakes could happen. If he could save one child from suffering the fate of his son, it would be worth it. "I'm in."

When McKenna smiled, warmth unfurled in his stomach. But he wasn't doing this because of her. At least, not totally.

"Terrific." Beaming, Selena shot out one hand. "Thanks, Dr. Castle."

"You can call me Logan, Selena." He ignored the twinge of trepidation as he shook her hand. What was he getting himself into? But he just couldn't sit on the sidelines.

Exhaustion forgotten, he couldn't wait to get to his laptop at home. There was so much he wanted to learn about Guatemala.

~.~

Going into that weekend, McKenna felt giddy. Logan was coming to Guatemala. On the heels of elation came a wave of reservation. What if her own enthusiasm had swept him into a situation he might not handle well? Could a man with a structured, squeaky clean life handle the grinding poverty and everything that came with it?

Bring it on. Best to know it now.

She was sitting in her office staring out at the leaves shriveling from the heat on the trees in the courtyard. The weather had been brutal. Her mind circled the Logan problem like the airless wind that sucked the air out of Chicago. Maybe she'd invite him to dinner. Give him a chance to opt out of the trip. Just a friendly chat.

But her body wasn't agreeing with the "friendly" bit. She squirmed in her chair, remembering brunch at his condo. The food wasn't uppermost in her mind. Goosebumps rose when she remembered his hands. Who knew they could be so talented? His wandering lips? Brought a damp rush to her lap. Her office chair squeaked as she shifted restlessly. She reached for her chocolates. After enjoying one dark bite thoroughly, she grabbed her phone.

"Want to hang out Saturday night?" she asked when Logan picked up.

"Hang out?" His tone indicated she'd invited to tour the morgue.

"Right, I'll make dinner. We can talk about the upcoming trip. Make our lists. You might have some questions." She was clutching the phone so tight her hand cramped.

"Um, sorry, McKenna. I have dinner plans Saturday. But thanks for the invite."

Disappointment swamped her. "Oh, well, sure."

"Sorry." Was that a smile in his voice? "What about golf Sunday? Practice our game."

Game? "Golf, right?"

"Of course? What else?" He was toying with her. She loved and hated it.

By the time they ended the call, she was wondering who the heck he was going out with on Saturday.

"What's up?" Selena lounged in her open doorway. "Girl, you look like you lost one of your best friends."

McKenna chewed on her lower lip. "I invited Logan for Saturday dinner, but he has 'plans.' Suggested golf Sunday instead."

Selena's cackle did nothing to ease McKenna's discomfort. "Good for him. You better decide what you want from that man, McKenna. The goal is to be the Saturday night date, not the Sunday filler. You gotta be the main event, girl."

"Hey, I don't need that, okay?" Selena was right and they both knew it. Every woman knows the Saturday night date ranks higher than Friday night. Sunday afternoons? For cripe's sake, they hardly ranked at all. McKenna was relieved when her phone rang. Answering the call, she could hear Selena's laugh as she retreated down the hall.

~.~

That Sunday they played golf at Logan's club. McKenna was eager to improve her game before the Foundation golf outing in August. The Marketing Department was doing a stellar job of promoting the event. Already they had signed three anchor sponsors, as well as dozens of gold and silver supporters.

But she really didn't feel like playing golf today. The day was hot and sunny, with not even a breeze for relief. The backs of her thighs stuck to the vinyl seat of the golf cart, and perspiration trickled from her upswept hair.

"Good thing we're not sailing." Moving restlessly next to her in the cart, Logan looked up at the leaves of a maple tree hanging listlessly overhead.

"Right, although a dip in the water would be nice."

Logan in a bathing suit. She had to blank that image out while they waited for the couple ahead to tee off. Play was so very slow. Mouth dry, her tongue stuck to the roof of her mouth. After picking up her now-empty cup of iced tea, she swirled the melting ice cubes. One glance at Logan and she knew that no liquid would slack her thirst.

"Maybe it's too hot for golf," Logan whispered, so close that she could see the perspiration beading his sculpted lips, could feel the damp warmth of his breath on her skin. "Maybe we should head back to my place?"

"My thoughts exactly."

Wait, what had she just said?

Without another word, he backed up the cart and headed for the clubhouse. They were bundling their clubs into the back of the Porsche when her phone went off. Logan's head bowed.

"It's the ER," she said, checking her phone. "Brody Lightcap."

"McKenna, we just admitted a patient named Angie Dowd," Brody told her, voice terse when she took his call.

"Right, Angie's in my natural childbirth class. I'm on my way. Brody, how bad is it?"

"We won't know the whole story until we run some x-rays and tests. She's beat up pretty bad, McKenna."

"Be right there."

"What is it?" Logan asked, ripping the car door open for her.

Sliding into the passenger seat, she didn't trust herself to say much. "A patient from one of my classes." Angie's pale face flashed in her mind as Logan tore out of the parking lot.

Bless his heart, Logan broke just about every law in the books speeding down the Eisenhower toward the city. Maybe the police saw his OB MD license plate because they didn't stop him.

When they reached Montclair, he left the car in the doctor's slot. The two of them slammed through the doors of the ER. Recognizing them, the receptionist waved them back.

Face stormy, Brody was coming out of the cubicle as they approached. "We're taking her to radiology, McKenna. Maybe she'll talk to you." His expression said it all and her stomach tightened.

"Really bad, Brody?"

"Some asshole broke her jaw."

Behind her, Logan expelled a breath. "I'll wait out here, McKenna." He squeezed her hand before she went into the cubicle.

Under the stark overhead lighting, Angie's slender form was covered with a white sheet, her baby bump a slight hope.

"Angie, it's McKenna," she said softly, fighting her own tears.

Although the girl's left eye was swollen shut, Angie's right eye fluttered open. A tear squeezed out, headed for a jaw visibly misaligned.

"You don't have to say anything, Angie, but you're going to be all right." She unhooked a stethoscope from the wall. Lifting the sheet, she listened for the baby's heartbeat. "We're going to do some tests, Angie, but the baby sounds good. For now."

Angie whimpered and McKenna's fists knotted. She wanted to kill the bastard. After checking Angie's IV for pain medication, she told her she'd be right back and slipped into the hall to update Logan.

"I'm going to stay here," she told him.

Logan nodded, pushing one tangled curl behind her ear. "Call if you need me."

"I'll be fine."

His knuckles brushed her chin softly. "No, I mean it. Call."

Logan's words bolstered her as she watched him walk away. He seemed like such a steady guy.

And that thought is totally premature. She returned to Angie.

Throughout that afternoon, she stayed with the girl, accompanied her to radiology and conferred with Jeff Botsford on the films. Angie's jaw and right arm were broken. They were still assessing any internal injuries.

Cindy came in to talk briefly with Angie, assuring her that she was not going back to that apartment. The women's shelter that Cindy had in mind was the same facility Fay Shriver, the Foundation Board member, had mentioned.

"But you're going to be staying here for a while," McKenna told Angie. "Cindy will talk to your boss at work. Don't worry about that."

In the afternoon, Logan reappeared with a carton of soup and a ham sandwich from Panera.

"How did you know I haven't eaten lunch?" she asked as she

wolfed down the sandwich in an ER consult room.

Logan grinned. "I know you. Patients first, food later."

His silent support was something she sure wasn't accustomed to but now discovered she needed.

Good grief. She was starting to need Logan Castle.

Chapter 12

While McKenna clucked over Angie like a mother hen, the battered girl continued to improve. With Cindy's help, three days later Angie was discharged to New Horizon, the women's shelter. Thank goodness Angie's baby survived the cruel attack. The short conversation McKenna had with Angie before discharge indicated the girl was torn. She realized she was in no position to raise a child. At Angie's request, Cindy put her in touch with an agency that handled private adoptions.

McKenna was thinking through other options for Angie when Logan called to ask her to join him the following Sunday on his boat. "Sounds fabulous." Humidity and heat bore down on the city. Flattered, she was still aware she was the Sunday date.

Wasn't this what she'd wanted? Her mind spun as she prepared a picnic lunch Sunday morning for Logan and her to enjoy later that day on his boat. As she layered thick slices of ham with brie and Dijon mustard, a bad case of jitters plagued her stomach. She was glad Logan had decided to join the Guatemala group, but she was still nervous about it. Would the trip into the wilds prove to be too much for Logan? Could he function successfully without a sterile operating suite for his use?

After pulling on a coral polo and white shorts, she finished packing the wicker lunch basket. Outside the kitchen window, finches competed with cardinals for seeds at the bird feeder—a scurrying bundle of feathers and high-pitched chirping. Comfortable on her window platform, Sasha followed their activities with great interest, tail twitching.

"Know how you feel, little girl," McKenna murmured. "Sometimes what you really want is just beyond your reach. Those birds would peck your eyes out if you got near them." Nibbling on one of the chocolate-covered strawberries, she knew Vanessa and Amy would laugh at her. What advice had she given both of them? "Be a babe."

Right now McKenna was terrified to follow her own advice. With a sigh, she threw some chocolate brownies into the basket.

The front doorbell rang and Sasha leapt from her perch, startling the birds from the feeder. After clicking the basket shut, McKenna crammed a baseball cap on her head and dashed for the door. Her rubber-soled shoes squeaked on the parquet floor she'd laid by hand.

When she threw open the door, Logan stood smiling in the glow of a summer day. Clean shaven and wearing a crisp blue and white striped oxford cloth shirt with his khaki shorts, he looked unbearably handsome. "Ready for a little sailing?"

"You bet." She gave him a quick kiss.

Minutes later, they were in the car and on their way down Lake Shore Drive. "How's your student doing?" he asked. "The girl from your class?"

"She's at the shelter now." As they drove, she filled him in on

Angie's condition.

"Thank God you took an interest," he said.

"If I didn't, who would?"

"Right, but today let's relax and have fun."

With a deep sigh, she settled into the leather bucket seat. "So things are hectic with you too?"

He shrugged as he shifted. "Just busy, with Priscilla coming on board. It's all good."

"So how's that coming?" she asked, angling her body toward him. Seemed like she was always running into Priscilla in the hospital. So perky and perfect. McKenna had shoved her in Logan's direction and now she wondered. Was Priscilla his Saturday date? McKenna would cut out her tongue before she'd ask.

Eyes on the road, he pursed those wonderfully sculpted lips. "Bringing someone new on board requires time. Pays off in the end. But we're going to forget all that today."

The parking lot at Dusable Harbor was crowded. On weekends, boat owners were probably eager to get out on the lake, Logan explained. Gulls cawed overhead and a playful breeze tousled the long curls that bounced from her cap as McKenna followed Logan to the office. The smell of the lake engulfed her, rich and damp. Within a few minutes, they were in a dinghy, and a young man named Mike buzzed them out to a blue-and-white sailboat with trim, clean lines. Larger than she expected and very Logan, except for the name.

"Wild Thing?"

"Surprised?" His eyes were unreadable behind those aviator glasses.

"Very."

"Don't judge what you don't know."

Okay, the shiver became an icy chill down her spine. Blond hair ruffling in the stiff breeze, Logan climbed the short ladder and helped McKenna aboard.

"Thanks, Mike," he said, taking the basket from McKenna's hand. The small skiff roared back toward the marina.

Taking in the neatly coiled ropes and spotless white surface, she settled onto one of the navy cushions. "This is one sweet boat, Logan. My brothers and I fooled around with a Sunfish when we were in our teens. Small stuff. What Seth would have given for one of these." As Seth would say, the sloop was loaded. High-tech gadgets were everywhere and Logan no doubt knew how to work them all. She wasn't surprised. Everything, from the ropes to the instrumentation, looked like it was kept neatly in place.

"What do you do if the wind dies?" she asked, tugging down her cap against the sun.

"Don't worry. The boat has a motor."

It didn't look as if they'd need it today and she turned her face into the bracing breeze. The hat wasn't going to work so she took it off and stroked her hair back into a scrunchie. After slathering herself with sunblock, she held up the bottle. "Want some?"

He shook his head. "Already took care of that."

Well, of course. So efficient. But her hand tightened on the bottle at the thought of smoothing lotion onto Logan Castle's skin.

Her imagination couldn't get past his shoulders and chest. Dropping the bottle back in her bag, she took a deep breath, eyes on the water ahead. Way safer than Logan's broad shoulders and muscled thighs.

Clouds ribboned across the blue sky. As a kid, she'd called them tiger clouds. She settled back with a sigh until the boat began to thump across choppy water.

"Once we get into the clear, it should be smoother going," Logan said, his eyes on the horizon. A few other sailboats skimmed the water while a speedboat cut through ahead of them, casting a wake ruffled with white caps.

When they pulled out of the channel, Logan rigged more sail and McKenna jumped up to help. Eyes checking his monitoring equipment and the breeze, he worked with the sails just as efficiently as he handled his practice. She followed his direction.

"You're a natural," he remarked with approval after they'd come around once and she'd ducked under the flying boom.

She grinned. "Thanks to my brothers."

"You're really close, aren't you." A wistful note laced his words.

"Most of the time. Sometimes they can be a pain in the neck."

"Not from what I saw that day. Must be nice to have siblings. You're lucky."

"I know." If she hadn't grown up with her brothers and sister, maybe she wouldn't want children so badly.

"Want to steer?" Logan asked, motioning to her after a while. Ready for any challenge, she scuttled around until she was next to him, the tiller jutting out between them. "If you want to go left, you turn right. It's easy."

"I remember that from my brother's Sunfish." She took hold of the tiller.

"You're a woman who likes control, aren't you?" Logan observed after a while.

"Is that a bad thing?"

He gave her a steady look before answering. "For me? Not at all."

"Good." The breeze caught her hair, teasing out tendrils. Exhilaration pulsed through her. What a great day. As the sun climbed higher, so did the temperature. Logan handed her a water bottle from up front. Soon she shed the sweater from around her neck. Logan lounged across the back seat, hair whipping back from a contented smile.

"You love it out here, don't you?"

His nod was filled with sleepy contentment. "Great place to get away and think."

About what? Would he mention the baby he'd lost? Until Logan shared that important piece, she didn't know if she could feel close to him. Anyway, McKenna was only his Sunday date. The thought that she'd brought this on herself rankled more than a little.

Logan busied himself with adjusting the sail, tugging on the ropes. The sun soon lulled her into silence. After a while, he took the tiller. Their comments flowed easily. Was she the only one who felt energy surging between them? In fact, her thoughts were downright disturbing and they had to do with warm skin, moist lips and a deep thirst that sips from her water bottle couldn't satisfy.

Cripes. She better not get ahead of herself with Hot Doc.

Better to set a safer course. "Will your grandmother come to the golf outing?"

"She golfs, so maybe. She'd beat the pants off both of us." Up above, the sail began to flutter. Logan was on it in a second, tugging on ropes and pulling in the slack. Her breath tightened just looking at him. The speed still didn't pick up. "The wind's dying. We might be sitting here for a while unless you want me to start the motor."

"Time for a swim?" She pulled at the hem of her polo. Was she steamy from the temperature or Logan? "Think I'll change into my suit."

"Changing room below." Logan nodded toward the back.

Grabbing the green and yellow striped beach bag that she'd had forever, McKenna made her way down the narrow steps. Keeping her balance was tricky as the boat lifted and fell on the swells. She blinked to see when she reached the bottom of the steps. Sunlight sifted into the space below from slitted windows that looked out over the deck. The main room was lined with dark blue cushions that could serve as beds. Blue and white blankets were folded neatly at the ends. Looked dry down here, but there was no escaping the smell of the lake.

The area felt so cozy, so intimate, a great place to nap when the sun got too hot. But the order in this area was anything but casual—no wet towels or rumpled clothing. Everything had its place, even the stack of extra beach towels folded neatly on a ledge.

She wasn't going to dwell on Logan's neatness thing. Not today.

Digging into the beach bag for her suit, she kicked off the rubber-soled shoes and took out her green flip flops. As she slipped into her new lime green bikini, she was glad she'd gone shopping. The old navy one-piece just wouldn't do it. Not for today.

Were her goose bumps from the cool air down here? Okay, the suit was showing way too much skin. From deeper in her bag, she pulled out a roomy white shirt. Men's shirts made great cover-ups and she owned one in almost every color. She slid her arms through the generous sleeves and rolled them up a bit, leaving the buttons open.

When she returned topside, a rogue breeze caught her cover-up and it billowed behind her like a spinnaker. Logan glanced up and the look in his eyes gave her chills. "Wow, what can I say?"

"'I like your suit' would do it for me," she joked, tossing her beach bag onto the seat. Suddenly shy, she tugged the corners of the white shirt tight around her middle.

Logan frowned while she worked on her knot. *"Like it…*more than covers it."

"Thank you…I guess. Why don't you change? We'll have an even playing field."

"Playing field, huh? You can sure tell you grew up with a bunch of boys."

Jumping up, he angled around her with a touch on her shoulder. Watching him disappear down below, she still felt the imprint of his hand.

Get a grip. Plunking onto the seat, she closed one hand tight on the tiller.

With the sun beating down, she enjoyed guiding the sloop through the water, even though they were hardly moving. Maybe Logan was right. She did feel comfortable being in control, but it was more than that. When she delivered babies, she was aware of being part of something much bigger than herself.

Eventually the wind died completely. They weren't making much progress. As she looked out over the lake, she slipped one hand up to her shoulder where her skin still hummed, either from Logan's touch or a bad case of nerves. The skyline of Chicago had receded in the distance along with other boats. It was just the two of them.

When Logan reappeared, she was thankful for her sunglasses. He couldn't see her gaping. He hadn't bothered with a shirt and the view was pretty spectacular. Broad shoulders narrowed to the striped swimsuit riding low on his hips. The pattern of his dusty chest hair followed that V.

"Level playing field?"

She snapped her gaze up and caught his sly grin.

"Maybe I could have some of that sunscreen now?" His eyes glinted over the rims of his sunglasses.

"Sure." She dug around in her bag for sunblock while Logan put the boat on autopilot. Seconds later, she was smoothing lotion across his broad shoulders in the places he couldn't reach. Her fingers were pale against the ridges and hollows of his back. "You must spend a lot of time out here." She splayed her hands wide on his upper back and drew them into his spine, applying pressure with the heels of her hands.

When he shrugged, muscles rippled under her hands and into her stomach. "I spend as much time as possible on the boat or golfing. I try to remember to wear a shirt. On the boat, it doesn't always work."

So he came out here alone? Now, wasn't that just the saddest thing? Her hands stilled for a second before taking up the rhythm again. Good Lord, his muscles were knotted tight, from neck to his waistline—although she hadn't gotten that low yet. That thought made her stomach roll like one of the swells thrown by a large freighter.

"Massage could be a second career, not that you need one." He pulled in a sharp breath when she hit a knot.

"Just give me a minute," she muttered, bearing down with her thumbs. When the stubborn muscle released, he groaned, unleashing a wave of heat in her thighs.

"I, uh, teach massage to the couples in my natural childbirth class." A languid breeze offered little relief. She tipped her face into it anyway. Anything to help cool her body. "Helps relax the muscles during labor."

None of her students moaned the way he did. His primal groan tugged at her tummy and lower.

"Makes sense," he gasped when she bore down.

Pulling in a mouthful of moist lake air, she moved up to the knots in his neck. His body fought her, and a line of perspiration beaded along his hairline.

"Loosen up." She gave his back a light pat.

"I am." But his shoulders drew up, tight and resistant.

"No you're not. We're on the water, for Pete's sake. No ringing pagers or phones. Deep breath and out."

"Yes, ma'am." After a couple of deep breaths, the corded muscles in his neck flattened under her fingers.

"Better."

"Thank you, teacher."

"Don't sass me now."

"Is this how you handle the students in your class? Or do they always fall in line?" he teased.

She laughed. "Most couples are so nervous they never give me any lip." As she worked with his neck, her fingers brushed the damp curls along his neck. She fought the urge to rake her hands into his thick head of hair. She licked her dry lips and imagined cradling that head in her hands and just...working out all those tensions. His and hers.

Dazed by the white bright sun, it was so easy to close her eyes and daydream. They'd go below into the damp coolness. A couple wet, heated kisses and Logan would work the thin straps of her top down her arms and cup her breasts. She'd shiver while his lips nuzzled the warm hollow in her neck and then trailed down to take their time with the beaded tips that hung heavy with waiting.

She moaned.

"What is it?" Logan asked, twisting his head to the side.

"Nothing." She sucked in a breath and held it.

"Don't hold back. Lay into it."

"Oh, I will." She gently pressed his head back into position, smoothing the pads of both thumbs over the base of his neck. "Don't bark orders at me, Dr. Castle," she murmured.

"Just do what it takes." He flipped his head to the other side.

She took up her work and the daydream reached for her like a dangerous undertow.

When Logan had finished with her breasts, left them full and throbbing, he'd hook his fingers in her bikini bottom and slide it slowly down her legs. Trembling, she'd fall back onto the cushions with a whimper.

Whimper? When have I ever whimpered?

But the dream flowed on. Reaching up, she'd skim her hands over his chest, following his happy trail until she cupped him gently. He'd moan. She'd increase the pressure. His trunks would come off easily and he'd spring up, ready and at such a good angle. Her fingers would begin to work.

Logan's gutsy groan ripped McKenna from the dream. He tensed, as if horrified by his own voice. She could hardly keep from laughing. Had Logan been indulging in his own naughty reverie?

"Enough. Time for a dip." Twisting free, he whipped off his sunglasses and tucked them into a side pocket. When he jumped up, he landed right on her foot. Good Lord. She shrieked with pain.

"Oh, my God. McKenna, I am so sorry." Face stricken, he dropped to a crouch at her feet. She'd never seen him look so helpless.

"I should have kept my shoes on. It's not your fault." She tried to wiggle her toes, but that right foot hurt like heck.

"Do you mind if I give it a feel? Your foot, I mean?"

Sitting back, she extended her right leg. Cradling her foot with one hand, he ran the other palm gently up over her heel and arch. Hot Doc had the magic touch, and his gentleness did not surprise her.

Now she knew why his practice was so busy.

"Where?" He'd jammed his sunglasses back on his head.

"Where what?" she murmured like a dazed dimwit.

"Where does it hurt?"

"Ah, the toes, in my toes." She attempted another wiggle. The throbbing pulsed.

How could a man have such cool fingers on such a hot day? But he did, except when he touched the joint of her big toe.

"Ah! Painful."

"Hmm." He sat back and, boy, she missed those hands. "Want me to tape it? That's about the only thing you can do with a broken toe. You can always ask Griff on Monday."

This was getting ridiculous. "Look, I'm sure it'll be fine. Let's get in the water." The sun bore down.

"Sure you want to swim?" He stowed his phone in a nook behind the seat cushion.

Hopping up, she found her balance. "Absolutely. Might be the best medicine." After checking her pager and her phone and seeing no messages, she slipped them both back into her purse and shoved it into a nice dry corner.

Logan dropped sail. The boat slowed and the heat descended.

"Use the stairs at the back of the boat to get into the water. Let's not get too far from each other."

He came to stand next to her. The scent of warm coconut sunblock made her head swim.

Their eyes locked and her head buzzed with heat.

"Think I'll take the direct route." Grabbing for his hand, she stepped gingerly onto the edge of the boat.

"Watch yourself."

Her body smacked the surface in a cannonball, feet tucked up tight. The water was oh, so cool, and she ignored her protesting foot. After Logan plunged in next to her, she kicked her way to the surface. Hair slicked back against his head, he bobbed up, his concerned frown easing when he saw her. "Foot okay?"

"Let's forget about it." She didn't want this day to be about her foot and she swiped at her face, hoping her nose wasn't streaming.

"You're one tough lady."

"Not really." McKenna didn't want to be tough. She wanted to be tender. Especially with Logan. Treading water with hair slicked back, he looked like an ad for expensive men's cologne.

"I'll race you around the boat." And she was off, leaving him sputtering behind her.

For the next twenty minutes, they raced each other in the cool water. The first lap, they were neck and neck so they decided to go for best of three. To her dismay, he won.

"You're very competitive," Logan said, tossing his wet hair from his eyes.

"You bet." Chest heaving, McKenna struggled to catch her

breath.

"Let's call it quits. Rest that toe." Concern tightened the planes of his face.

God, the guy was gorgeous.

"Good idea." Her arms felt fatigued, the toe was throbbing and she was famished.

But her he-man sandwiches weren't going to satisfy the need tunneling through her body.

Chapter 13

McKenna opened the picnic lunch while Logan rustled up some frosty beers below. Not being on call had its advantages. She could count on some relaxing time. But with Logan? Maybe not so relaxing.

Suit still wet, she felt comfortable in the sun but tugged the shirt tighter. "I freckle really badly," she threw out, handing him a sandwich. His eyes deepened as they found the deep indentation of her cleavage. She forgot to chew. Shivered as her nipples peaked.

"Your skin is so creamy, McKenna." The catch in Logan's voice brought an even stronger reaction. "You should protect them…it."

She laughed while a furious blush surged up his cheeks. He popped open his beer and took an audible gulp. Loving her Hot Doc's discomfort, she rocked back. "You sound like my mother, talking about sunblock." She ran slow fingers across the top of her breasts. He looked away and she chuckled.

"Having fun yet?" His frown didn't fool her. He was enjoying this too.

"Let's eat."

"Good idea." Logan took a huge bite. The conversation they'd had weeks ago in the Purple Frog about people's eating habits came back. His expression told her he remembered too. Bite by bite, nibble by nibble, they matched each other. The sail boat lifted on a swell when a large cruiser motored past.

She loved the fact that they were in tune and he sure didn't seem intimidated by her boldness. This day was so perfect, but she'd come with a purpose. "Logan, I hope you don't feel railroaded into this mission trip. It's a tough week."

About to take another bite, Logan put his sandwich down. "What? You don't think I'm up to it?"

"Not at all. It's just that we need your heart as well as your clinical skills."

His flush told her she was only making things worse.

"Wish you'd give me more credit, McKenna. Are you afraid I won't measure up?"

"Logan, that's not what I ..."

"Think I've eaten enough." He stowed his sandwich in the baggie.

Now she'd hurt his feelings. "How about chocolate?"

"Dessert?" The smile was back. So was the playful glint in his eye.

"Exactly. We need chocolate." She pulled out a container and popped the lid. The sun beat down as they sampled red strawberries dipped in dark chocolate.

"Delicious." Logan finished his berry in two bites and reached for more.

"You bet. Lordy, it's hot." Shrugging out of her shirt, she grabbed another strawberry.

His lips slowed, shiny wet and smeared with chocolate.

"Sweltering."

Her fingers closed over the treat in her hand.

Logan kept chewing, lips moist and eyes registering her response.

Her throat closed and the chocolate in her hand became a squished mess. "I like to make it last longer…the pleasure," she explained, opening her fingers and eyeing the destroyed berry.

Silence stretched between them. "Always a good goal." His throat worked. Tossing back the last of his beer, he crunched the can in one hand. "Want another beer?"

She shook her head. "Think I'll stay with the strawberries." Her head swam—either from the heat, the beer or her hormones.

His wide shoulders lifted and settled. "Guess I should take a pass too."

"Lighten up, Logan. Two beers won't turn you into a drunken sailor."

"You think?" A slow smile tilted his lips.

"Absolutely. "And she slapped her bare thigh for emphasis with the hand that wasn't chocolate.

His eyes dropped to that thigh and shifted back to her messy hand. He tossed the can to the bottom of the boat. "I don't really want another beer." Wiping the perspiration from his upper lip, he lifted his glinting gray eyes to hers. It was like being stung by a laser.

Later she never could recall just how she wound up on his lap. Their bodies slid together so naturally. His lips took hers in a slow kiss and her hand closed over the strawberry. When Logan pried open her fingers and began licking the chocolate mess, she nearly lost it.

Oh, so naughty. And amazing.

When his lips circled back to her, they tasted like chocolate—the expensive dark stuff with a bitter edge. Forget polite conversation and collegiality. Felt like they'd been waiting for this all day. Their lips explored and teased until she was gasping and her head spun.

The sun stoked her need. She wanted him so bad.

But hadn't he taken someone else out that Saturday night?

"Stop!" She pressed both hands against his chest. Even if he weren't playing the field, time and life had made her cautious.

Getting physical was easy. Getting close? Something else entirely and way more important.

Logan's eyes blinked open, and drooped half closed, like a toddler who doesn't want to wake up from his nap. "Why?" His fingers worked her back.

"Because. Logan, I've been down this road before. I want to be careful."

"So do I." His sweet little boy grin settled into concerned lines. Oh, cripes. She brushed her fingertips over his frown lines and they eased. His sandy eyelashes fluttered and his eyes closed. With a groan, she melted. He nuzzled her throat, his tongue on her pulse. The boat rocked as a speedboat roared past, a cooling spray splattering them in its wake. "Get a room!" some kids called out.

~.~

Shoving back, Logan felt like a total idiot. He'd been so determined to hold it down today. Establish boundaries. The last thing he wanted was for McKenna to feel this was all about the sex. Some docs might operate like that, but he wasn't one of them.

Besides—and this made him feel almost silly—but was *he* ready? Funny but with her he was wondering what it would all mean. Pulling away from her luscious body in that tiny, teasing bikini was torture. McKenna blinked up at him, greenish brown eyes clouding. His stomach plummeted when she sat back and slowly pulled on that damn shirt. "Guess we should get back," he murmured, half hoping she'd disagree.

"Suppose it's time." In silence McKenna packed the food away in her basket and he rigged the sails. Didn't take long. The sun was setting. The wind had died, and they weren't going anywhere. Eventually Logan had to start the motor, which for him was admitting defeat.

"Want to get something to eat?" he asked when they reached the harbor.

McKenna wouldn't meet his eyes. "I have to work on some lesson plans for my natural childbirth class."

"Maybe another night."

"Sure. Right."

On the way back to her apartment, they hardly spoke. Had he blown it? Had he over thought this whole damn thing? That would really piss him off.

They kissed good night at the door. That pissed him off too.

~.~

McKenna was in countdown mode for the trip to Guatemala. Usually she was energized and ready to go. But this year, every time she thought about that week, her stomach did a slow slide. The day on the boat had been confusing, and they hadn't gotten anything settled. Would the week in Central America help or just add more tension?

What if Logan hated a mission that gave her great satisfaction? In many ways the trip might be a turning point and that thought kept her awake more than one night.

Because Bethany would be the only midwife left in the office, one of the other midwifery practices would provide coverage for that one week. Fortunately only two births were on their calendar, but babies often didn't arrive on schedule. As she prepared for her class the Wednesday night before their departure, McKenna was preoccupied. At three o'clock, she had to break for a meeting. The Day in the LDRP event was scheduled for August and the planning committee was meeting.

As she stood in front of the elevators, her mind was a million miles away. A familiar voice made her look up. Amanda and Connor were strolling toward her, hand in hand.

"McKenna!" Amanda colored.

Connor looked from one to the other, his face a question mark.

"Are you coming to visit me?" Drats. Had she missed a message from them? Amanda shook her head, a telling blush deepening. Always a man of few words, Connor was studying his running shoes.

Giving her husband a let-me-handle-this look, Amanda said,

"We just came from seeing Logan again."

"Again?"

Amanda nodded. "We've been preparing for, well, in vitro maturation that Logan does in his fertility clinic. And this was our day for a good retrieval. In four days or so, the eggs should be ready." Her words came fast and jumbled, while McKenna's brother turned the color of the red exit sign.

"That's wonderful." McKenna threw her arms around Amanda and gave her a quick squeeze. Gosh, how she wanted this for her brother and his wife. But caution dampened her enthusiasm. They'd been disappointed so many times. "Maybe this time."

Connor shifted his shoulders. "Yeah, well, we'll see."

Amanda gave her husband an admonishing glance. "We're hopeful. And Dr. Castle... Logan...has been great. Thanks for recommending him."

All McKenna could do was beam. "Gotta run. Keep me posted."

With a wave, they continued to the parking garage while she took the elevator down to the overpass and hurried to the OB unit.

Jack Frazier had taken the lead with the committee plan to host a Day in the LDRP. He reported that all the vendors were in line, and their sample products should be there on time. The event was slated for the end of August. The summer was slipping away.

Priscilla sat taking notes. Logan couldn't make the meeting. "But of course I'll keep him up to speed," Priscilla said pointedly as the meeting wrapped up.

McKenna hated the sharp spear of jealousy. Was Priscilla

Logan's Saturday night date?

"Logan's so excited about the trip." Priscilla caught up with her as McKenna left the meeting.

"Do you mean Guatemala?" McKenna asked. *Trip?* For her it was more a mission.

"He's been telling me all about it." Did her tone suggest more than a mere conversation?

"We're so happy that he could join us." McKenna hardly recognized her prim and proper voice. Priscilla was becoming known as the Blonde Bombshell around the hospital. McKenna detected the faint scent of hair spray when Priscilla waved good bye and bustled in the direction of the OB unit.

McKenna was going to put this all on hold. Departure day was only days away. She had more important things to take care of, like Sasha's care, although Vanessa had assured McKenna that her precious cat would be safe with Bo. Her little boy was delighted that they would be cat sitting for that week.

~.~

Early Saturday morning Logan and McKenna stood together in the airport, waiting to board the plane. Overhead they were announcing flights. The scent of Logan's spicy aftershave hung in the air. The thought that they would be living in close quarters for one week made her suck in a deep breath. How would she handle that? She clutched her boarding pass tighter.

Logan ploughed one hand through his thick hair. "Wonder if I should get a cup of coffee before we board. You want one?"

"Not really." As McKenna watched him gallop toward

Starbuck's, Selena caught her eye and quirked one brow. McKenna just shook her head and made herself relax into the black vinyl seat. Everything would be all right. An important mission lay ahead—one that stayed uppermost in her mind for months after they returned. That should be her focus, not Logan.

For the past week, she'd helped Selena organize the equipment they planned on taking. Boxes of stethoscopes, broad blood pressure cuffs and baby scales were packed, along with medical supplies and medications donated by pharmaceutical companies. The rural midwives were often left to improvise. Hospitals often weren't adequately stocked in this part of the world, much less the midwives.

Logan made his way back to the waiting area, checking his phone as he sipped his coffee. The man was totally oblivious to the admiring glances women cast his way. With his blue shirt and jeans, he looked boyish today. When he caught her staring, McKenna felt the warmth of Logan's grin clear to her toes. He'd tucked a paper under his arm, but he set it aside when he took the seat next to her. He gave her hand a quick squeeze, his palm warm from the cup of coffee. She wanted to curl up in that heat. Feel it expand.

But not now.

When their flight was called, it felt good to push forward. Felt good to leave those darn worries behind in the waiting area.

Right—as if she could do that.

The first leg of the flight took them to Tampa, Florida, and a three-hour layover that seemed endless. She braided her hair into pigtails and reapplied her coral lipstick while Logan watched, that secret smile playing across his lips. Nerves on edge, some of the group used their iPads. Where they were going, there would be no hookups and many were leaving final messages for loved ones who wouldn't hear from them for a week. From there, they boarded a smaller plane for Guatemala City.

"A nap sounds good," she said, getting settled on the small plane. "This may be the last air conditioning for a while."

"Yeah, I figured that." Logan let his head loll back, lashes feathering across his cheeks. Scrunching down in her seat, she remained way too aware of his muscled thigh next to hers. As she drifted off, she wasn't sure if the breathing she heard was her own or Logan's. She slept fitfully.

When they reached the airport in Guatemala, heat shimmered from the tarmac. All they could see through the small window was the runway and hills rising in the distance behind a small yellow building.

"Look around. Don't leave anything on the plane," Selena warned. They scrambled from their seats, pulling luggage from the overhead bins.

Grabbing their duffel bags, they inched down the small aisle. Heat blasted them as they deplaned. Eyes gritty and body still working out the knots, McKenna pulled her sunglasses into place. Logan was behind her. She wouldn't have been surprised if he bolted back onto the plane but he fell into step next to her.

Once inside the small airport, McKenna scanned the waiting area. "There's Teresa, the midwife who helps organize the trip."

Logan grinned as he took in the squat older woman, hands

clasped over an ample stomach and face creased into a smile. "Looks like she's been doing this a while. Does Teresa still deliver babies?"

"Yep. Many of the midwives, or *comadronas*, as they're called, practice until they can't physically do the job. Hardy women," she added, closing the gap and giving Teresa a big hug.

"McKenna, you always come back." Teresa's arms encircled her. The woman smelled of sun and earth. She turned to welcome the rest of the group. "Selena, welcome. Terry, Janet." How amazing that she remembered their names. Then she came to Logan.

"Teresa, I want you to meet a new member of our group, Dr. Logan Castle," Selena said.

Teresa gave Logan an appraising glance. "*Un doctor. Bienvenido a Guatemala. Encantado*," she whispered, rising on tiptoe to hug him.

To McKenna's amazement, Logan repeated the words to Teresa. Hands reaching up to his shoulders, the old woman accepted him right then. In Guatemala, the relationship between doctors and midwives was rocky. But not for this pair.

Together they trooped toward the baggage area. "Juan is waiting for us," Teresa told them as they grabbed their bags. They followed her outside into the blazing sunshine where a wizened older man missing most of his teeth stood outside a battered van, straw hat in hand.

"*Hola, Juan!*" The group chorused and his smile widened. After packing their bags into the back of the van, they clambered inside, two crammed onto each bench seat.

When Logan dug for seat belts, McKenna shrugged. "We just hang on and hope for the best."

She was relieved when he gave her a rueful smile and settled back, one arm stretched around her shoulders. Stubble patterned his cheeks and chin, and the heat had already raised a sheen of sweat on his skin. When Juan threw the van into gear with a lurch, Logan braced himself with his long legs. He might turn into her mountain man before this trip was over.

Only he wasn't hers, was he?

"How many times have you been here?" Logan asked as the bus bumped down a rutted highway.

Dust seared her squinted eyes when McKenna turned to him. "This is my third summer trip." Pulling her rubber bands from her hair, she attempted to rebraid them. It was hopeless. She might as well accept the frizzies for the next week. Warm humid air bathed their faces but brought no relief from the heat. Logan propped one elbow in the open window. He looked like a teen on his way to summer camp.

Trepidation coiled in McKenna's stomach. This sure wasn't summer camp.

~.~

Logan smiled, looking at McKenna in those pigtails. "When do you take summer vacation?" he asked, bracing himself when the driver took a curve. This bus sure didn't feel safe, although the older guy seemed to know what he was doing.

"This *is* my vacation, Logan. Sounds weird, but you'll see."

She was amazing. Most women preferred a five star hotel with room service rather than a developing country that might not even have a working bathroom.

In the seats ahead of them, heads bobbed and people napped. The newbies were glued to the windows, and he was one of them. The air was sharp with diesel fuel as the bus skirted the city. The acrid smell reminded him of Europe. Soon they left the clutter of homes and shops behind. On either side lay open fields, occasionally broken by stands of pine that thickened when the road began to climb. After a while, his ears popped and Logan worked his jaw. Evening came and darkness fell, but the heat held. He squirmed against the torn vinyl seat. Felt like he'd been wearing this shirt for a week. Next to him McKenna seemed perfectly content, her body rolling easily as Juan navigated the bumps in the road.

They climbed higher and higher. "Will you look at that," he said under his breath when they'd reach a peak. Green hills undulated below. In the distance, a stream meandered through the countryside, foaming white as it fell. God, this was gorgeous. The route took them through small villages. Dogs followed the van, barking at the unexpected intrusion. One arm out the window, Juan waved and called out to people he must know. Women dressed in simple skirts and faded blouses watched from doorways, children clinging to their legs.

When Juan honked the horn, they all waved.

"People here don't have much. The rural areas have the highest poverty rate," McKenna explained. "Most don't go to school, even if there is a teacher. They work the fields like their parents, scratching out a living, if they're lucky."

"Some of the children look frail," Logan said, his gut clenching when they passed clusters of kids. These were the children whose photos had drawn him to this mission. Well, their faces and McKenna's passion.

"Undernourished," McKenna said shortly. "It's endemic. UNESCO and other international groups have made inroads but there's still much to be done."

This environment was so different from the lakeside high rises of Chicago. McKenna had grabbed a bottle of water in the airport, and now she twisted it open and took a swig. But the water only offered warm wetness. The air blowing through the open window smelled damp and earthy. Bright birds flitted through the rich greenery and the distant chatter of monkeys echoed in the tall trees.

As the night sky turned darker, Teresa passed around a basket with tortillas filled with cooked beans and corn. "Eat. Soon we will be there."

Logan considered the modest supper cupped in his hand. He was starving. The smell of food was irresistible and he wasn't disappointed when he bit down. Corn and beans had never tasted this good. Even the hot peppers that brought tears to his eyes were welcome.

After they finished eating, McKenna's body slumped onto him. Even though she added to his own body heat, he didn't mind. In fact, he relished her curves and quickly fell asleep, his head resting on hers. Some time later the sound of grinding brakes startled him awake. The van had stopped.

"El Limar," Juan announced with a flourish, as if this were

Palm Beach and they were on tour. The old man made Logan smile. Beside him, McKenna gave a sinuous stretch, pulled away and peered out the window. Rubbing her eyes, she shot him a sleepy smile. The doors slapped open with a rusty screech.

"Home, sweet home…for a week," Selena announced, jumping down from the bus.

In front of them sat a low adobe building that may once have been yellow. Now the paint was peeling. The long wooden bench in front of the building was warped, one end held up by cinder bricks. McKenna massaged her neck while Logan tried to work the kinks out of his long frame as they stood in the crowded aisle.

She nodded toward the low structure. "That's the clinic. And the bunk house."

He figured as much. "Let me take your duffle."

"Absolutely not." She hoisted what looked like a heavy bag onto one shoulder. "Down here, it's every woman—and man—for himself."

"Is that a warning?"

"Just the way it is." She stood in the narrow aisle looking like a woman who could take on the world.

"Do you ever let a man help you?"

A shadow passed over her face and, damn, he regretted those words. "Didn't mean anything by that, McKenna. Just a thought."

"And I hear it." The frown stayed on her face.

When had hot and sweaty ever turned him on? With McKenna, the combination became an aphrodisiac.

After grabbing his own bag, he ducked his head and followed

her down the aisle. The hum of insects filled the air as he eased down the steps, along with periodic cries of some bird, a lonely sound that chilled him despite the heat.

"Thank you, Juan." McKenna turned to the bus driver. "See you tomorrow?"

"*Si, si.*" And then he pointed to Logan. "Come with me, *no?*"

So, that's how it was? Logan glanced back at McKenna, who fluttered her hands, pushing him toward the old man. Well, that question was answered. So they wouldn't be bunking together. His concentration level might improve.

When the others filtered into the bunkhouse that also served as their clinic, Teresa bustled over. "Logan, I thought you could sleep with Juan." Her shoulders pulled up as if she were defending the honor of the women. In some ways, Teresa reminded him of his grandmother.

"No problem." Sleeping near McKenna may have tested his patience at a time when he needed his sleep. He had to have his wits about him this week. With a regretful backward glance, Logan grabbed his bag from the back of the van and followed Juan down the road. The image of McKenna standing in the doorway stayed with him all night.

Chapter 14

The next day, the tantalizing smell of coffee pulled McKenna awake. Stiff from a night in a hammock, she slipped on her sandals and headed outside to the latrine.

"Feels almost like home," joked Sherry Barry, waiting in front of her.

"Right." In the early morning dampness, McKenna's gray sleep pants and T-shirt felt like a second skin.

Profound stillness surrounded them as early morning light crept through the dense undergrowth. When they returned to the sleeping area, Teresa was bustling about in the kitchen corner with her quiet competence. Logan hadn't arrived yet. Or had he bolted and asked Juan to take him back to the airport? Her stomach turned over as she unhooked the hammock from the ceiling. Logan was made of stronger stuff than that and this week could provide proof.

"Patients are already lined up outside the door," Teresa told them.

McKenna wasn't surprised. The need was so great in the highlands. Midwives or *comadronas* took care of general health for the women and children. The people here were mostly Mayan, indigenous to this area. Sadly, they were not always welcome in city hospitals, even if they could make the trip. Often skilled in herbal remedies, they sometimes needed modern medicines that could make a life or death difference.

Fortified by coffee, McKenna quickly consulted with Selena.

"Juan has gone back to Guatemala City to pick up the boxes of equipment and pharmaceuticals," Selena explained. "If patients need medications, they will have to wait."

"Did Logan go with him?"

Selena frowned. "No, Juan can handle it himself."

"Of course." McKenna shook off her qualms. She'd come here to help, not to evaluate Logan's abilities to work in a less than sterile setting. This was stupid. Why did this matter so much to her? But it did.

Yawning, Logan wandered into the clinic. "Did you have something to eat?" McKenna asked.

"Yep. Had a couple of the packaged meals I brought with me." Logan looked rumpled but alert. A worn blue T-shirt outlined his broad chest, and faded jeans were slung low on his hips. The pungent smell of his new leather boots filled the small room. When she glanced up, he was grinning. "Did I do good, Mom?"

Her cheeks flamed. "Teresa has coffee."

"Good. Smells great in here."

That determined jut of his chin? Logan was in the game. Teresa beckoned to him with a tin mug of coffee.

After a quick breakfast of warm beans and cold cornbread, they converted the sleeping area into private exam cubicles with sheeting strung from the hooks that had held the hammocks, now bundled into corners. Midwives would arrive midweek for a training session.

"Do I have any volunteers to go about two or three hours farther up into the highlands?" Selena asked. "Teresa tells me that an older *comadrona* could use some help training other women to take her place. How about it?"

Hands shot into the air, and two of the women prepared to leave. McKenna, Selena and Logan would stay in El Limar with Sherry, the nutritionist, and the four remaining midwives.

The day started. With Teresa's help, women filed into their makeshift exam rooms while their children played out front. In addition to checking pregnant women, the group of clinicians was also dealing with problems resulting from inadequate care in the hospital. In one morning, McKenna sent two of the women to Logan to repair a poor episiotomy. One young woman's C-section incision had not healed and her baby was three months old. Vaginal tears, fistulas, incontinence—by the time they broke for a quick lunch, McKenna's stomach was churning. Troubled, she sought out Teresa for an explanation. "Teresa, I've got to ask…why are so many women going to the hospital for delivery if the care is so poor?"

Teresa's face twisted with disgust. "Criminal, no? Most hospitals will not allow midwives. But if anything happens with that delivery, of course it's blamed on the *comadrona*."

Frustration choked McKenna. She grabbed another cup of coffee. Eyeing the closed curtain of Logan's cubicle, she hung around like a mother waiting for her child to come out of kindergarten on the first day. His patient emerged with a grateful smile before Logan stepped out. His shirt rode up when he stretched, and she enjoyed the view. "Everything okay?"

"Fine." He followed her eyes and she yanked her gaze north. "See anything you like?"

"What if someone heard you?" she whispered, glancing at the curtained cubicle.

"I think they'd get a good laugh. The proper Dr. Castle."

So he knew what the staff thought of him. A dozen denials leapt to mind, but they died on her lips. They wouldn't be true.

He chuckled, studying her face. "How about you? Good so far?"

"This is pretty much what I expected."

Logan had never looked sexier, leaning on one shoulder against the cinderblock. "Guess I didn't have many expectations," he finally admitted, jaw shifting. "I'm new to all this. Kind of taking it all in. Tell you one thing. Don't think I've ever had patients more grateful than these ladies. It's humbling, McKenna."

"I agree." Heart lifting, she wanted to hug the man. His eyes danced, almost as if he knew what was running through her mind. But time to get back to work. Another patient was following Teresa back to McKenna's cubicle.

By early afternoon, the sun had climbed high in the sky. Heat rose in puffs of dirt on the road outside. The desultory cry of birds pierced the drone of insects. With flat straw hats jammed on their heads, women waited outside, some holding a *serape* over their small children to protect them from the sun. Inside, moisture beaded on the cinder block walls, evidence of the last rain.

Although McKenna couldn't see Logan, his calm voice drifted over the white sheeting. At times, she thought she detected an edge of frustration, but it was the situation, not the women that frayed his patience. One glance told her that much when he burst from his cubicle, looking for more bandaging. They merely nodded to each other. So much work ahead, and the people had come so far.

The parade of maladies always took a toll, but McKenna's heart positively tore when dainty Ana Lena stepped into her cubicle. Perching timidly on the edge of the cot, the young woman held a large baby with a startling shock of dark hair. From the way she sat, McKenna knew she was far from comfortable.

"*Hay dolor?* Pain?" McKenna asked.

"*Si. Mucho.*" With halting words, Ana Lena explained about her three-day labor and the difficulty delivering her son. "*Pepito es tan largo.*"

Indeed, Pepito was a very big baby. If he was twenty-two pounds now, he must have been a good fifteen when he entered the world. Panicked when the baby hadn't arrived after two days of hard labor, her husband had carried Ana Lena for three hours until they reached the city. McKenna could only imagine that trip.

Teresa came to take Pepito while McKenna examined Ana Lena. As she murmured reassurance to the younger woman, McKenna struggled to keep her face from reflecting the horror ripping through her. Ana Lena should have been given a C-section. Instead, the young mother's entire pelvic floor had been damaged. McKenna didn't need a pediatric specialist to know that the child with his sunny smile and empty eyes had been affected by the hours of slamming against Ana Lena's pubic bone. Under usual conditions, a C-section would have been done but they had waited too long in an area not served by a *comadrona* and the hospital was so far away.

Dark eyes shadowed by too many disappointments, Ana Lena looked to her for some sign of hope. McKenna smiled encouragement. *"Hay un doctor con nosotros."*

Ana Lena shrank back, no doubt thinking of the doctor who did this to her.

"Un momento," McKenna told her, holding up one finger. *"Y no te preocupes."* Telling Ana Lena not to worry was useless. Her unremitting pain was a constant reminder.

McKenna sought out Logan. Hunched over in his cubicle, he was scribbling on a pad of paper. No electronic medical records here. Seeing McKenna, he tossed the pad onto the cot. "This is no way to chart patient care."

Was Logan reaching his limits? Struggling past her own worries, she explained the situation.

"Sure, I'll take a look," he said, grabbing the antibacterial gel and scrubbing. He snapped up two surgical gloves from the box. "Couldn't be any worse than the fistula I just saw."

But it was. She could see that by his clenched jaw as he examined Ana Lena. Slowly and gently, he asked questions, nodding encouragement through her sad tale. Then with McKenna's help, Logan told her how he could help. The poor young mother may not totally have understood Logan's words but there was no misinterpreting the compassion in his eyes. Tomorrow he would perform surgery. Janet Johnson, one of their midwives, had once been a surgical nurse, so she would assist.

"I'll be there too," McKenna assured Ana Lena, who turned to her with big dark eyes.

Teresa called for Logan and they had no chance to discuss the case further.

The day spun on, one case after another, often presenting a longstanding ailment that had worsened over years. Proud and resilient, the villagers relied on herbal treatments learned in childhood, but some health issues did not respond. Many problems had become critical by the time the villagers made their way to the clinic.

McKenna's back and neck began to ache, along with her thighs. The cots were low, and she was still tired from the long trip. As the heat climbed, the humidity pressed over them like a warm sponge. Her scrubs clung to her body, and ringlets were teased from her pigtails no matter how often she brushed them back. Still, the women's patience and gratitude kept her going.

Later in the day, she found Logan in the kitchen, foraging through the cabinets.

"What are you looking for?"

"Sterile wipes." Hair mussed, he looked incredible. Felt totally inappropriate to think of him this way under these circumstances, but there it was. Yanking a warped drawer open, she handed him a pack. "Please level with me. Can you help Ana Lena?"

Expelling a tight breath, he propped a hip against the counter.

"The entire perineum needs reconstruction, but I think I can repair it. It's worse than anything I've seen in the states. I'd just like to meet the butcher who did this to her." A muscle worked in his jaw.

Teresa was making her rounds. "*Hay una problema?*"

McKenna shook her head. "Dr. Castle and I were just discussing a patient."

In her faded blue skirt and colorful woven top, Teresa stood stolid in her huaraches, pushing back wisps of gray hair. "*Por favor*, do not become discouraged. The work you do here... *es muy precioso.*" Almost like a blessing, she placed both her hands over Logan's.

"I only hope it's enough." With an angry hitch of one shoulder, Logan turned to go back to work.

Watching him disappear behind the white sheet, she whispered to Teresa, "He'll be fine."

"Your *novio* is a good man." When Teresa smiled, deep lines radiated from her brown eyes.

"Oh, he's not my boyfriend."

"No?" Teresa's wise eyes told McKenna she didn't believe her.

Any further denial stuck in McKenna's throat. She didn't know what Logan was to her. With every patient he treated, her protective barriers weakened, leaving an uncomfortable vulnerability.

Teresa brought in another young mother with worried eyes. "*Buenos dias,*" McKenna greeted her, seeing the eyes clear. "*Como estas?*"

When shadows lengthened, Teresa turned on three stark light

bulbs that served the area. A patient had just left and McKenna stretched, feeling the tight knots in her back resist. Her eyes stung and rubbing them didn't help. Outside the clinic door, villagers still stood patiently, feeding their children with food kept in their serapes.

Finally, Teresa called a halt, stepping outside to explain that they would be seen tomorrow. The patients quietly dispersed. "Where will they go?" McKenna asked.

"The people of this village will take them in. Or they can stay in the church." Teresa pointed up the road, past the mothers who leaned in doorways. The tiny mud-yellow church had quickly become the recovery area for any women having minor procedures. Then her face lightened. "Juan has returned with the supplies. Can you help unload them while I prepare food?"

"Of course." Together with Logan, Selena and Sherry Barry, McKenna lugged the boxes into the back room and began to organize the medical supplies. The aroma of cooking food soon filled the air. "I'm starving," she murmured, her stomach growling.

"Double that." Logan's arm brushed hers while they were filling a cabinet with wipes, bandages and ointments.

How twisted was it that she could be wildly attracted to a guy who smelled like he'd spent the day in the gym? McKenna swallowed hard and ran her hands down her wrinkled scrub pants. Didn't matter if he was a mess, Chicago's Hot Doc had never looked more gorgeous. His hair was lined with sweat ridges from combing it back with his fingers. And that chin darkened with a two-day beard? She wanted to run one palm along it. Strike his body like a match and feel the heat.

One corner of his mouth quirked up when Logan caught her staring. "Hungry?"

She gulped. "You bet."

Their eyes locked. The moment stretched. Her body gave her all kinds of disturbing signals.

"Smart ass," she finally whispered. His lop-sided grin split into a smile.

This was the Logan she loved.

Really? The impact shook her. Thank goodness he'd turned back to stacking supplies in the cupboard and didn't witness her confusion. When had she fallen in love with Logan Castle? Was it when he'd taken the cold tortilla from Teresa or when he assured Ana Lena that he would help her? After quaking with nervousness and holding him off for weeks, the country club doctor had inched his way into McKenna's heart with small acts of kindness.

Oh, man. The new revelation knifed through her.

Love upped the ante. Brought consequences she hoped she could handle.

By then Teresa was spooning warm beans and rice into tin plates, and they grabbed bottles of pop. Taking the food outside, they slumped onto the weathered bench. For a few seconds, everything fell silent. Night sounds hummed all around them.

"Questions? Comments?" Selena asked between mouthfuls.

"Hey, why don't you step off that soapbox and enjoy your complex carbohydrates?" Sherry joked. "Everything went fine."

A couple of them rolled their eyes. At times today, the cases were anything but fine. They compared notes, discussed issues and offered suggestions. McKenna much preferred this informal setting to case conferences in one of the hospital meeting rooms. Of course, having Logan close beside her was a plus point. The task was huge and the time remaining, short. This was like trying to empty Lake Michigan with a teaspoon, for cripe's sake.

Here in Limar, they were the only hope, at least for now. Teresa pointed out the small ways the midwives helped the women, like suggesting olive oil to help the skin stretch easier during birth. They had brought cases of donated packets of olive oil to avoid vaginal tears during childbirth.

For the next two days, they continued to see patients. In the back corner, often assisted by Janet, Logan worked silently, lips pressed tight. He never complained. But with each day, he withdrew into a world McKenna couldn't enter. As she trembled with the new knowledge that kept her awake, Logan became increasingly quiet.

Maybe when he went back to Chicago, he would be relieved. Maybe he'd be sorry he'd come and he'd turn to Priscilla Preston and her pristine world where women's obstetric and gynecological problems were handled in sleek offices with plasma TVs and educational videos.

Snap out of it, McKenna. Time to focus on the work and not Logan. Time to rein in her growing feelings. Sure. Like she could do this.

The day with the Guatemalan midwives was one McKenna would never forget. Almost twenty came, some wise from years of practice and others still new to the field. A cooling breeze blew from the mountains that day and heavy dark clouds threatened rain.

These sessions dealt with more complex issues, like how to determine when a woman needed to be transported to a hospital. Because of the tension between hospitals and midwives, the women viewed a transfer as a necessary evil. They feared it but might have no choice. The death rate for both infants and mothers with complications was high.

With Teresa interpreting and another woman translating into Mam, the Mayan dialect, McKenna took them through the various stages of labor. She explained what complications might indicate a real problem. Although Logan would have done a good job with this subject, it was important that they see a woman authority figure. "If a woman doesn't dilate or if the baby's head doesn't drop into the pelvis after hours of labor, then it's time to think about the hospital."

Unease rippled through the group at the mention of the hospital. One new midwife admitted she'd lost a woman only last month from uncontrolled hemorrhaging. In that case, transport to a hospital might have saved her life. The women settled down with stern faces.

"Most babies are born within three hours of pushing. If progress doesn't seem to be made, again it's time to evaluate transporting the patient to a hospital." McKenna took them through other indications. They all needed to understand these signs to ensure the safety of both mother and baby. Their distrust of a health care facility twisted something deep in her gut. But they had no other recourse. Although Logan could have used the time to take a break, he stayed in the back, slugging down a bottle of pop and listening.

Terry White had been primed to address family planning needed so desperately in these far-flung regions. The cities had access to resources like birth control but in distant villages, knowledge was limited and large families contributed to the poverty. The Guatemalan midwives listened carefully to Terry's presentation.

At lunch, Sherry passed out posters written in Spanish illustrating the dietary needs of women and children. Starvation stalked children in this area, but poor parents had no lands to plant with crops. Meals were often unbalanced and limited.

"What we offer is just a drop in the bucket," Logan murmured as the day's session wrapped up.

"We'll never be able to solve all their problems, Logan. Took a couple of trips for me to come to terms with that. But our support is appreciated. We can make life-changing interventions for some of these women. Isn't that better than nothing?"

"Guess it has to be." Logan's eyes were shuttered.

A cool chill worked its way down McKenna's spine. The night before they'd taken a walk away from the clinic after supper. In the cool darkness, he'd kissed her. Need unleashed through her body with a wicked snap and she'd struggled for control that just wasn't there. She wanted him so badly.

Logan's heavy panting told her he felt the same.

But she wanted more than this, and the realization opened a chasm between them.

After the session with Sherry was over, they walked down to the church where Ana Lena was resting following her pelvic floor repair. McKenna had glimpsed Logan with Pepito, dangling objects in front of the baby. Pepito reacted only to a voice not a keychain or a stethoscope, unless it made noise. Although Logan kept a tight cap on his feelings, she wished she could read his mind. Was this work a sad reminder of the son he'd lost and would that prove a barrier for Logan?

Later in the day, McKenna saw Logan walking down the dirt road that went into town, nodding to people who came to their open doorway to see *el Americano, el Doctor.* Her concern eased a bit. Maybe everything would be all right. Maybe Logan would realize that their work was valued. That they could never address every need, but it still had tremendous worth.

Logan was scheduled for two additional pelvic floor reconstructions toward the end of the week. Word of Ana Lena's operation had traveled quickly. So far he had done five hymen reconstructions. The girls had looked penitent and hesitant, but once they realized Logan and the crew weren't there to judge them, they emerged from the procedure smiling.

But Wednesday night as she lay in her hammock, McKenna was awakened by the sound of rolling thunder that reverberated clear into her stomach.

"What the heck?" Sherry muttered from the next hammock. "Sounds like the sky is falling."

McKenna listened for the patter of rain on the leaves of the trees outside. "That's about right. Up here, rain is serious. Tropical rainfalls can wash out roads and flatten huts."

The clouds must have opened just then. The roar of the downpour made sleep impossible..

Chapter 15

Rain pummeled the roof all night. Juan snored and although Logan had packed ear plugs, there was no blocking a buzz saw. Instead of sleeping, he listened to the rain and thought about the week, which had been totally amazing. He felt he'd made a difference and was glad he'd come. Studying McKenna as she worked with the patients gave him a deep appreciation for her skills and compassion.

Come morning, Juan handed him a black trash bag he'd slit for Logan's arms. Logan tugged it over his head. He hadn't showered all week and for a second he considered just walking down to the clinic in the rain. But then he'd be soaked and uncomfortable all day and he had too much to do.

Slogging down the muddy road in his trash bag, he was glad he'd picked up these work boots for the trip. Thunder broke overhead and water poured from the sky with no sign of letting up. Even the trees looked discouraged. When he reached the clinic, McKenna's expression stopped him at the door. "Do I look that bad?"

She shook her head. "Nope, Dr. Castle, you look that good."

He would have kissed her but Sherry and Teresa were talking nearby. Except for one evening, they'd had almost no time together alone.

"I've never seen anything like this." One elbow propped against the door frame, he studied the driving rain that seemed to melt everything into a brownish green river. "Sure doesn't look good. And we can't afford a down day. The women need recovery time. I want to check them before we leave."

McKenna threw him a guarded look. "I told you this would be difficult, weather included."

"Hey, just an observation. I'm fine and this..." He gestured outside. "This is fascinating."

She visibly exhaled just as Teresa bustled out from the back. Sometimes he felt he was walking on eggshells with McKenna. He followed her back to the kitchen. The pigtails were growing on him and she'd never looked more beautiful.

By that time, he worried that Sunday would come too soon. There was so much more to do. Teresa clucked encouragement, serving generous slices of cornbread and strong coffee for breakfast. He needed both. As he ate, he wondered if the women would even make it to the clinic today. The murkiness started to lift but the rain didn't relent. Tin cup in hand, he walked out to the waiting room and stood in the doorway. The sight that greeted him would remain with him a long time. Heads bowed and trailed by older children carrying babies, mothers slogged through the water with only worn capes for protection. Teresa quickly crowded them into the waiting area at the front.

Logan fell back, humbled. How often had his patients canceled because they didn't want to ruin their hairdo in the rain or were worried about getting tied up in traffic? Some of these women must have started out in the middle of the night. They were that eager to be seen. Putting aside their mugs, the staff greeted patients with warm smiles and encouragement.

"These are some tough ladies," Logan murmured to McKenna, who was organizing her supplies.

"Aren't they? So strong with such spirit." Without a bit of makeup, she glowed, totally in her element.

"They're like you, McKenna. Spirited. Unbreakable." She flushed and looked away before ushering her first patient into her makeshift cubicle.

Mid morning, Teresa appeared with Pepito in her arms. Logan had just finished with another fistula and was grabbing a cup of coffee. McKenna also stepped out from behind the sheet, eyes lighting up when she saw Pepito. "Let me take him," she said.

What a picture. He had to take a sip of coffee to hide his confusion. Rocking the baby, McKenna hummed the lullaby that played over the PA when babies were born at Montclair. Pepito nestled close and McKenna looked so happy.

She was a woman who should have children. Lots of them.

Could he give her that?

Uncertainty stunned him. Logan blinked, forcing himself to focus on the baby, not his own uncertainty. What did the future hold for this little guy, who obviously would have special needs?

Running one hand over the baby's soft hair, McKenna murmured, "So big but so tiny. And such big challenges ahead." She kissed the top of the baby's head and looked up.

Logan shifted his attention to the windows. Rain blew in

although they'd tried to tape papers over the open windows. "These women are such troopers."

"You're exhausted. Why don't you take a break?"

When would she stop hovering? "I can sleep next week."

~.~

Her heart stuttered when their eyes caught. One of Pepito's chubby hands wandered up to her face. When she kissed each tiny finger, the baby cooed.

"Amazing child." Voice raspy, Logan caught each movement.

"I will take him. *Precioso bambino, no?*" Teresa had bustled over and McKenna gave up her charge. She had to go back to work. Anything to keep busy so she didn't grab Logan and wring him like a wet towel for answers.

That's exactly what she'd done with Nick, she now realized. And look at how well that had turned out. But the stakes hadn't been this high. She had to shelve that thought.

The day wore on, dark and wet. It was almost impossible to tell when night fell, except her aching shoulders told McKenna she'd been working for hours. After a quick slab of cornbread, Logan disappeared down the road and she tumbled into the hammock and dreamless sleep.

When the rain let up the following day, the midwives who had gone farther north returned with their escorts. Tired but exhilarated by their adventure, they told tales of tough women working under impoverished conditions.

Thank goodness the sun came out on Saturday, but humidity pulsated in the small enclosure. Their time here was winding down much too quickly and it was hard for McKenna to picture going home. She felt the familiar tugging on her heart that plagued her every time she left Guatemala. Chicago and all its conveniences seemed so distant.

The villagers always prepared a feast Saturday night to thank them. As they wrapped up on Saturday, McKenna felt a sense of accomplishment, even greater than her earlier visits. This trip had presented more difficult cases and a broader reach for their teaching opportunities. The grateful smiles of the patients and local midwives made it all worthwhile. Behind them, they would leave not only good wishes but also boxes of medical supplies. The relentless work had kept her from her preoccupation with Logan. But soon she'd have to deal with him.

Their exchanges had been brief and truncated. He had been so quiet. Was she the only one restless with need?

She loved Logan. And love creates need.

Just what she'd been trying to avoid.

After Logan left for Juan's, McKenna gave herself a sponge bath with bacterial wipes. She was drying herself off, when Selena slipped into the cubicle. "So how's it going?" Selena's dark eyes snapped with curiosity. "You know, the two of you."

"Your guess is as good as mine." Taking her unkempt braids apart, McKenna vigorously brushed her hair out.

"He's done amazing work."

McKenna wielded the brush more slowly. "Yes, that he has. The man seems to be made of steel. Who knew?"

"I think you knew. But heck, I sure didn't." Selena's raucous chortle bounced off the cinderblock walls.

"Stop. The others will come running." Pulling her hair back into a claw clip, McKenna twisted some curls along her neckline. Sure wasn't easy to fix her hair without a mirror.

Selena gave her a silent shoulder bump. "So what do you think? A keeper?"

McKenna turned thoughtful. "He's definitely tougher than I figured. But I just don't know, Selena." She was not about to parade all her fears.

"Stop, McKenna. Time to get gussied up." She threw what looked like an embroidered cloth at McKenna.

"What's this?" Shaking out the fabric, McKenna held up a scoop neck blouse decorated with a flower pattern in intense colors of mauve, orange and green. "How gorgeous!"

"Present from Teresa. We all got one. Put it on," Selena tossed over her shoulder, heading out. "Time for celebration."

McKenna smiled as she slipped into her gift. The neckline dipped low, and she shivered. Tracing her fingers along the tops of her breasts, she remembered how Logan had looked at her in her green bikini that day on the boat. Seemed like a lifetime ago. She'd been so uncertain then. Not any more. Now she was in the game, but she had no idea how Logan felt.

The rain had stopped and the air caressed her skin, warm and inviting. Time to relax.

Darkness was falling when their group of volunteers reached the cave not far up the road from the village. The women laughed softly, dressed in the hand-embroidered blouses Teresa had provided. Celebration floated on the night air. The recent rain had awakened all sorts of rich, earthy smells. McKenna breathed deeply, listening to the night sounds along the way. A soft breeze had come up, the air fresh and new against her skin. Her hair was slipping from the clip, springing into long copper curls on her shoulders.

A fiery glow beckoned from the cave when they drew closer. The tantalizing scent of food reminded her that she hadn't eaten much that day. Her stomach had been too nervous. The trip was ending. She prided herself on being able to forge ahead, no matter what the circumstances.

But now she knew she'd fallen in love with Logan. She had a lot more on the line.

Tortillas and cobs of corn along with what smelled like pork sizzled on a large open hearth. At the back of the cave stretched a long table decorated with red and fuchsia wildflowers. The scene was elemental and beautiful. She'd attended many hospital banquets, but nothing could top this simple elegance. Torches mounted in sconces lit the interior of the cave. Dressed in one of his blue shirts and fresh jeans Logan stood talking to Juan in the flickering light. His clothes might be rumpled but somehow he'd shaved and his hair curled damply at his collar. As she approached, his gaze caught hers in the darkness.

One glance and she knew he saw it all—the long hair, the blouse. She rolled a shoulder as a tease and caught the glint in his eyes. But this was a group trip, so she took a seat between Sherry and Janet Johnson. Logan ended up at the other end of the table with Selena.

With quiet smiles, the villagers served dinner. The steaming plates were heaped with tortillas stuffed with a mixture of beans and rice seasoned with spices that made her stomach growl and her eyes sting. Strips of wild boar were piled next to hunks of some kind of fowl. She was ravenous. The villagers filled earthen goblets with an amber liquid that sent fire to her belly before it mellowed out. She tossed back another gulp.

Moving to the front of the group, Teresa began to speak. "As usual, your visit was a blessing for all of us. The gift of your talent is beyond measure."

Both men and women applauded. For a second, McKenna's eyes brimmed. Had she ever felt so grateful for her career? On the other side of the long table, Selena carried on an animated conversation with Logan, probably signing him up for next year.

"Now, please eat!" Teresa held up her hands. McKenna ate voraciously, making up for a week of beans and rice eaten on the run. A villager kept filling their goblets. While comparing notes with Sherry and Janet, McKenna felt Logan's eyes on her. When she felt her top slip from a shoulder, she took her time pulling it back into place.

By the time the music started, she felt full and pleasantly mellow. A small group of villagers played guitars, accompanied by drums and some kind of melodious whistle. The strings sang to her and she could feel the percussion instruments throb throughout her body. When the villagers began to sing, their words spoke of pride in their country and love for each other.

After a native dance presented by the women, the men joined them, while the children stood clapping. McKenna smiled over at Ana Lena sitting on a blanket with a large attractive man who must be her husband. The man was holding Pepito, who looked happy and well loved.

Family bliss. She was so caught up in the picture they presented that she was surprised when Logan touched her shoulder. "Dance?"

He didn't wait for an answer, tugging her to her feet. Some of the other midwives began to dance with each other, and laughter filled the air. Excitement rippled through McKenna's body when he pulled her into his arms.

"I'm not a good dancer, but I'm a great leaner," he whispered.

"I can follow." She fell into him, her body finding its place.

"You follow?" His chuckle tickled her breasts. "Who are you kidding, McKenna Kirkpatrick? You're a leader, and you know it."

"Takes one to know one."

"Um, hmm." He nuzzled her neck. Heat siphoned off reason and she clung to him. The sway of their bodies took on its own rhythm. All she could hear or feel was Logan, the tensile strength of his body intoxicating.

"You should wear your hair down more often." His fingers played with her curls.

"Ah, my hair started in an updo."

"Changes are good."

"Most of them." They kept dancing.

"You love all of this, don't you? This week, I mean." Angling back, he studied her face.

"Always wish I could do more." She glanced over at Ana Lena.

"Right. I know what you mean."

But right now, she wanted to think only of him. McKenna's arms twined around his neck and she pressed shamelessly against him in the darkness. The flares threw deep, friendly shadows. The unmistakable press of his erection made her crazy. If she weren't careful, she might start to grind against him and wouldn't that be embarrassing?

Finally, with an exasperated groan Logan took her hand and gently pulled her toward the road back to the village.

She balked. "What will everyone think?"

"Do we care? They've had us all week." Logan dropped a kiss on her forehead. "Selena seems to have worked magic tonight."

A red flag went up. "What kind of magic?"

His laugh was a confident chuckle. "Apparently Juan is spending the night in the church—and Selena tells me he's happy about it too."

"So that leaves you alone?"

"Oh, I don't plan on being in the tent by myself." His arm tightened around her shoulders.

Every nerve in her body tingled. But as they walked, Logan seemed pensive.

One of her sandals skidded on the loose rocks in the road but he caught her. "Whoa, steady." Logan's hands squeezed her elbows. Heads down, they kept walking.

"You're so quiet. What's on your mind?" she probed.

"The women and the children, especially Pepito. What lies ahead for that little guy?"

"To be loved by these villagers," she offered, wishing it could be more.

His steps slowed and stopped. Turning, he took both of her hands. In the darkness, his eyes held a wet glimmer. "McKenna, I had a son."

The blunt statement startled her. She reminded herself to breathe.

"Hardly lived when he died." Logan's voice broke.

"Oh, Logan." Her arms around his waist, she pressed a cheek to his thudding heart.

"And I blamed midwifery for it. Rebecca, my wife, believed in the process and labored way too long. I was taking my boards. She didn't want to bother me. Bother me!"

A wind wailed high in the trees and a chill chased down McKenna's spine.

"Pepito could have been my Ricky." He began to walk again, as if he could outpace his words and she stumbled to keep up. "But my son died. The doctor told me the long labor wasn't to blame, but I thought otherwise."

They were at the hut. When he turned to face her, his eyes held a question. She cupped his face in her hands, his skin warming her palms. "I'm so sorry, Logan. So very sorry."

Pressing his face into her hand, he kissed it. Heat coursed through her hand and into her core. "This week I could see that accidents aren't always caused by bacteria or bad judgment. There are a gazillion other factors. And like Pepito, it just happens. The parents do the best they can and go on…somehow." A bleakness swept his features. To see this competent physician humbled like this tore something inside her.

"I wish life were a safe place, but frankly, it just isn't." She thought of all the patients she'd seen that week and the problems that weren't their fault.

"You've shown me that. You've been wonderful. But McKenna. I don't know if I can ever do that again."

Her mind blanked. "Do what?"

"The children thing. I have to be honest." He dropped his hands.

Her mind clamored in protest, but she shut it down fast. This wasn't the time to peel his words and consider consequences. Her body wanted only one thing tonight. Sometimes logic and reason had to take a backseat.

McKenna couldn't see a thing when she nudged him into the hut. The smell of damp earth and burlap assailed her nostrils. From somewhere, he grabbed a high-beam flashlight and clicked it on. The light etched his face into angles that framed his burning eyes. Their kisses became a race against time. While she unbuttoned his shirt, he slid her native blouse over her head. She heard the sharp intake of breath when he saw her bra. "Black lace in the jungle?"

"A girl can hope." Black lace doesn't take up much room in a knapsack. His eyes told her it had not been foolish at all. She kicked off her sandals.

Thumbs hooked in the waistband of her jeans, he edged them

down over her hip bones. "You are so beautiful," he whispered.

Her hands found him and he groaned. "I think you've outgrown these jeans." She popped the top button and the zipper rasped down. Stepping out of the pants, he kicked them aside. "These too." She reached for the black jockey shorts.

Her body jerked when he took her face in his hands. "Thanks for bringing me here."

She cupped his hands. "You wanted to come, right?"

"Of course. The week was life changing."

Questions careened through her head, but when he bent to kiss her, all thoughts stopped. The two of them entered another world. The week had been so busy. In this hut, it came down to one man and one woman. She wanted nothing more.

McKenna had never needed a man like she needed Logan Castle. And she would have him.

He flicked off the light. Hands and lips found each other. Their bodies raged, slick and hot with uncontrollable need. When she kissed his chest, she thought her lips might sizzle.

"Oh, baby," he managed as her tongue circled one nipple and then the other.

Stretching out on the cot, he tugged her down on top of him. Her hands tunneled through his hair, and she brought her mouth down hard. But she wanted more than a kiss. She wanted the taste of him. Sitting back on her heels, she explored his body, tasting the saltiness, grazing the wiry hair that patterned his chest. She gloried in his moans.

"Enough," he finally said, gently easing her up.

"Not quite." With a slow smile she sheathed him with her body. Oh, yes. This was Logan Castle and she loved him. The knowledge burned in her chest, banishing the truth he'd shared.

She didn't want to know it. Not now.

"Ah, McKenna, McKenna," he whispered. As she settled, his lips relaxed into a smile. His hands molded to her body, sliding over her ribs, the thumbs grazing the lower fullness of her breasts before his palms cupped them.

"So good," she said.

Moving his hips, he swung her into a rhythm.

Angling her body back, she pressed onto him. "You...never cease...to amaze me."

"Too much talking." He closed his eyes, hands tight on her waist as he moved.

They couldn't pace themselves. Not this first time. All too soon the end was within reach. She pressed toward it while Logan surged beneath her. The release rocked her to her core. He followed fast behind her with a deep shudder.

Never had it been like this for her. Never.

Her feelings filled her and spilled over. "Logan, I love you," she murmured, collapsing over him. His body tightened, and she squeezed her eyes shut.

Damn. If only she could reel back those words.

Chapter 16

The trip home was blurred by fatigue, but McKenna couldn't sleep. She was probably the only one of their group awake. Turbulence kept them snapped into seatbelts, and she felt every dip of the wings. Logan was wedged between the seat and the window, sound asleep. He hadn't said much since she blurted out the L word the night before.

Her skin crawled when she thought about that moment. Couldn't the man say something...anything? That one word felt lodged between them. The rest of that long night? Her thighs still ached.

Darkness had fallen on Chicago when they touched down at Midway Airport. By that time McKenna had worked out an escape plan. While Logan was heaving his duffle from the overhead compartment, she scrambled down the aisle, streaked down the gangway and hightailed it toward baggage claim.

She'd been downright naive and stupid. When Logan finally shared the heart wrenching story about his infant son, McKenna decided all systems were go. She'd never been one to hold things in. Logan's lack of response whipped her back to a similar proclamation of love with Nick. She'd had feelings for the guy. But McKenna always felt Nick's eventual declaration of love had been pulled from him like a stubborn wine cork.

Now here she was, living all that again. She thought she'd gotten smarter. When she reached the baggage claim area, McKenna was panting. The carousel was still empty, but her mind wasn't. Why had she opened her heart to Logan when obviously he didn't feel the same? What seemed meaningful to her in the darkened hut may not have meant the same to him. Her head ached from overthinking this. Fatigue weighed on her while she waited at the baggage carousel.

Finally luggage spilled onto the conveyor belt. When she saw her bag, she leapt forward.

"Hey, where'd you go? I'll get your that for you." Logan came up behind her.

"No need."

"Fine, I'm going to get a newspaper." Logan wandered off.

Finally her black bag with the hot pink tag swung past. Lurching forward, McKenna hefted it off. From the corner of her eye, she saw Selena rushing to meet Seth. Her brother's arms opened as he came through the rotating door.

That's what McKenna wanted from a man. Open arms. Ready smile. An uncomplicated relationship.

She started to run. "I'm going to hitch a ride with Selena and Seth," she called over her shoulder.

When Logan's head jerked up from scanning the headlines, his stunned expression should have stopped her. But it didn't.

"Selena, Seth, wait up!" Waving, she rushed toward the couple, the black duffle thumping against her leg.

"Hey, McKenna! Have a good trip?" Seth looped one arm around her.

"Can I get a ride?"

Seth squeezed her shoulder. "No problem, big sister."

Ignoring Selena's questioning look, McKenna pushed ahead of them. The Chicago summer heat felt dry, unlike the highlands. She'd come home. As she jammed her bag into Seth's trunk, she definitely was not the person who'd left here a week earlier.

On the ride home, she sat silent in the back while Selena told Seth about the week. At one point, McKenna pressed one hand against her chest. Her heart felt shredded.

~.~

After a sleepless night, McKenna felt relieved to return to the hospital Monday morning. Bethany had held down the fort, despite the fact that two babies came early, bringing her total deliveries to four for that one week—a full schedule for a solo practitioner.

"Are you exhausted?" McKenna asked her after Bethany had brought her up to speed.

Eyes ringed with bluish-gray circles, she shot McKenna a smile. "Of course. To make matters worse, Sarah Bachman had a difficult time."

"Tell me about it." Sliding into her chair, McKenna pulled up Sarah's chart while Bethany filled her in on the problem with Sarah's blood pressure. The delivery had ended up in the OR.

McKenna looked up. "Did Gary take the call?"

Bethany shook her head. "No, Priscilla."

McKenna stopped reading. "How'd that go?"

"Great. Priscilla handled it well. Sarah had the prettiest little girl. Amber Bachman came into the world a little early but beautiful."

Back to Priscilla. "Well...does Priscilla follow the same protocols as Gary...or Logan?"

Tilting her head, Bethany appeared to be thinking back. "Smooth, professional. Very reassuring." A huge yawn halted her recap just as Selena showed up.

"How did it go last week?" Selena clapped one hand on Bethany's shoulder.

Bethany began her recap again while McKenna reviewed Sarah Bachman's chart. Priscilla's detailed notes made Logan's looked like a brief overview.

Bethany moved on and McKenna sat back. Her mind wandered from the data on the screen to that last night in Guatemala. Could their crazy lovemaking with Logan might be chalked up to that crazy drink or the romantic lighting from the torches. Whatever it was, it hadn't followed them back to the states.

The week picked up speed and McKenna threw herself into work. The Foundation was in countdown mode leading up to the golf outing that would benefit the new OB projects. Jack Frazier had taken an active lead along with Dennis Heckman, chairman of the Foundation Board.

Their goal was rather modest but enough to seed the new unit. Warren had indicated that the Foundation was capable of supplying the rest of the funds, but board members did want to know the hospital community was behind it.

"We decided on a date for the Day in the LDRP," Jack Frazier commented at their next meeting. Logan was conspicuously absent. He'd sent a short email and McKenna had taken over.

"The employee open house is going to be really exciting," Priscilla said. "Jack has the most creative ideas. Can't wait to see how it all comes together."

Oh, that cheery prattle might fool some. But McKenna had seen Priscilla's clinical notes. This was definitely not a frivolous woman. She felt embarrassed for ever thinking that. After the meeting wrapped up, McKenna walked out with Priscilla. "So you golf?"

"A little. Fourteen handicap," Priscilla told her.

Fourteen? Pretty darn respectable. McKenna would have to spend some quality time with Vanessa on the golf course.

Although she got a quick glimpse of Logan in the hall midweek, she quickly made a detour to avoid him. Confusion roiled in her chest. By the end of the day, she felt both jetlagged and overcome. Dorothy had rescheduled a lot of their appointments from last week to this week. McKenna's mind cranked slowly. To top it off, her phone was malfunctioning. Some of the mission group had this problem last year due to the change in humidity upon re-entering the states. Flipping to a temporary phone only added to the pressure. Dorothy forwarded her calls, but McKenna felt like she was always playing catch-up.

At the end of the week, McKenna sat slumped at her desk, going through the pile of mail Dorothy had slit and set neatly on her desk.

"Catching up?" Bethany stuck her head in the door.

McKenna nodded. "Probably take another week. By the way, how did the natural childbirth class go?"

"Nothing unusual. It's a good group." Bethany slipped into the chair opposite the desk, folding one leg under her. "Angie really missed you."

"Anything new with Angie?" *Like a bruise?*

"No, she's got a couple months to go, right?" Bethany rubbed the heel of one hand into her eyes. "Oh, and Cindy stopped by. Asked you to check with her when you got back."

McKenna's antennae shot up. After Bethany left, she grabbed her purse and her keys. In the outer office, Dorothy was getting ready to leave.

Selena's office light was still on, and she called out as McKenna passed, "Hey, not so fast."

McKenna tried to edge away. "Gotta get to Cindy before she leaves."

But Selena was hot on her trail. "Just one question. What was going on last Sunday night at the airport? You sprinted toward us like an assassin was on your trail."

McKenna's keys bit into the palm of her hand. "Just wanted to get home."

"What about Logan?" Selena's eyes narrowed. "I saw the expression on his face."

McKenna gnawed her lip. She didn't want to sound paranoid but she'd made a mistake, one she wished she could retract.

"McKenna?" Selena persisted.

"I used the L word. Okay?" McKenna winced, remembering. "Heat of the moment and way too soon."

Selena shook her head slowly. "I understand but you're not a girl who tosses it around."

"Ah, I don't think Logan thought so. Silence, Selena. The man never said a word."

"Stop beating yourself up. Logan's an internal processor. Everybody knows that. He likes to think things through completely before speaking."

"We have some major differences."

Throwing her hands up, Selena said, "All couples do. Sometimes people can change. Don't be a piece of hard porcelain, McKenna. Be a piece of clay that can be molded."

"I'm a girl who tends to break molds," McKenna said on an exasperated sigh. "See you tomorrow."

The walk over to the hospital cleared her head a little. But the pristine tiled floors, original art work and subdued overhead lighting made her think of the stark working conditions in Guatemala. They'd sweltered and the air-conditioned comfort at Montclair felt so wrong. And yet the patients in that Central American country remained so cheerful. Their gratitude kept them close to McKenna's heart.

Despite that, heaviness continued to weigh on her. The sun was shining. She had a great career, family and friends. How could she make herself so miserable about Logan when she had so much? Sometimes her mind sorted through feelings way better than her heart.

When she got to Cindy's office, the social worker was just leaving. "Hey, where's your tan?"

"Well, you know those cabanas," McKenna shot back. "I spent most the time under a sun umbrella. Bethany said you wanted to see me. Something about Angie?"

"Walk with me. I'm on my way out." Grabbing her briefcase, Cindy snapped off the lights and they headed for the elevator. "I wanted you to know she's considering giving her baby up for adoption. She knows this isn't the time for her to be raising a child. She wants to go to trade school. Said something about becoming a paralegal."

"Sounds like a woman with a plan. Thanks for your help, Cindy."

Cindy touched her arm. "No, thank you for identifying the problem. You always have a good eye."

The social worker's words stayed with McKenna as she drove home. Did her good eye apply to her personal life? Or was she blind when it came to Logan?

It wasn't until much later that evening when she was cleaning up the kitchen and giving Sasha a cat treat that it hit her. She'd been so caught up in her own misery about Logan that she wasn't putting two and two together. Anyone could adopt Angie's baby. That's when she picked up her landline.

The weekend loomed and she told herself she was glad to have a clear schedule. After all, she was on call. No time for dating anyway. But she couldn't ignore the emptiness in her heart. From past experiences, she knew the healing power of time. But she'd really had hopes.

When Leticia Sloan went into labor Friday night, McKenna was almost relieved. After all, sleep had eluded her. Lake Shore Drive hummed with traffic and bright lights as she drove to the hospital. Every time she came to a stoplight, she looked around. Couples sat in the front seat of almost every car, talking, laughing and sneaking quick kisses. Date night, and everyone seemed to be going somewhere with someone. Gripping the wheel tighter, she tried to push that thought from her mind.

Really grated on her that she'd been perfectly fine before Logan. She'd had a full life on her own. Now? She'd turned a corner and there would be no going back.

When she reached the hospital, Leticia had already been admitted and was waiting for her in the birthing suite, husband Tyrone hovering at his wife's side.

After a quick check, McKenna could see the young mother was well on her way. "Six centimeters." And she gave the couple a thumbs up. "Want to get in the pool?"

Eyes wide, Leticia nodded and her husband helped her ease into the warm water. It was always miraculous to her how a pregnant woman's entire body seemed to relax into the water birthing process. The music Leticia and Tyrone had chosen was jazzy blues. Tyrone was a sax player, and he'd taped this sequence just for his son.

The birth went smoothly and two hours later, Abel Sloan came into the world. Hearing the baby wail and seeing his tiny arms flail about, McKenna felt that old tug, only now it seemed stronger than ever.

And totally out of reach.

When she put Abel in Leticia's arms, Tyrone cupped one hand gently over the tight curls on the baby's head. McKenna's throat swelled at the simple gesture. She hated that she was getting so sentimental. After the proud father cut the cord, McKenna delivered the placenta. One of the pediatric nurses stood nearby, ready to tend to the infant.

McKenna's mind went back to Guatemala and the limitations faced by those women. Of course, they knew little of birthing pools and soothing music. In her head, she worked on ways to make their trip even more productive next time. If she kept her mind on Guatemala, she wouldn't obsess about Logan.

Although she didn't need any caffeine since she wanted to sleep when she got home, McKenna stopped in the staff lounge. Only the quiet whirling of the air conditioning greeted her. She ambled over to the huge plate glass window. The view was so amazing at this time of night—the tiny lights marking Chicago's shoreline. In the murky darkness, the lake looked so mighty and mysterious. Then she saw him. Huddled in the corner, Logan sat hunched over the slate he often carried with him. Maybe it was time to face him. She took in a nervous breath when he lifted his head.

"McKenna! Where have you been?" Flipping the cover over his iPad, he stood and stretched.

"Did you have a delivery tonight?" She kept a distance between them.

"C-section." Scratching his head, he sent her a rueful smile. "I thought of Guatemala the entire time."

But obviously he hadn't thought of her. The past five days, she'd been so preoccupied with him. He couldn't even call?

His eyes darkened to coal as he came closer. "You haven't answered my calls."

Her hand went to the phone on her hip. "Oh shoot. My phone has been on the blink. Dorothy got me a temporary and I thought all calls had been forwarded."

"That explains a lot." By this time he was close enough to trace a line down her arm.

But she just couldn't do this. She wanted to go back to the safety of a life she could control because she didn't care about anyone. "Logan, I..."

"What's wrong?" His brows drew together.

She began backing away, the new phone a welcome vibration on her waistband. Grateful for any interruption, she peered at the number. "I've got to go."

Logan's brow furrowed. The man was not happy. "McKenna, what's going on? We are going to have this conversation."

"Of course. Fine." Taking another step back, she nearly fell over the coffee table. "About those words I said that night..."

He looked stricken and her heart spiraled into her clogs.

"Of course you know it was just the heat of the moment."

"Really?" The frown deepened.

Enough. Waving her phone, she headed for the door. Her chest felt like it might explode when she burst into the hallway. When the door swished closed behind her, she doubled over, hands on her knees. Felt like the time she'd caught a ball in the stomach playing softball.

The page had come from the OB floor. In her dazed state, she hadn't completed her care notes. With a sense of relief, she took the steps to the unit and threw herself into documentation. The process cleared her mind.

Too bad the activity didn't work on her heart.

On Saturday morning, she called Amy and asked if she could visit.

"Absolutely. Gianna changes so much every day. You won't believe how big she's gotten. Besides, I was just about to call you. Mallory had to go back to Savannah on business. Feels so lonely without him. Vanessa is up at the lake with Alex and I don't feel like driving up there."

"I'm on my way."

Thirty minutes later, McKenna stretched out in a lawn chair under a huge oak tree in Amy's backyard. On her back in a netted playpen, Gianna swatted at a quilted mirror that reflected her beautiful little face.

"How was your trip to Guatemala?" Amy asked, handing McKenna a frosty lemonade. "You look tired."

"I'm exhausted." She launched into an animated retelling.

"Wow, you never realize how lucky you are," Amy said after McKenna told her about Ana Lena and Pepito.

"Exactly, but the people are amazing, Amy. So much strength and love in those families. So much endurance."

Her friend tipped her head, eyes speculative. "How did it go with Logan on the trip?"

McKenna stabbed her straw into the ice. "He did great work. I don't know what we would have done without him, especially for cases like Ana Lena."

"That's not really what I'm asking. How are you and Logan?"

McKenna lifted her gaze, trying to stop her darn lips from trembling . "Oh, Amy, I'm absolutely miserable. I told him I loved him."

Amy's face lit up. "But that's wonderful!"

"No, it's not. He didn't say anything." The emptiness of that moment felt even worse now.

"Give him time. You always like things tidied up and settled. Men aren't like that. Sometimes they need time to think things through…especially when it comes to love. Didn't you say he was married before? That complicates things. Mallory was like that, remember?"

Looking back to Amy's exciting trip to Italy with Mallory, who was a stranger to her at the time, McKenna swallowed hard. She'd sure given Amy a lot of advice about how to handle the Savannah gentleman. Mallory's reticence had just about spoiled everything.

"But things worked out great for you." The backyard of the Oak Park home Mallory had purchased to keep Amy close to her family looked so homey. The scent of cut grass filled the air along with the tart smell of the potted geraniums stationed around the patio. "I hate to ask, but when are you going to Savannah?"

"Soon. Probably in the early fall. Mom and Caitlin are so busy with their new businesses and the work they're doing with Mallory that they won't even know I'm gone. You'll have to visit us. After all, Harper's down in Savannah."

At the mention of her younger sister, McKenna smiled. "That would be great. I miss Harper, and always enjoy Savannah."

"Call me with a status report," Amy joked when McKenna left an hour later.

"Sure will. But don't expect too much." Hugging her friend, McKenna kissed Gianna on the forehead. That sweet baby smell stayed with her as she drove down the Eisenhower Expressway toward the lake, along with Amy's words of caution

Chapter 17

McKenna welcomed the fast pace of the following week. In addition to her clinic, she worked with Jack Frazier on Day in the Life of the LDRP. Showing employees what was coming in the new unit was bound to bring them all on board. Warren believed that informed employees were any institution's best advertising. McKenna wanted a lot of buzz about the new unit, and she wanted it all to be good.

At home, she took her frustrations out on her golf swing in her small backyard. McKenna had to be ready for the Foundation fund raiser. No way was she going to make an idiot of herself on the golf course. She'd already done that in a hut in Guatemala.

"You running a track meet or something?" Selena asked one day when McKenna streaked past her in the office hallway.

"Still trying to catch up." She avoided Selena's gaze.

"I don't know what happened that night in Guatemala with Logan but get over it. This is so not you."

McKenna swallowed hard and edged away. "Late for my interview with a meditation teacher for our natural childbirth class."

"Sure you are."

She was grabbing at distractions, glad that there were plenty this

week. Amanda called with amazing word about Angie. "Connor
and I don't know where this in vitro maturation will take us but
we're moving ahead. Meanwhile, Cindy contacted us about a girl in
one of your classes. She's going to set the adoption wheels in
motion, if Angie agrees."

"Of course Angie will love you, Amanda. I'm thrilled for you."
One way or another, it looked as if Amanda and Connor would
finally have a baby.

"This couldn't happen without you, McKenna. I just can't thank
you enough."

Amanda's news set McKenna off on another path. Her mind
brimmed with plans. She'd call Harper when the news was final
and together they could plan a baby shower. Harper always
welcomed any excuse to visit Chicago. Together, the sisters would
cook up a terrific event to celebrate Amanda's impending
motherhood.

While McKenna's mind worked overtime, the golf outing
loomed. She spent the weekend before smacking balls, moving her
practice shots to a driving range. The swinging motion loosened
her shoulders but couldn't budge the ache in her heart whenever
she thought of Logan.

"This really sucks," she told Sasha when she arrived home, hot
and sweaty. Grooming herself on the windowsill, her cat ignored
her. Vanessa had taken Sasha while McKenna was in Guatemala.
Sasha was still ticked about her owner's absence.

McKenna's phone had been repaired so her old number was
again operational. Logan called twice, but she sent the call directly

to voice mail. Avoiding a problem wasn't her style. But the baby news had caught her off balance. In so many ways the trip with Logan had been a revelation. Their night together took her to a place she'd never been with any man,.

And then she'd ruined it. In typical McKenna style, she'd launched onto untested ground instead of taking baby steps. And he'd answered with stunned silence. That was after an announcement that still echoed in her heart. Maybe they both needed some time apart. She dreaded a conversation that might only confirm heartbreak.

If Logan wasn't her forever man, she had to move on. Smart women did that. After watching him with the children in Guatemala and hearing his story about his own baby, she had a deeper understanding of his family issues. Could she even envision a future without children? For her, marriage meant family. She'd totally understood Amanda's pain when pregnancy didn't happen for her. Babies weren't an option in the Kirkpatrick clan. They were a necessity.

~.~

The day of the golf outing dawned sunny and warm but without the stifling heat that often came with August days in Chicago. Unfortunately McKenna seemed to have picked up a cold. A cough had kept her awake all night. She tucked some cough drops in her golf bag along with a pack of tissues and some cold pills. Getting dressed was an effort. Her mind said yes but her body was telling her to go back to bed. The new pair of white shorts flattered her figure, and the moss green visor matched her polo shirt. After tying

her hair back in a ponytail, she jammed the visor on her aching
head, determined to make it through the day. With almost two
hundred golfers playing, maybe she wouldn't run into Logan.

"McKenna, you look ready for the day," Warren Mitchell
greeted her as she pulled up to the bag drop. A young man hustled
to take her clubs and she handed her keys to the valet.

"As ready as I'm ever going to be," she answered with a sniffle.

"You feeling okay?" Warren peered down at her with concern.

"Just a cold. Not to worry."

Usually dressed in a suit, Warren looked cute in khaki shorts
and white polo with the Montclair logo on one sleeve. "Logan's
been telling me about the great work you did in Guatemala," he
said, walking with her toward the clubhouse. "He thinks we should
do more. In fact, he's gathering a team of specialists to return with
him next summer."

She blinked. "He is?"

Eyes twinkling, Warren nodded. "You've been good for him,
McKenna. Got him more involved in the world."

"He was incredible in Guatemala, Warren. Other doctors might
not even consider putting in those long hours under far less than
perfect conditions." She thought of the operating room updates
he'd wanted so badly for Montclair. Yet, he'd been amazing with
basic equipment.

"The efforts Logan described to me this week are ambitious.
I'm behind him one hundred percent. We can talk about that later.
See you on the course."

McKenna watched the CEO walk away. Turning his surprising

news over in her mind, she gathered her information packet and bought a mulligan ticket for a much needed extra shot. Scanning her outing information, she froze, golf shoes suddenly rooted to the carpet.

Logan was her partner? Putting her materials down, she took out a tissue and blew her nose. Perfect. Just perfect. Straightening her shoulders, she grabbed the packet and marched out to the cart path. Might as well get it over. According to the listing, Cecile Montclair and Priscilla completed their foursome. McKenna looked forward to meeting Logan's grandmother, but this was going to be a long day.

"Hi, McKenna." Priscilla glanced up at her from under a blue visor that matched her eyes. She was arranging her clubs in her bag. "Don't you look cute?"

McKenna always wondered who would wear one of those tiny golf skirts. Now she knew. Priscilla Preston's legs went on forever.

"Finally I get to meet you, McKenna!" The older woman seated in the other extended a veined hand. "I'm Cecile Montclair."

Finally? "Good morning, Mrs. Montclair. So pleased to meet you. I have a cold so I hope you don't mind if I don't shake your hand."

"Of course, dear. How considerate." In a lilac polo and white capris that showed off a trim body, Logan's grandmother was a study in aging. The family resemblance felt a bit disconcerting. One glance and McKenna felt like she was looking straight into Logan's piercing eyes.

"Call me Cecile," the older woman said crisply. "I've heard so much about you, dear, during our Saturday night dinners. Hope you didn't mind but the only way I could capture Logan's full attention was by making a date."

McKenna was stunned. This was Logan's Saturday night commitment?

Cecile's glance traveled past McKenna and brightened. "Ah, here he is. Logan, darling."

"Good morning, ladies." Logan gave McKenna a guarded glance. "So you've met my grandmother?"

McKenna nodded. "Yes. We were just chatting."

She was relieved when Dennis Heckman took the mic, welcoming them to the outing and taking them through the schedule for the day. "Let's have a great day in honor of the innovations coming to the Obstetrics Department."

A cheer went up. The golfers' enthusiasm reminded McKenna why she was here, and the turmoil in her chest settled down. As Logan swung onto their cart, smelling of fresh air and coffee, her pulse speeded.

"Phone still broken?" Logan asked.

"Not really. Just busy." Bending over, she tied her shoes tighter.

"We've got to talk."

"Absolutely." Grabbing the scorecard, she wrote in their names and tucked it back on the steering wheel clip. Then she tugged a tissue from her pack.

"You okay?" Turning fully, he studied her.

"Just a cold. Sorry." Her nose was probably red.

"Probably shouldn't be playing."

"I'm fine."

He didn't look convinced.

They pulled up to the starting hole. Jumping out, Priscilla took the first shot. The woman had power and form as she posed on the green. Grabbing her driver, McKenna was up next. Her shot connected and she was more than pleased to see that she'd outdistanced Priscilla.

"My, oh, my," Cecile trilled. "Isn't this going to be an interesting day?"

The older woman played a measured game, and she was quick to laugh at her own mistakes. Wasn't hard to like her. Logan clearly adored his grandmother. Even though the silence in their own cart felt uncomfortable, McKenna began to relax. Since they played the best ball in a "scramble," the pressure wasn't on her to perform. With Logan, she strived to keep the conversation on work.

"Warren mentioned that you plan to gather a group of specialists to return to Guatemala next summer." McKenna hit on a safe subject while they were waiting for Cecile and Priscilla to tee off on the fifth hole. "I guess Guatemala really impressed you?"

His hands tightened on the steering wheel. "Why would that surprise you after what I told you about my son?"

"I think it's great, Logan," she said softly.

"Pepito did it for me." His eyes grew distant, as if he were thinking back to the Guatemalan highlands. "Anything we can do to make life better for these children—especially those with special needs, I'm all for it."

Admiration surged through her. "A lot of people might talk

about helping but not everyone takes action." She almost added "I'm proud of you," but that would have been condescending. And it would have sounded very possessive.

She had no claim on Logan Castle.

Easy to think, but hard to feel in her heart.

They'd reached his ball and Logan swung out of the cart. "For me, it's an ultimatum."

Watching him position himself for his next shot, McKenna fought the feelings coursing through her. Admiration. Love. Lust. And sadness. All in that order. She knew she wanted more than passionate nights with Logan. But she didn't know if he could give any more…to any woman. Not with his tragic history.

"Don't look so serious. It's just a game." Priscilla came to stand with her.

McKenna tightened her grip on her club. Ahead of them, Cecile had apparently asked Logan a question and now he was giving his grandmother a short lesson about her stance.

"She's really something, isn't she?" Priscilla mused with admiration.

"Logan adores her, doesn't he?"

"They've always had a close bond. She's a good friend of my grandmother's. They play bridge together. Cecile hasn't changed a bit over the years, even though Logan's mother, well, she hasn't been around much."

McKenna had a lot of questions about Logan's parents, but she wasn't about to mine Priscilla for information. No wonder Logan had hired Priscilla so quickly. He'd grown up with her.

"Guess we're up," Priscilla said, adjusting her visor.

Hole after hole, their foursome cheered each other on. A breeze helped make the heat bearable. McKenna began to feel a little better. Maybe getting out in the sun had been a good idea.

The day improved with every hole. With great effort she left her useless worrying behind. Her future would unfold, somehow. And she'd learn from her mistakes. She knew that much about herself.

By the end of the day, McKenna was sunburned and exhausted. Logan had picked up the pace, and they had a decent score. Probably wouldn't win any awards, but they'd had a great time. By the time they played the back nine holes, her stalwart acceptance was weakening. Every touch, every look—she felt drained from keeping herself in check.

After the last hole, Priscilla and Cecile took off for the clubhouse. Logan tallied their scorecard, and they drove in silence to drop off the cart. McKenna perched on the edge of the seat, ready to spring out. But when Logan pulled the cart into line at the club, he turned to her with such sweet intensity burning in his eyes. "McKenna, I—"

"Logan! Logan and McKenna!" His grandmother waved to them from the doorway.

McKenna waved back. "Looks like we better join the party."

"Fine. But we will talk later. Are you sure you're feeling well enough for this dinner?"

"Absolutely." She swung out of the cart.

This project was her baby, and she had to see it through. Hair a frizzy mess, McKenna went in search of a ladies room.

"Oh, there you are!" Cecile Montclair grabbed her hand when McKenna emerged from the restroom and tugged her into the dining room. "Now, come and sit next to me. We can have a nice chat."

Held firmly by Cecile's deceptively delicate hands, McKenna smiled. Cecile was so darn cute. "You want to talk to me?"

"Well, of course, dear." Taking a seat, Cecile motioned to the chair next to her. This was a woman used to giving orders. "After all, you've brought the spark back in my grandson. And you got him to go on that wonderful mission trip to Guatemala. Good for you."

"It wasn't a pleasure trip," McKenna pointed out through her surprise. "Logan worked hard."

"Oh, I love to hear you defend him, McKenna. That's when he's at his best, you know. Helping people." Cecile whisked her fingers through silver blond hair, delicate gold earrings winking at her ears. "About time he gave up that brooding. Of course, we all felt terrible about the baby, but there you have it. That's life."

How did his grandmother know that McKenna was aware of Logan's loss?

A waiter took their drink orders. After he left, McKenna's eyes drifted to the front of the room where Logan was examining the silent auction items, Priscilla at his elbow.

Cecile followed her glance. "Beautiful girl, isn't she?"

"Absolutely."

"Talented too. And she's been through so much. That awful husband. Not as strong as you, I dare say. These days women need to be strong, or they end up coming home." With a tsk, tsk, she nodded toward Priscilla.

So that's how it was? Sympathy readjusted McKenna's assumptions about the new member of Logan's practice.

Cecile pursed her lips, as if she'd already said too much. "What a good man. Thank you," she murmured as the waiter served their ice tea. "Anyway, here he comes."

Logan was headed their way. When his eyes sought her, the heat could have melted the ice cubes in McKenna's glass.

"Now, don't tell him we've been discussing...you know," Cecile murmured.

"Oh, of course not." McKenna was still turning Cecile's words over in her mind.

"Hungry?" With a light touch on her shoulder, Logan slid into a seat next to her.

"And who's this lovely lady? Heard you burned up the fairways, Cecile." Warren had joined them and, by heavens, began flirting with Logan's grandmother.

McKenna hardly knew what she ate that night. Besides, with her cold she couldn't taste a thing. Under the tablecloth, Logan squeezed her hand. Every logical thought fled while awards were given out and silent auction items distributed to the highest bidder. Lots of laughter, lots of camaraderie. The event was a huge success and enthusiasm ran high for the OB unit and all the planned improvements in the OR.

Her head began to throb from all the applause. By the time the activities wound up, she felt this day had really been too long. The crowd filtered out of the banquet room into the foyer. Priscilla's smile had seemed genuine when they'd said good-night. She was taking Cecile home.

"See you again soon, I hope." Cecile gave McKenna a tight hug. "So nice to meet you."

Cecile glanced at her grandson. "Better take this girl home and give her some of your chicken soup."

Logan nodded with a grin. "Good idea. I'll walk you to your car," he told her as they waved good-bye to his grandmother.

"You don't have to do that."

"I want to." When he took her hand, she was too exhausted to protest.

"Your grandmother is something else," she told Logan as they strolled in the summer evening. Katydids sang in the tall grass along the back of the parking lot.

"She wants to have you over for dinner soon."

"Really?" Seeing Logan's ancestral home would tell her so much more about him. But did she really want to know more? Wouldn't that make this whole thing harder?

He backed her up against her jeep, still warm from a day in the sun. "I don't want you overwhelmed by my family."

"Family? Who else, beside Cecile?"

"Occasionally my mother stops in." His eyes were gray velvet and his lips, warm as the summer breeze when he kissed her. "She'll want to know everything."

"Everything, huh? And what is everything?"

"Look, McKenna, I needed to think about things after, well,

you know…"

"After I told you I loved you." She wanted all the cards on the table.

He tipped her chin up. "Right, you caught me off guard. You're outrageous and funny. Bossy and brilliant…"

"You could give a girl a big head."

She was joking but Logan's expression was so serious. The katydids seemed to stop, along with the rest of the world. "I love you, McKenna. You caught me by surprise but of course I want everything for us together."

She sucked in a breath and he kissed her. "You're going to get my cold," she murmured against his lips.

"Doesn't matter. I'm going home with you to whip up some chicken soup."

She shook her head. "You don't have to do that."

He tipped her chin up. "I want to. That's the point. That bossy part in you? Get used to me doing stuff for you. You don't have to take on the world alone, McKenna Kirkpatrick."

The idea felt disturbingly new. And nice.

One hand on his chest, she pushed back and swallowed. "Logan, I have to tell you. My future includes kids. Just the way it is for me." She could hear the tears in her voice and clamped her lips shut.

"I wouldn't have it any other way. Trust me. You've brought hope to my life." When Logan grinned, his entire face lit up. "Of course I want children, McKenna Kirkpatrick, and I want them with you. Sassy red-headed gremlins who poke their fingers into food."

"Oh, Logan." Relief and gratitude left her limp as his lips found hers. His cheeks felt warm and scratchy from the long day in the sun. Good thing night was falling and the valet had parked her car in a far corner of the lot.

He pulled back. "Have patience with me?"

"Just pick up the pace, okay, Hot Doc?"

"Sometimes I'm a slow learner."

She laughed. "You? Really?"

"For both our sakes, I wanted to take the sure and steady route with you. But you're not a girl who goes slow. With me, that's probably a good thing. Don't ever give me too much time to think. I might get into trouble."

She snuggled closer. "Trouble, huh? Tell me when I get too bossy. I just thought I was a self-actualized woman."

McKenna could feel his chuckle. Oh, how she wanted to have these arms around her for the rest of her life. "So we're both looking for new ways to do things?"

"Absolutely. I like to do research. Let's enjoy getting to know each other."

The car blazed warm behind her back but Logan's lips felt hotter. She stilled his roving hands. It wasn't that dark out here. "We're definitely making a scene."

"And I definitely don't care. You've been so distant since we got back."

"I'm about to close that gap." She wrapped her arms around Logan, so glad she wasn't on call.

Epilogue

Eighteen Months Later

Mounting the platform at the foot of the birthing bed, McKenna grabbed the snap-up rail for support. "With this bed, you can take a lot of positions or you can deliver in the birthing pool if that's your choice." The group of visitors craned their necks. If she counted right, this was the seventh tour coming through the Open House for the new Labor, Delivery, Recovery and Post Partum unit.

"When are you due?" one of the pregnant mothers asked.

Running one hand over her taut belly, McKenna smiled. "In about a month."

She hobbled from the bed and pointed to the next room where they could see what looked like a tub with a glass viewing panel. "Every room in this new unit has a birthing pool. You can use it as a Jacuzzi to ease your labor or remain in the water and deliver your baby. Up to you."

A ripple of wonder ran through the group. It was such fun to introduce so many new parents to the concept. "My sister-in-law delivered twins a couple of months ago. Water birth, and I assisted. It can be done." McKenna smiled as she remembered. Amanda and Connor were now settling in with their new family of three children. They'd adopted Sean, Angie's little boy, only to discover that, with Logan's help, Amanda was pregnant with twins.

Slipping through the door, Logan hovered in the back of the room. "There's my husband. Do any of the guys have questions?

Logan gave a small wave. God, he was one hunk of a handsome man and he'd make a great dad. Logan was now lobbying to have a childcare center in the hospital. The summer before, he'd brought huge changes to the summer mission trip to Guatemala. Ana Lena and her husband had agreed to come up for an evaluation arranged by Logan. To Selena's delight, specialists were now on board with the program.

Sitting on the edge of the birthing bed while couples asked Logan questions, McKenna marveled at how her husband advocated for the new unit. He'd done a complete one-eighty in his views about water birth and had even brought portable birthing pools to El Limar last summer.

He'd changed and so had she.

The tour group moved on to the next room, where Selena picked up the tour.

"Happy?" McKenna asked after Logan had found a quiet corner to give her a kiss that was definitely not part of the tour.

His relaxed smile widened. "More than happy. You will never know."

"I'll give you plenty of time to explain," she whispered.

"Might take a while."

"Gosh, I hope so." The baby inside gave an impatient kick when McKenna's Hot Doc turned up the heat.

Rescuing the Reluctant Groom

A Windy City Romance

Follow the exploits of Selena Ruiz, McKenna's good friend and colleague, in *Rescuing the Reluctant Groom*.

A cold sun batted its head against the frosted bedroom windows. Winter in Chicago and the temperature hovered around ten degrees outside. Somewhere in Oak Park, church bells tolled. The weather might be freezing but contentment warmed Selena's heart. Rolling over in bed, she traced a finger down Seth's back. The man barely moved. Cocooned under the quilt, she snuggled closer to his heat. *Madre de Dios*, this felt good.

If she poked her nose above the covers and exhaled, her breath might form a cloud. Outside, car tires whined, spinning on the ice. Selena sure wasn't anxious to get out there. *Que bueno* that today was McKenna's turn to be on call for their midwifery practice.

Like always, Seth had kicked off the comforter. The man was a walking space heater. He lay curled on his tummy like a baby, except babies didn't have muscles like his. Seth Kirkpatrick was a babe, not a *niño*. The man was strong enough to load a stretcher into an ambulance himself, gentle enough to calm an accident victim. Her man was all heart.

Dark stubble accented his square chin and framed his sculpted lips. The auburn Kirkpatrick hair was shaved shorter on the side.

Oh yeah, he was a bad boy and Selena should feel darn lucky. Instead, frustration chipped at her peace, like an ice scraper against the frosted window.

"*Te amo*, you maddening man," she whispered. Bells still rang in the early morning air, happy as wedding bells. Her hands and heart felt restless. She danced her fingertips over Seth's strong nose, skimmed the full lips.

Wedding bells and babies?

What was with her today?

With a sleepy mumble, Seth hugged her tight. Face pressed against the pillow, he was dreaming. She chuckled when he wrinkled his forehead, like he was trying to tell one of his stories. Most times, he couldn't remember the punch line. Seth got so mad when that happened. Pushing up on an elbow, she watched him.

Que guapo. Her man was so gorgeous.

Was Seth hers? Sometimes she wondered. Sure, he could talk about medical conditions with patients. *No problema.* But when it came to feelings and their relationship? Not so good.

The words she'd been waiting for? Selena heard them only in her dreams.

Eyes still closed, he ran a warm hand from her shoulder to one hip.

"Oh, *mi amor*." She squirmed with pleasure.

"Sissy…" he breathed.

"*Sissy?*" Selena sprang up so fast, the quilt slid to the floor. Frigid air seared her skin like dry ice. Had her heart stopped beating? She swatted at him. "*Qué dices?* What did you just say about

Sissy?"

Rubbing his eyes, Seth mumbled, "Sissy who? Sissy Hanson?"

Sí, I'm having a heart attack.

A frown appeared above his dark eyes. The bells had stopped. All joy had been sapped from the room. "What are you talking about, babe? Huh? Come here, Selena."

That husky morning voice usually worked Selena like a loofah sponge. Not this morning. *Sissy?* The name still rang in her ears. Blonde hair, blue eyes and a body that even made that navy EMS uniform look sexy. Standing beside the bed, Selena felt stiff as a cemetery stone. She crossed her arms across her heaving chest.

Then she got mad.

"You! *Idiota! Mi madre me dijo que…*" Words that would make her mother blush flowed like lava. Still wasn't enough. Grabbing a pillow, Selena started swinging.

"Hey, stop! What are you doing?" Seth struggled to sit up.

She tossed the pillow but not the anger. Selena pressed her trembling lips together. No way would she let Seth see her cry. Reaching down, she grabbed her clothes from the cold hardwood floor. Woke her up fast, that's for sure, and made her madder than ever.

"What are you doing?" Sitting up, Seth scratched his head.

"I'm leaving. You never tell me you love me. *Nunca.* Never. I'm a fool. And now this Sissy thing? Really?"

"Sissy Hanson?"

"Ah, hah!" Leaning over, Selena stabbed his chest with one finger, wishing her nails were longer. "So you admit it."

"Admit what?" He ran a hand across the muscular chest now imprinted with her fingernail. How could that one move turn her on? Selena's anger kicked up a notch.

"So you like her blonde hair, eh? That cute dimple? How long has this been going on? All those nights together working the late shift?" How could a man look so adorable when his hair was a mess and he had sleepers in his eyes?

He shoved up onto an elbow. "What are you taking about, woman?"

"First word out of your mouth this morning. Sissy. Oh, Sissy." Lips pursed together, she gave a great imitation, even though Seth hadn't said the name *quite* like that.

Seth's lips moved but no words came to comfort her.

Shoving her head into her sweatshirt, Selena swept two rubber bands from the night table and yanked her hair into pigtails. "*Perfecto*. Deny it, go ahead. Tell me you're not fooling around with her."

Seth looked at her like she'd grown two heads. "Selena, baby, I'm asking you… what *is* going on?"

Normally Selena would melt when Seth blinked those long eyelashes that no man should have. Not today. She held up two fingers. "*Dos años*. Two years together and you still can't use the L word. But you can moan about Sissy. Oh, sure. *See-see*. Well, she can have you!"

Ah, hah! That got him up. Trying to find his jeans, he hopped around on the cold floor. Seth's muscular legs flexing in the dim light almost made her weaken. But not this time. Instead, she kicked his jeans farther under the bed.

"Selena, honey, that's not true. Stop being so crazy."

"*Loca?* Me?" Grabbing the cowhide purse he'd given her for Christmas, she raced for the stairs. "We are over. *Finito.*"

She should have done this a long time ago. Should've left him the first time she told him she loved him and he just looked at her. Right, he'd stared at her like she'd ordered a meal not on his menu. Clutching the bannister so she wouldn't fall, she gulped back her tears. No way would she let him see her cry.

Maybe Seth Kirkpatrick never would settle down. Maybe he'd always be a ladies' man, the *muchacho guapo* every woman wanted.

Shoving her feet into her suede boots, Selena tore her silver quilted jacket from the front hall closet. Stumbling to the head of the stairs, Seth was having a hard time getting into his jeans. "For cripes' sake, Selena. Wait."

Glancing into the kitchen, she saw the red Fiesta dishes she'd set out last night. The ones she'd bought him for Christmas, so bright and cheerful for the holidays. McKenna, Seth's sister and Selena's good friend, had teased her. "You got dishes for my brother? That's so cute, Selena. Is this part of his hope chest?"

Cute. So perfect for a couple on Sunday morning—plates for eggs and toast, the red mugs ready next to the coffee machine.

Grabbing one of the plates, she turned.

Now halfway down the steps, Seth came to a halt. "Selena?"

A flick of her wrist sent the dish soaring like a frisbee. He ducked. *Qué lástima.* Barely missing one of his Frank Lloyd Wright sketches, it shattered against the wall. Seth's hands shot out, palms up. "Selena, honey. Please."

A mug felt so good in her hand. Heavy enough to hurt. "Please? *Please, Selena,"* she mimicked him. *"*I love to hear you beg."

This time she took aim. The mug hit his arm and ricocheted to the bannister before crashing to the floor. But hurting Seth hurt her. She paused, but not for long. This morning, her own pain felt worse.

Seth picked his way over the broken pieces. "Ouch. Crap. Are you crazy?"

"Loca, sí!" Crazy enough to fall in love with you. Another mug. But he dodged again. For a big man, Seth could be quick on his feet. *Crash.* She smiled and considered the sugar bowl. That piece had been hard to find. And he was close to the bottom of the staircase.

Racing from the kitchen, she yanked open the front door. Icy air blasted her face. Jacket not zipped, she didn't even feel the cold. After she slammed the door behind her with a bang, she heard Seth swearing a blue streak. Taking a deep breath, she smiled.

A frozen world greeted her. Snow fell softly, catching in her hair and squeaking beneath her boots. She tried to be careful hurrying to her sports vehicle. At least it started. Leaving the engine running, she popped the back open, grabbed a brush and cleared the windows. Cold snow blew back into her face. They didn't call Chicago the Windy City for nothing.

Tears blinded her by the time she climbed back into her car. Seth hadn't come after her. Clutching her chest, she breathed in and tried to calm her breaking heart. Then she floored it.

Seth's front door opened just as she squealed away from the

curb.

"Selena! Wait!" Is that what she heard?

No more waiting. The SUV fishtailed and then shot down the street.

Sunday morning and the streets were quiet under the fresh mantel of snow. Newspapers were embedded in white lawns and driveways. Eyes blurred with tears, she eased up on the gas. Last thing she needed was a ticket or an accident. When she reached Harlem Avenue, she turned north toward the Eisenhower Expressway. It was too early for bumper-to bumper traffic. The leaden gray sky was turning pearl pink. Sniffling back her tears, she switched on the radio. Thank goodness the song that blasted was Adele. Something about burning so bad after she broke up with her man. *Perfecto.*

Selena ratcheted up the music until her ears rang.

She'd broken those expensive dishes. Really? She busted out laughing.

Right now Seth was sipping coffee at his breakfast bar, watching sports highlights on TV. He probably thought she'd get over it, like always. He'd grab the dustpan and sweep up the broken dishes, along with pieces of her heart.

Later he'd stop over, lean in her doorway like the hottie that he was and give her an I'm-so-sorry smile. Embarrassing, but that had worked in the past. Her anger always melted like snow in March.

But this was January.

What made this different, besides the Sissy thing?

They were at the two-year mark. Within two years, a woman

knows if he's a keeper. Well, Selena knew. She wanted Seth Kirkpatrick for the rest of her life. But maybe he didn't feel that way. How that hurt. Popping her console open, she grabbed a tissue.

Did she think he actually had a thing with Sissy, the cute EMT on his emergency medical services squad? Not really, and some of the pain eased with her sigh. Still, the fact that he'd used Sissy's name, even in a dream, made her head pound. Stoked up again, anger flowed through her, igniting every nerve ending along the way. She banged her hands against the steering wheel to ease the pain in her heart.

But she better watch it. Her palms throbbed. These hands delivered babies, her life's work.

Only one place for her this morning, so she headed for Montclair Hospital. No way could she go home to her apartment and sit there alone on this cold Sunday. At the office, she could update the charts Dorothy had left on her desk. Hardly any traffic clogged the Magnificent Mile when she hit Michigan Avenue. Trees strung with tiny white lights, the area always looked like Christmas.

This year the holidays had brought so many good things to the Kirkpatrick family. Her good friend McKenna had become engaged to Logan Castle, the head of OB at Montclair. Sure, she was happy for McKenna. Six months and Logan popped the question.

Selena wanted to be next. She envisioned a ring on her finger that said Seth loved her forever. But she might have gray hair before he said those words. Sure, sometimes he'd toss out a "Love ya" before they hung up. How she longed for a lot more than that, but she'd be happy with "I love you, Selena. Will you marry me?"

She couldn't wait forever.

The ache in her heart pooled in her empty stomach. Maybe she'd never eat again.

She drummed her fingers on the steering wheel, waiting for the light to change. Collars turned up against the winter wind, visitors strolled past sparkling windows. But Selena couldn't feel the joy. Her mood felt as heavy as the parking meters. Had she wasted two years with Seth Kirkpatrick? After all, she was twenty-seven. She sure didn't want to be like McKenna and reach thirty with no prospects in sight. Babies didn't always come easy. Look at Connor, the oldest in the Kirkpatrick clan, and his wife Amanda. Getting pregnant had taken over five years and left them broke.

This past winter they'd adopted a baby whose young, unmarried mother had been in McKenna's natural childbirth class. Meanwhile, the in vitro treatments at Logan's infertility clinic finally kicked in for Connor and Amanda. They were pregnant with twins and suddenly Kirkpatrick babies were everywhere.

But not for Selena.

When she reached the parking garage of the hospital, she took the ramp slowly to the top level, where snow mounded around the wheels of McKenna's red jeep. She must have had a delivery last night. Jumping out of her SUV, Selena listened to the waves rumbling below. Lake Michigan thundered against the ice floes that formed along the shore, heavy, dark and cold.

Cheeks prickling from the icy wind, Selena wiped her nose on her jacket sleeve just like her *mamacita* told her never to do. Today she felt like breaking every rule.

Wasn't she made of tougher stuff than this? All those hot summers detassling corn and picking cherries as a migrant worker had taught her one thing. She could survive anything. With or without Seth Kirkpatrick, she would have a better life. Turning on her heel, she locked her car with one click and hurried toward the elevator shaft.

Her phone pinged and she checked it while she waited. Sure. Seth would now bombard her with texts. The silver doors opened and she crammed the phone back in her pocket.

Taking the elevator down to the third floor, she marched across the overpass and into the medical office building attached to the hospital. The empty hallways spooked her on weekends. Unlocking the door of For Women, she entered the deserted waiting room, now lit by one lamp they left on for the cleaning staff. Chairs lined the walls, along with low tables stacked with magazines full of Hollywood gossip.

Stretching along the far side, a huge bulletin board was papered with snapshots of babies—their Wall of Fame. She never got tired of looking at those pictures. During the week, this room was crowded with women. This morning, no patients waited to register at the high counter where their receptionist Dorothy usually sat.

The practice was growing. For Women had three midwives, two nurse practitioners and two medical assistants, all drawn by natural techniques like water birth. She headed back into the exam area. When she saw the light on in McKenna's office, her steps slowed.

Facing McKenna right now might be hard. But her office was empty and relief flooded through her. Head down, Selena continued on and unlocked her own door. Unzipping her jacket, she tossed it over a chair, dropped her purse on the floor and collapsed into the desk chair.

How had Seth become such a heartbreak?

Turning on her computer, Selena scanned the admissions. Yep, Melanie Turner had her baby last night. Their patients rotated through the practice, eventually seeing all three midwives. But McKenna had been Melanie's main contact. Melanie and Richard were a cute couple who had waited a long time for this baby, kind of like Connor and Amanda.

But Selena was getting ahead of herself. Why worry about babies when she couldn't even land the man? She was reading the Sunday memo from Warren, their CEO, when the outer door opened. Five seconds later, McKenna stood in her doorway. Selena's throat closed just looking at the woman who would never be her sister-in-law. Man, she couldn't even get the words out. No way would she cry on McKenna's shoulder, but she sure needed her advice.

McKenna's smile slid from her face. "Hey, girlfriend. What's going on?"

A sniffle was all Selena could manage.

McKenna's arms opened. Pushing back her chair, Selena walked into her friend's warm comfort. She was seriously in need of some sisterly love. "Hate to tell you, McKenna. But it's Seth."

"No way. What has he done?"

"Sissy Hanson. That's what or who he's done."

McKenna's loud gasp could probably be heard in the main building. "No way. Seth would never do that to you. Where did you hear this?"

Taking her seat, Selena poured out the sad story. "You're probably right, McKenna. This may have been just a dream— although I think he should dream about me. But things aren't looking good."

"My younger brother can be a knucklehead." Stunned didn't quite cover McKenna's expression as she plopped into the wingchair and listened to Selena's story about shattering the new dinnerware in an all-out assault on Seth.

"You mean the ones you just gave him for Christmas?"

Selena wiggled her eyebrows. "Bad right?"

They both laughed until tears came.

Then the chuckles died in Selena's throat. "Seth's not coming around with a ring like Logan. He's not even offering me the L word."

McKenna's jaw dropped. "Are you kidding me? Selena, that's crazy. You are gorgeous, funny and smart. I can think of maybe ten other guys who'd stand in line for a date with you. Go for it."

And this was from Seth's own sister? "What are you saying?"

"Seth doesn't even tell you he loves you? He's going to be thirty, for Pete's sake. The boy better take a good look at his life and what he wants."

A rock plummeted to the bottom of Selena's stomach. "Guess it's not me."

Grabbing Selena's hand, McKenna squeezed hard. "Trust me, he *does* want you. You just have to remind him of that."

"How?"

McKenna's lips tilted into a devious smile. "Plotting Seth's wake up call will give me something else to think about..."

"Right. Besides your wedding? *Caramba*, McKenna. That should be your main concern right now, not my problems."

McKenna's engagement to the hottest doc on staff made Selena so happy. She'd been with them on their mission trip to Guatemala the summer before, the week that really sealed their romance. Why couldn't Seth have Logan's certainty?

"Seth never tells you he loves you?" McKenna's forehead wrinkled.

"It's more a 'Love ya, babe' thing."

The sound from McKenna's lips gave Selena the giggles. She did the best strawberry ever.

"And the worst part is, this isn't the first time I've broken up with Seth. He might not take me seriously." Selena couldn't resist looking at her pinging phone, where texts kept popping up.

Still mad at me? Don't be. Please.

And also:

Hated to get out of bed this morning without your wakeup call.

Uh huh. She knew exactly what Seth meant and her body reacted.

Finally:

Want to come over and watch the game this afternoon? We can talk.

Right. Talking during a basketball game. That would never

happen.

Seth wasn't good at talking. Period.

"Show him you mean business." McKenna's face brightened. She was such a great idea person. The specialized birthing unit now under construction had been her brainchild, although at first Logan had fought it. As head of OB at Montclair, he could be conservative.

"How can I show him anything? I told him I never wanted to see him again."

Of course she would see Seth again. Every time an EMS Limited ambulance pulled into the Montclair ER, there was a good chance Seth would be on it. She couldn't avoid him forever.

Getting to her feet, McKenna strolled to the window and began to etch hearts into the white frost. Despite the maintenance department's work, the windows in this building continued to frost over. "Stay in his face, Selena. Don't give up, okay?"

"I'm not a quitter."

"That's right. Resilience. That's what you teach those women in Guatemala." McKenna smiled at her window handiwork. "And you're a good friend. You even come to Sunday dinner at my parents' house."

"When Seth and I were together. I'm not coming today."

"Why not?" McKenna tried to look all innocent.

"Because I can't? Because I'd like to pick up a kitchen knife when I think of Seth and Sissy."

McKenna's chuckles echoed in the small office. "Make it uncomfortable for him."

Selena's phone pinged again and her chest tightened. "I don't know if I can do this. Not today."

"Maybe you're right. Give my family time to needle him. They know the drill with Seth. Growing up, he had to have everything the other boys had. If Connor got a new lunch bucket, Seth had to have one too."

"But Connor's the oldest."

"Seth never got over it. A middle child who had some, er, issues." McKenna stumbled a bit but before Selena could get a question in, her friend roared on. "He'd gripe to my mother and usually got what he wanted."

"Reenie does fuss about him." Selena loved the family's nickname for Maureen Kirkpatrick. "I like to hear how it was with your family growing up." For Selena, the rowdy family seemed almost magical.

McKenna shrugged. "We're like most families, I think."

"How can you say that? Growing up, I never went to one school. You were at St. Edmund's from first grade to fifth grade, right?"

McKenna shrugged. "Sure. We all were. Even my mom went to that school."

They were talking about different planets. Time to set the record straight. "We moved all the time, McKenna. Like any migrant family, we followed the crops from Texas to Michigan and then back down again. We were always changing schools. I never had a best friend."

The last comment brought a gasp. "Oh my God, Selena. I knew

you worked on a farm but..."

"Not a farm. Many farms." Had she said too much? This felt so embarrassing but McKenna was her best friend, the one she never had growing up. "If we stopped at a store for bread and peanut butter after working all day, people would stare at our dirty clothes. When my mother spoke to us, our names confirmed what they suspected. We were 'illegals' in everyone's eyes. For a while I even considered changing my name. Selena, Rafael. Our names made us different."

"But I love your names. They make you special."

And that's why she adored McKenna. "That's not how the rest of the world sees it. Anyway, here in Chicago I felt like I finally belonged." For the first time in her life, she fit in and she wanted it to stay that way.

Remembering those early years took effort. The adrenaline drained from Selena's body and she felt so darn tired. What a good time she'd had with Seth the night before. They hadn't done anything special. Just watched an action movie on Seth's big-screen TV, the one the family camped in front of for every sporting event or race.

The Kirkpatricks always made her feel welcome. Bringing her crockpot over, Selena would make a huge pot of her mother's Mexican chili, bubbling with tons of hot peppers. In fact, that crockpot was still in Seth's cupboard.

Uncoupling wasn't going to be easy.

"Seth always loved my chili," she murmured, twining a curl around her finger.

McKenna's boisterous laugh lifted Selena's spirits. "He's gonna miss way more than that."

Snatching Seth's photo from her desk, Selena shoved it into a drawer. "Oh, I hope so."

~.~

Pushing open his parents' front door, Seth stamped the snow from his boots before stepping inside. The smell of his mother's pot roast reminded him that he hadn't eaten all day. Food? Last thing on his mind. Toeing off his boots, he left them on the mat along with the others. His mom had cooked one of his favorites and he wasn't hungry. Maybe he had the flu.

Who was he kidding? This thing with Selena had him worried. She hadn't answered her phone or texted him back all day. And that mess at home? It took him a while to clean up the broken dishes.

What a woman. He'd never seen her this angry. In a weird way, it turned him on.

"How's my handsome boy?" Hurrying from the kitchen, his mom wiped her hands on her apron before lifting her cheek for a kiss. She smelled like onions and *Charlie*, the perfume she asked for every Christmas.

"Hi, Mom." He tried to smile.

She peered closer. "What's wrong?"

Dammit. "N-nothing." He gave her a tight hug and backed off.

"Seth? What are you keeping from me?" She had him by the forearms, but no way did he want to mention this thing with Selena. With any luck, he'd have everything sorted out in a few days.

"You worry too much, Mom. Nothing."

Thank God Mark and Connor, two of his brothers, arrived just in time from the back family room. "How's the boy?" Connor cuffed him on the shoulder. The squalling upstairs was probably from Sean, Connor's newly adopted son.

"You're not looking so good." Mark narrowed his eyes. "Big night out?"

"Nope. Not really." Enough of this. Escaping, he marched into the living room where two of his sisters-in-law were having a heart-to-heart on the sofa. Girl talk. Bad timing.

With a wave, he escaped to the kitchen. Big mistake. McKenna was cleaning the carrots at the sink. Last person he wanted to see. Sugar-burned carrots were one of his favorites. Not today.

"How's it going, little brother?"

"F-fine." As if to prove it, he grabbed a carrot and munched down. His stomach did a weird twist but he kept chewing.

"You're really going to tell me everything's fine?"

So the word was out. Damn. He could hardly swallow.

His mother bustled into the kitchen behind them. "What's going on?"

McKenna's eyes skewered him. "You'll have to ask Seth."

With a growl, he barreled toward the family room, high-fived his dad and said hi to Logan.

"Hey, how's it going?" Logan looked up.

"Don't start." Grabbing a can of pop from a bucket of ice in the corner, he plopped onto the sofa.

Feet up on a hassock, his dad looked as amazed as his future brother-in-law. "Get up on the wrong side of the bed, son?"

A retired fireman, his father had never been good at heart-to-heart talks. Seth was not about to go into the Selena thing with him. And Logan? If he hadn't asked McKenna to marry him last Christmas, Seth wouldn't be in this situation. He wouldn't be here alone.

This was all Logan's fault. He grabbed some pretzels from the bowl on the coffee table and crunched down hard. The TV blared but his dad and Logan weren't even watching it. Instead, they were giving him weird looks.

"Could we just watch the g-game?" Pretzels in hand, Seth settled in, just as he did every Sunday. But everything felt different. "What's the score?"

His dad was still giving him the fish eye and Logan? Was that a grin?

Amanda appeared in the doorway behind the sofa. Sean, her adopted son, was cradled in her arms. Four months pregnant with twins and she already looked like she could deliver any day. Connor came up behind her, crooning at his new son. He'd never seen his brother like this. The whole place smelled of baby powder and poop, and Connor was all googly-eyed.

"Where's Selena?" Amanda glanced around.

Seth jumped up so damn fast he made the baby cry.

"Hey dude, baby in the house." Connor took the baby from Amanda and started patting him on the back.

"Sorry, Amanda. Connor." Feeling terrible, Seth wished he

could comfort the baby. But he couldn't. Not today. He'd probably drop the kid.

From the look on Connor's face, Seth knew he'd be given the third degree later. Connor took his role as oldest in the family seriously. Seth started to sweat. Why did his parents always pump the heat up so high?

Downstairs where the pool table was set up, the kids' voices rose above the crack of the balls. Usually Seth liked hanging out with his nephews and niece. Today the noise was getting on his nerves.

Wheeling around, he headed back into the kitchen. "You look like you've seen a ghost, son." His mother was tending the carrots sizzling in the pan. Smelled like biscuits in the oven, another one of his favorites. His stomach growled but nausea made it impossible to think of eating.

"Aw, Mom. I don't think it's a ghost that's bothering him. Is it, Seth?" Lifting the cover of the slow roaster, McKenna poked the meat with her fork. Her sly grin told him she knew. Cornered, he felt like he was in a speeding ambulance and the patient wasn't responding.

"Nothing is bothering me, okay?" Maybe he needed a beer, not pop. Tossing his empty can into the trash, he grabbed a beer from the refrigerator, twisted off the top and took a cool sip. It tasted like vinegar and his stomach lurched.

He should have stuck with the pretzels.

"What's the matter, Seth?" A smile played along his sister's lips. She was loving his discomfort. Had she told their mother anything?

That would be out of bounds.

He did what any man would do. Kept quiet. He was edging toward the door when McKenna turned, "Hey, how's Sissy Hanson doing?"

His mother's head jerked. "Who is Sissy?"

"N-no one. Just someone I work with."

"Long blonde hair," McKenna murmured while his mother's mouth fell open. "She wears it in a braid down her back. Does she ever unbraid that thing, Seth?"

Spatula in hand, his mother fisted her hands on her hips. "Seth Michael Kirkpatrick, what have you been doing?" Looked like she just might use that spatula on him, the way she did years ago when she caught him raiding the cookie jar.

"Nothing." His arms flew out, sending the damn beer all over the kitchen.

With a smug smile, McKenna handed him a roll of paper towels. "That's about right, Mom. He's been doing absolutely nothing. Better clean up your mess, Seth."

About the Author

Barbara Lohr writes heartwarming romance with a flair for fun and subtly sexy love scenes. In her novels, feisty women take on hunky heroes and life's issues. Family often figures in her stories. "No woman falls in love without some family influence, either positive or negative." Her series include *Windy City Romance*, which includes jaunts to Savannah and Italy, and *Man from Yesterday*, which launched in 2015. Dark chocolate is her favorite food group, and she makes a mean popover. When she's not writing, she loves to bike, kayak or golf. Barbara lives in the South of the USA with her husband and a cat that insists he was Heathcliff in a former life. For more information on the author and her work, please see:

www.BarbaraLohrAuthor.com

www.facebook.com/Barbaralohrauthor

www.twitter.com/BarbaraJLohr

Acknowledgements

Many thanks to Romance Writers of America and Central Ohio Fiction Writers. My core of fellow writers have been invaluable. Also a huge thank you to the other writers on the loops that share their wisdom, addressing writing and publishing issues on a day-to-day basis. On a more personal level, Sandy Loyd and Marcia James, can't thank you enough for your sage advice and sense of humor. I look forward to enjoying this journey together. Thanks to Kim Killion for covers that rock. For this book, a grateful shout out to Dr. Wayne Lippert, technical advisor on the obstetric clinical questions. Any misinterpretations would be mine!

For my daughters, Kelly and Shannon, reading has always been a shared joy for us, from Judy Blume to Janet Evanovich. I am thrilled to have you as my "advisors." My grandchildren, Bo and Gianna, you bring me such joy and often pop up in my work. Both of you experienced water birth first-hand basis, although you didn't realize it! To my husband Ted, words aren't adequate to thank you for your love and support. You're my rock who quickly steps into the role of IT guy when emergencies arise. May we have many more wonderful years together that include trips to Leopold's for ice cream.

Other Works by Barbara Lohr

Windy City Romance series

Finding Southern Comfort

Her Favorite Mistake

Her Favorite Honeymoon

The Christmas Baby Bundle

Rescuing the Reluctant Groom

Man from Yesterday series

Coming Home to You

Made in the USA
Columbia, SC
26 October 2020